AVAILABLE DARKNESS: BOOK TWO

SEAN PLATT

DAVID W. WRIGHT

STERLING & STONE

For Todd.
April 1970 – April 1996

AVAILABLE DARKNESS:
BOOK TWO

Previously on Available Darkness...

Thousands of years ago, Earth was once connected to a world called Otherworld, a place of great technology and magick. During a civil war waged by the technologically advanced North upon the South, several people came to Earth via portals, looking to start anew. They called themselves Pioneers.

However, when their magick threatened to corrupt the natural development of the human race, a rift soon divided the group, with the self-appointed Guardians making it their goal to protect humanity from the influence of either magick or alien technology.

The Guardians destroyed the portals home and waged war on the other group, the Harbingers, who aimed to influence humans with their knowledge, and to reunite the worlds.

A truce was formed with the Guardians agreeing to let the Harbingers live peacefully, so long as they didn't attempt to interfere with humanity's development. The Guardians soon infiltrated the highest rankings of government, where they've been a mainstay for many years, with varying degrees of assistance when deemed necessary, but maintaining their secrecy outside of very close ranks.

BROTHERS DIVIDED

Around 30 years ago, a new portal appeared, very briefly, carrying over a woman and two children. The woman was fleeing Otherworld, and her husband, king of the Valkoer, people infected by an alien race of parasites which live within them. Over time the parasites turn their hosts into vampire-like creatures who absorb the life force (or soul) from their victims, along with their memories.

The woman and her two young sons, John and Caleb, were soon hunted down by her third son, Jacob, a few years older than his brothers. Jacob killed her out of jealousy of being left behind with his cruel father.

Jacob spared his siblings and spent years living among earthlings, feeding off of them, hoping to someday find a way back, as his portal was one-way only.

Caleb, the older of the two boys, was adopted by an FBI agent at the request of Duncan Alderman, a Guardian and Pioneer who is not only a billionaire, but also pulls the strings of much of the government, and the FBI in particular. Duncan recognized the boys as being from his world, and needed to know more about how they arrived on Earth. He also soon developed a bond with Caleb, who he came to regard as the son he'd never had.

Caleb's mind was wiped of his origins and he was able to live as a human for many years.

John, however, was infected with the Darkness, another name for both the parasite, and the powers it offers its hosts. Much like the mythical human vampires, the Valkoer can be killed by sunlight.

John spent much of his youth separated from his brother, put in facilities by the Guardians who tried to both heal him, and at other times tried to harness his powers and turn him into a soldier for their cause. This hypocrisy, that the same group who would destroy magickal artifacts from Otherworld would also utilize the same magick and even try to create a magickal vampire assassin, disgusted John, turning him off to both Duncan and the Guardians.

John eventually escaped, and found a way to squelch the Darkness within him and live among humans. During this time, in the 90s, he fell in love with a woman named Hope Barnett, and they lived together in St. Augustine, Florida. She knew nothing of his past, aside from the stories he made up. Nor did she know of the monster inside him.

Everything was going smoothly until bodies started showing up burned and John was having dreams, and fears, that he was somehow taking lives at night as he slept.

Together with Larry, his personal private eye and apprentice magick-user, John realized that his brother Jacob had found him and was trying to find Caleb as well.

Jacob discovered that he could harness the power of the three brothers to create a portal to Otherworld, which he eagerly longs to return to.

THE GUARDIANS

The Guardians, who control the secret FBI Omega division, cannot let this happen. If Jacob gets back home, there's a good chance he can keep the portal open. An open portal to Otherworld could spell disaster if Harbinger, or the Valkoer on the other side, decide to utilize it and invade Earth, enslaving its people.

The Guardians wanted to kill John, who is hard to find, but if they had to, they would instead kill the unwitting Caleb whom they have in their employ, to prevent Jacob from activating the portal.

John, sensing the growing danger on all fronts, decided to have Hope's mind wiped clean and give her a new life somewhere safe, without any memory of him.

Larry's mind was also wiped of Hope's location to assure her safety.

John and Larry were going to find Jacob and kill him, but soon realized that the danger was too great to Caleb, so they went into hiding for more than a decade.

A DECADE LATER…

In 2011, Duncan found John, informing him that the Guardians were growing restless. Jacob was gaining strength and it was only a matter of time before he found John, and through John, found Caleb.

Duncan forced his hand — sacrifice yourself or your brother will die. Duncan also showed John a picture of Hope and delivered the threat, "We know where she is."

John agreed to sacrifice himself.

He had Larry and a magick-user named Adam perform a spell to revert him to his vampire self, and then bury him in a special coffin. After the spell took effect, two days later, they would raise the coffin and open the slot built into the lid, allowing the sun to kill him.

Once John was dead, the portal could never be opened, and the world, along with Hope and Caleb, would presumably be safe.

However, Larry betrayed John, not wanting to lose his friend, and the person who showed him so much magick — a person who helped him feel less like a loser. Larry and Adam returned to the grave to raise the coffin, but instead of opening the slot and allowing John to die, Larry had Adam wipe John's memory. Larry then shot Adam dead and apologized to John as he slid a paper into John's coffin with an address to Larry's safe house.

John awoke with amnesia, thanks to the memory wipe, unaware of who or what he was.

He wound up accidentally murdering a man named Randy Webster. To John's surprise, he found that Randy was keeping a child in his closet as a sex slave — an 11-year-old named Abigail whose parents died years ago. She was sold by her trashy uncle to Randy and had nobody to care for her.

John wound up taking her with him as he tried to piece together his identity and past.

MEANWHILE...

Caleb was following leads on a serial killer who burned his victims alive. Among those victims, his wife Julia, more than a decade ago. Soon, Caleb found out from his superior, Special Agent in Charge Bob Cromwell, that this killer was no ordinary killer, but rather an alien vampire.

Cromwell manipulated Caleb, never telling him that the alien is his brother, and that in reality, John didn't kill Julia.

John, on the run from Harbinger agents who were now working for Jacob, wound up in a shootout which resulted in Abigail being mortally wounded. John saved the girl, instinctively, by infecting her and turning her into a vampire, too.

John immediately regrets saving her, feeling as if he's sentenced her to an immortal curse which will force her to live life forever as a child, and forever having to kill in order to survive.

Soon, John's mind wipe faded and he remembered everything — including Larry's betrayal. John and Larry got into a heated fight and Larry apologized, begging for forgiveness. Abigail convinced them that with Jacob and the FBI closing in on them, they needed to stick together now more than ever.

Larry recruited a gangster he knows, a giant of a man named Tiny, to put together a small army to go after Jacob.

However, Jacob managed to kidnap Abigail and held her hostage, demanding that John find Caleb and bring him to his compound where they can finally create the portal and Jacob can go home. In exchange for helping him get home, Jacob promised to let Abigail, John, and Caleb all live.

John agreed to the plan while secretly concocting a plan to defeat Jacob once and for all. It began with a blast of truth to his brother, Caleb.

Turns out that more than a decade ago, Jacob and John's presence so close to Caleb who was working the murders in St. Augustine, triggered the parasite laying dormant in him. He woke to himself feeding on his wife. John and Adam discovered him after the act and proceeded to wipe his mind of the event, and the self-torture which would haunt him. They also managed to return him to his normal status, forcing the parasite to go dormant again. Adam built a phrase into the mind wipe, however, which would erase the fabricated memories if ever needed.

John delivered that phrase to Caleb to wake him.

Caleb, now aware of his nature and at least part of his past, was led to Jacob's compound where he followed John's lead and helped open the portal. Caleb, using a knife given to him by his boss to kill John (and which can be used on any Valkoer), was going to kill Jacob the first chance he got.

However, a battle broke out between John's army of

gangsters, led by Tiny who agreed to be turned into a vampire to help even their odds going against the monsters and soldiers that Jacob had accumulated.

In the chaos, Jacob escaped through the portal. Caleb, determined to kill him, followed.

John saw his brother go after Jacob, but his first priority was saving Abigail, who was locked, fittingly enough, in the casket he woke in.

By the time John got to the woods where she was buried, Abigail was gone, though.

She'd been taken by the Guardians, who left a note for John to meet with Duncan Alderman.

Duncan met with John and informed him that they'd sent people into the portal, but nobody has returned. He asked John to work, temporarily, for Omega and help track down any and all Harbinger agents so they can try to figure out how to get Caleb back, or at least prevent an invasion from Otherworld.

John said he doesn't want to be Omega's assassin. Duncan said if he won't, they'll turn Abigail into a soldier for them. She has already demonstrated remarkable feistiness, after all.

John agreed, so long as Abigail was set free, and they continued to leave Hope alone.

John secured Abigail's safety and asked Larry to look after her until such time that his job is over.

Now, we pick up one year later with *Available Darkness: Season Two*...

Prologue

SOMETHING WAS WRONG.

Emilia wasn't sure exactly *what* that something was, but a chill or a scent or a feeling curled through the air like a whiff from distant fire. She could almost feel it bleeding from the creaking branches, whispering in the angry breeze as she and her daughter walked their dog down Crestview at dusk.

It had been more than five years since their move to the burbs, but some instincts born on concrete never left and barely faded, even after you traded asphalt for grass.

Like the inescapable feeling that something horrible was about to happen.

Emilia looked up and down the block, casting her eyes across both rows of overpriced, two-story homes and equally exorbitant vehicles lining either side of the street. Nothing seemed out of place. Lights were on, families were

1

eating dinner and kids were playing outside. A few neighbors were trading gossip on their lawns, leaning over their picket white fences.

Yet, even with nothing out of place, Emilia couldn't shake the vibe.

"Stay close, honey," she called to Kayla, her 7 -year-old daughter, who was walking Mocha, their pain-in-the-ass Chihuahua two houses ahead.

"Okay." Kayla slowed her gait and pulled back on Mocha's leash. The Chihuahua tugged back hard, wanting to go faster, probably so he could piss all over the fire hydrant a half block up.

Emilia reached into her jeans, wrapped her fingers around the zapper Leo bought her the year before when that sex offender moved in down the street, then looked up and down the avenue, guiding her eyes from window to window. They weren't near the offender's house yet, but Emilia couldn't shake the feeling of being watched.

She felt vulnerable, and exposed, out on the street at dusk, even though she shouldn't have, surrounded by the sprawling lawns of Luxury Lane. The temperature seemed to suddenly drop, maybe 10 degrees, agreeing with the wind's sudden momentum and swelling her desire for home.

Mocha moved to the sidewalk, and Emilia hoped the damned dog was finally ready to do his business. Mocha sniffed and pulled away.

Nope, not there. He has to get to that damned fire hydrant down the street.

"Come on, dog," Emilia said through a sigh.

Kayla laughed. She loved the stupid little barking rodent, and didn't care if the tiny beast took 25 minutes to eliminate. Kayla was patient, like her father. Of course, it was easy to be patient when you saw your kid once every two weekends and didn't have to care for the world's most annoying canine.

Emilia never wanted a dog, but if it was a maternal must, then she wanted a *real dog* — a big, sturdy animal to protect them. Not a hyperactive rat. Which is probably why Leo went out and bought Mocha for their daughter's sixth birthday. He got to be the good guy, and give his daughter a "cute" dog, while inserting another annoyance into Emilia's world.

Leo was gone, but his mark, like the dog's territorial pissings, remained.

It could be worse. Be glad he's gone and you got Kayla.

Emilia forced herself to smile, thinking of her annoyingly happy friend Susan's constant advice, "Always smile and never forget to count your blessings."

Emilia counted her blessings; she was healthy, had a job and a happy, well-adjusted child. But she still couldn't shake the creeping dread. As if the weather were reading her mind, smoky clouds began gathered ahead at an almost alarming speed. An icy wind started to scream.

Something's wrong. Get back home.

"Come on, Honey."

Mocha started barking like crazy as Kayla turned. "What is it, Mom?"

Mocha ripped himself from Kayla's grip and tore into a run, dragging the leash behind him as he raced up the street toward the oncoming storm.

"Mocha!" Kayla screamed, chasing her dog.

Emilia's heart pounded as she called after her daughter, a dozen horrible scenarios racing through her mind — from the dog getting hit by a car to Kayla meeting the bumper's front instead, plus another several she couldn't bear to think on, lest she tempt fate into turning them true.

"Kayla! Stop!"

Emilia screamed louder, but her daughter kept running after the dog.

Emilia followed, racing as fast as she could as the clouds above turned swollen and black, rolling through the sky.

Tornado!

Wind howled, growing angry, as the highest branches began to violently whip the air. Thunder boomed. Lightning crashed, all too fast, inky clouds swirling through the street and casting her quickly shifting world beneath a pall of dark fog.

Emilia couldn't see her baby girl. She ran forth, screaming, "Kayla!"

"Mom?" Her daughter's call was a whisper ahead, but Emilia couldn't see her through the darkness.

She pressed on into the swirling chaos, pelted by chunks of hail and God-only-knew what kind of debris. "Kayla!"

She squinted, peering through the pall, churning like a freight train above and around her.

She caught sight of Kayla in the distance, running down the street and straight into the thick fog. It billowed forth and back on itself before being sucked into a vortex that appeared in the center of the street for a moment, before it disappeared.

In its place was a perfect circle of light suspended in the air a foot off the ground, measuring maybe 20 feet in every direction.

The world was still, so calm that Emilia could hear her breath as she approached the disc in confusion, awe, and fear. The disc, she discovered, wasn't made of light, nor was it a disc so much as a window revealing an impossibility on the other side: her street replaced with rolling woodlands basking beneath a brilliant sun.

4

Kayla and Mocha were nowhere.

"Kayla!" Emilia screamed, racing toward the giant window. Closer, she realized it wasn't a window, but a hole in the world.

What the hell?

Emilia slowed her approach, hearing and feeling a buzzing, growing in volume as it vibrated around the hole. The forest on the other side was deep and lush, real as anything Emilia had ever seen.

She felt like Alice, staring through the Looking Glass.

This can't be real.

"Kayla!" She moved closer, looked up and down the street to see if anyone else noticed the giant, floating hole in the world. Mrs. Ferguson and Molly were standing in the street, a quarter block away, mouths hanging half to the asphalt.

So I'm not the only one seeing this. I'm not crazy.

Emilia stepped closer, close as she dared, battling every instinct to run into the hole, just as her daughter seemed to do. She hadn't seen Kayla step through;, she'd seen her rushing in the fog before disappearing completely. Perhaps, Emilia told herself, Kayla was on the hole's far side, where maybe the street continued.

She circled the floating orb, keeping her eyes on the woods beyond, scanning for any sign of Kayla or Mocha. She finally reached the circle's edge and saw that the street did continue on the other side, though the floating hole was so thin you couldn't see it from the opposite end. Just a thin, jagged black line floating like a zipper.

As Emilia slowly rounded to the other side, her heart leaped in her throat, her eyes falling on the forest again, this time from a different angle. The sun lit a soft blue horizon with a wicked flicker of orange.

Something surfaced through the tree line.

"Kayla!" she cried out, inviting her daughter into her parted arms. "I'm here!"

Words were spilled from her mouth before she realized the shape wasn't her daughter, or her dog.

It was nothing she'd ever seen — something that looked like a man, but wrapped in angry swath of swirling darkness.

She stopped mid-wave, afraid to draw further attention from the whatever-it-was. But she was too late. The creature was a blur of fast-moving darkness, soaring toward Emilia. Two seconds later it stood at the aperture's edge, its bright blue eyes almost glowing as they stared into her soul.

It reached out, stretching an arm from its impossible world into hers.

Emilia screamed, turned, and tore down her street as fast as she could, away from the darkness, glancing back just in time to see the dark shape fully emerge from the hole and step onto her street.

She spun from the asphalt, stumbled onto her neighbor's dewy grass, and ran through her yard, desperate to lose the *thing* before it found her.

Emilia never saw what tripped her, sending her to the ground and under a blanket of black.

ONE

John

LATER THAT NIGHT

BRANCHES SWAYED in the breeze like bony fingers scratching the wind as John waited in the mobile command unit, shifting uncomfortably in his seat, staring at the bank of monitors displaying ugly news, interviews with frightened residents and Homeland Security officers explaining to the public — without any actual explanation — why an entire neighborhood was being evacuated and cordoned off.

In the first moments following the event, the news anchors pondered the possibilities: terrorist attack, chemical spill, or another in a long line of mass shootings which seemed to punctuate the news every month or three. But none of them came close to the truth. The portal had opened — an extraterrestrial, magickal event. The Army had been called in to erect a tented barrier around the portal, to prevent prying eyes from seeing inside, and anyone else from accidentally walking through, at least from this side.

While the first portal, created a year earlier, was contained in Jacob's compound, hidden from the public, this one had split open in the middle of a suburban neighborhood and spilled its horror in plain sight.

Within an hour, jittery, blurred cell phone footage caught by neighbors was being played on every channel.

Everyone wanted to know what in the hell this *thing* was.

Experts were trotted out, calling it everything from a wormhole to a government experiment gone awry to some sort of freak natural phenomena. Wormhole was the most accurate description, of course, though no one could possibly know what John and Omega knew — that this was a portal created by magick, a link to Otherworld, and in all likelihood, the swirling wellspring of a gathering threat.

"So, who do you think did this?" Commander Mike Mathews appeared behind John. "Someone on this side or the other?"

John stared at the monitors within the barrier, showing the portal with various colored overlays measuring the surrounding energy and other stuff John didn't understand, despite working with Omega for a year.

"I don't know who on this side could do it. Is anyone left in Harbinger who could even do this?"

"So you think Jacob did this from over there? And if so, can he create more?"

Mathews stared at John as if John was stashing secret knowledge and not sharing. Mathews was a short muscular man in his late 40s, and one of the most deft John had ever seen in shifting gears. One minute he was smiling and working reporters like a used car salesman unloading a lemon. The next minute, always behind closed doors, he was an intense, brooding, control freak on the verge of snapping. John tolerated the man because they worked well enough together, at least so far, but he could see their harmony grinding to a halt the minute Mathews woke on the wrong side of bed.

John sighed. "I don't know. If he created this, then yes, I'd say he can make more. But isn't the bigger question, *why?*"

Mathews' phone buzzed from his pocket. He turned from John, fished it from his pants, and brought it to his ear. "Mathews."

Brow furrowed: "Really? What does she remember?"

"Okay, set up an interview in Unit Seven. Make sure no one sees her."

Mathews ended the call and dropped the phone in his pocket. "The passed out woman's come to. Said her daughter's missing and someone came through the portal."

"Came through?" John leaned forward.

"She doesn't remember much. So we're going to question her in the Seven truck. See what she can tell us."

"Jesus." John's heartbeat gathered speed, the dread of something bad, like his brother Jacob, coming through. But there was also some excitement at the thought that his good brother, Caleb, also lost in the portal might have found his way home. "You think it's Caleb?"

"I don't know, but we're gonna find out."

Omega had people sitting watch on the first portal for a full year, waiting for anyone — or *anything* — to come through. They even sent three of their people in, though none returned. It was six months since anyone had attempted to cross through. John wondered if maybe one of their men had finally made it back, and if so, what they might have to report.

Mathews said, "Assuming the worst, Jacob's mounting

forces, and has sent someone through. If so, we've gotta find whoever crossed over — before shit gets bad."

~

MOBILE COMMAND UNIT Seven was Omega's designated interview truck, a 30-foot vehicle outfitted the same as their other units, but with an interview room where they could question witnesses and hostile suspects out of sight from others.

John stood in the corner of the windowless interview room as Mathews pulled out a chair for the woman, Emilia Serraben, so she could sit at the table across from him.

"Can we get you anything?" Mathews was pleasant, almost saccharine. "A drink or something to eat?"

"No, thanks," she said, blowing her red nose into a white tissue. "I just want to find my daughter Kayla."

"That's why you're here," Mathews smiled, continuing his calming, caring facade. "I'm going to ask you some questions which will help us get to the bottom of this."

"What is that thing? Have you seen it before?" Emilia's eyes brimmed with tears, desperate for solace, clearly hoping Mathews might offer a branch to grasp — anything to help the woman believe her daughter was safe.

"We have our best people on it," Mathews lied. "We hope to have your daughter back as soon as possible."

John swallowed his disgust, loathing Mathews' manipulation of a scared and shaking mother, but also fully aware that they had to mine as much information as possible from her to help them find whoever stepped through the portal.

Emilia explained how she and her daughter were walking their dog when a storm appeared from out of the blue. Next thing she knew, her daughter was racing into a fog. It vanished, leaving behind a "hole in the world," but no trace of the girl.

"Do you think it's possible she didn't go through? That she's still out there somewhere, lost?"

"Anything is possible," Mathews said. "And we have more than two dozen agents and officers out there combing the neighborhood to find out. We'll find her, Mrs. Serraben, I promise you."

His smile was pure comfort as he extended a hand to Emilia. She took it. Mathews squeezed, then lowered his voice, "You told one of our agents you saw someone come through the portal. Can you describe what you saw?"

She withdrew her hand to blow her nose, then shook her head. "It all happened so fast, everything is a blur. I didn't get a good look who or *what* came through. One minute, I was standing, then the next, I was flat on the ground. I came to in the ambulance. That was when one of your agents asked me to speak with you."

"You said 'who or what' came through. You saying it might not have been a person?"

"I don't know. I mean, I *think* it was a person. It was tall like a person, and standing upright. But it was so *fast*. At least it seemed that way, but I don't know if that's because of the hole, and the person only seemed fast ... " Emilia's voice cracked. "Or what."

The woman sounded less certain by the word. Mathews continued encouraging her to recount the story, repeatedly, using different words each time, hoping to elicit some small nugget of information, but the man was getting nowhere. She was scared for her little girl and growing more restless by the moment, looking past Mathews and John, at the door, wanting to go search for her daughter.

"Can I please go now? Every minute I'm in here is a minute I'm not looking for Kayla."

Mathews maintained his calm façade. "Certainly. Just give us one moment, please." He smiled at Emilia and ushered John from the room. Door closed, Mathews met his eyes. "I need you to get the info from her."

John swallowed, unsure he'd heard correctly. "What?"

"I need you to find out what she saw. Extract the memory."

"I'm not killing her. Can't we get Skinner in here? He can get her memories without burning her to death."

"We don't have time. Skinner's in New York chasing a lead on something else. We have no idea what came through the portal. And we need to get on top of this now, John."

"We're not killing a civilian! She just lost her kid for Christ's sake!"

Any pretense that John was close to Mathews' equal faded as his boss's face twisted into a display of impatient anger. "If we don't find out what happened, many more civilians could die, and likely will. You know what we're up against, John. You know what Jacob is capable of. We're talking about the greater good here. Must we *really* have this conversation *again*?"

"There's a difference between killing Harbingers and a civilian!" John tried to keep the growl from his voice. "I'll be the company hitman, fine, but not if it means killing innocents."

"I'm not asking, John. Get in there, *now*."

The look in Mathews' eyes was the only threat given, or needed. Omega held the trump card — Hope. They knew where she was. John didn't. They'd already made it perfectly clear that they would do whatever they had to if it meant keeping John in line.

He glared at Mathews.

One slave, and one master. So long as Omega held Hope over John, the equation would never change.

He went back through the door, and looked back at Mathews as if to ask, *Will you be joining me?*

Mathews turned his back to John.

Pussy.

John returned to the room alone and met the weeping woman's tormented eyes. The concern inside them had deepened, as if sensing his hesitancy.

"What's happening?" she asked.

John approached the table and sat opposite Emilia. Her eyes found his gloved hands, and she looked back up. "Did you find her? Did you find Kayla?"

John shook his head then opened his mouth. His voice wore the slightest crack. "Is there anything else you can remember about who came through the portal?" He hoped she would remember something, anything, which might allow him to spare her life.

Emilia's face flushed with frustrated anger. "I told you all everything I know. Please, can I leave now?"

John slipped off his gloves, and Emilia's eyes fell to his hands, as if somehow sensing the danger in his empty palms.

He held out his hands, without saying a word, hoping she'd take them as she'd taken Mathews'.

She reached out, her fingers stretching to embrace his.

No!

He yanked his hands back, startling Emilia.

"What the—"

John ignored her, jumped out of his chair and stormed through the doorway, back into the hallway where Mathews stood, staring past John into the room.

Before Mathews could open his mouth, John shook his head. "I'm not doing it."

Mathews gritted his teeth, then pushed past John and went back into the room. *What is he doing?* John turned just as Mathews retrieved his gun from inside his jacket and fired at Emilia, directly into her chest.

John screamed, then raced into the room, his hands ready to suck the life from Mathews.

Mathews' gun fell to the floor as an onyx blade dropped from his sleeve and landed in his palm. He thrust the blade out between himself and John, a warning for John to keep his distance.

"You know what this will do to you. So I suggest you get to work. Draw her memories before she bleeds out."

John swallowed his anger and fell to his knees beside Emilia, sprawled on the ground, looking up at John, confused and crying as her body emptied.

John whispered, "I'm so sorry" and set his hands on her head. He wished there was a way to do this that didn't hurt the victims so badly. If only he could kill with a gentle touch, to offer a painless exit.

They bonded, his fire spreading through Emilia, sending her body into convulsions, her eyes into giant balls bulging from her head. Her mouth opened wide enough for a scream, but none escaped. Her body blistered. John felt Emilia's memories surging through him in a tsunami of rolling emotions.

He closed his eyes, focused on the torrent, and tried to ignore the overwhelming fear and pain coursing through her and into him, searching for the memories required from the million inside.

He found them — reliving the woman's final moments, experiencing her creeping unease as the weather changed, fear turned to terror as Kayla chased the dog, then her unflinching horror as the portal opened before her.

He watched as something appeared on the other side

of the portal. Whatever it was moved fast. Large and dark, its form too blurry. John slowed the memory, watching as the blur grew to barely more than a shadow.

It was a man, but not a human: His brother, Jacob, back on Earth.

But why?

And where is Caleb?

John stared into the memory of his evil brother's eyes, feeling as if he were staring at death incarnate.

Is Duncan right? Is whatever waiting on the portal's other side gathering forces? And if so, why?

No one was safe until Jacob was found.

TWO

Abigail
———————

"IS THAT HER?" Abigail stared through the binoculars at the woman standing outside the nightclub with a small huddle of partiers, laughing and smiling like she hadn't murdered her 2-year-old son four years before. "She looks so different than she does on TV."

"Yup," Larry nodded, staring through his own binoculars beside her in the van, a block from the club. "That's *the* Karen McKenna."

Abigail zoomed in on the child killer. She didn't look anything like the sad-faced mother in the orange jumpsuit Abigail had watched on the news footage she found online. Looking at the woman now, with her well-tended blonde tresses and pretty new dress, from the diamonds around her neck to the shiny shoes on her feet, you'd never know she was a monster. She looked so *normal*.

Abigail looked at the people with her, two men and a woman, all of them laughing and smiling like Karen. "Do you think the people with her know who she is?"

"*Everyone* knows who she is. She's a fucking celebrity."

"How can they stand to be with her? Do they think she's innocent?"

"Well, she did get off. But I don't think it matters much to people like that. She's famous."

"She's famous for killing her child!" Abigail said, laying down her binoculars and looking at Larry. No matter how many bad people they'd killed, and no matter how many horrible things had happened to Abigail in her 12 years on the planet, she was still surprised by the dark depths of humanity.

"Fame is fame," Larry said, still peering through his binoculars. "Ah, there he is."

Abigail raised her binoculars and followed Larry's line of sight until it ended at the muscular bald man standing behind Karen. He was wearing a dark suit and a Bluetooth ear piece, as if he were Secret Service, rather than Murder Mommy's bodyguard.

"Think we can take him? *Without* killing him?"

Larry looked over, grinning. "I dunno, he's got one of those douche bag Bluetooths, isn't that an offense worthy of punishment?"

Abigail laughed, even though she was too hungry for Larry's humor. "If that were the case, we'd never run out of people to feed on!"

"Yeah, you really need to relax the rules a little, Abi. I say we add ironic hipsters to our list. We could hit the Apple store, Starbucks and that vegan place that just opened up on Crouch Avenue and stock up for the year."

Abigail looked through the binoculars again and saw Karen's bodyguard retrieving a Mercedes from the valet.

"Looks like it's showtime." Larry set his binoculars on the seat and keyed the engine. "You sure you're up for this?"

Abigail turned to Larry, waiting for his eyes to meet

hers. "Yes, I'm sure. Besides, I don't know how much longer I can go."

Larry looked Abigail up and down. Though he hid his reaction well, she could tell he was concerned. Her skin was almost gray, like it always got when she went too long between feedings. And while she wasn't staring at the edge of death, as she had been once five months before, the hunger weakened her significantly. And it hurt — a pain that she somehow felt both in her head and her gut, though she wasn't actually eating people, but rather their life force.

"Okay," Larry said, putting the van into drive and drifting into the street to follow the notorious Karen McKenna from the club.

They were tailing the Mercedes for nearly 10 minutes when Abigail finally asked what she knew Larry was dreading to hear — a question he'd answered a dozen times before.

"What if she didn't do it?"

"She did," Larry said, holding his eyes to the road. "We've gone over this, Abi. Several times."

"But the jury must've had *some* reason to let her go."

"Juries fuck up. All the time. In this case, everyone fucked up. From police botching evidence, to prosecutors being too stupid to work around it to the judge. Hell, I wouldn't be surprised if her daddy paid off half the jury!"

"Yeah," Abigail sighed. "I guess."

"Guess nothing. She did it. Goddamn, she practically did a Google search for 'How can I, Karen Theresa McKenna, murder my child and get away with it?'"

Abigail chortled, this time a sincere, deep belly laugh.

"You're right," she said. "You know how I get."

Larry's sigh said far more than any words. Abigail

looked down at her gloved hands, then back up at Larry, "I'm not gonna wimp out this time. I promise."

"I don't mind if you do. I know you don't *want* to kill anyone who doesn't deserve it. I get it. That's what makes you so much better than all these fuckers, Abi, believe me. If it doesn't happen tonight, I'll find someone else."

Abigail shook her head. "No, I don't want to put you in danger again. We'll kill her. Tonight, I swear."

A promise followed by a swear. There was no way she could back out now.

~

THEY SAT outside Karen's house — one of many her father had scattered across the country — waiting for the bodyguard to return to his car after walking Karen inside and presumably checking the place out. She'd been free for more than two years, and out of the news for one, yet judging from her bodyguard's actions, you'd think there were constant threats against her life. Maybe there were.

Abigail remembered the red anger burning from the sea of faces in the footage Larry had shown her from when the "innocent" verdict was read. The murder happened in Miami, and they were clear across the country in California, but the case drew international attention, mostly because of Karen's father, Peter McKenna, billionaire owner of the globally recognized timeshare company, McKenna Resorts. Abigail figured some other people wanting to see justice had probably made threats on her life, though she doubted many would go to the lengths she and Larry would to dispense justice.

They'd spent months researching Karen's case. Larry reached out to his network who knew people involved — always keeping enough of a distance to avoid an eventual link back to Karen's murder, of course. He'd also done some black hat-type research, hacking into Karen McKenna's cell and computer records, and finding several interesting tidbits that hadn't even made the relentless press coverage, which made Larry all the more suspect of Peter McKenna paying people off.

Larry said that there was zero doubt in his mind that Karen McKenna murdered her son. For Abigail, that would have to be enough. Tonight, she would feed. And tonight, Karen's son, Kyle, would finally find justice — once they took care of the bodyguard.

ABIGAIL APPROACHED THE BODYGUARD, sitting in his car on the street outside Karen's house. She was wearing black pants and a purple long-sleeved shirt to cover her ungloved hands. As she moved close enough for the guard to finally notice her, she pulled her long dark hair away from her face to display her tearstained cheeks.

"Please, help me, Mister," Abigail cried out as she broke into a run toward the car.

The guard lowered his phone and looked up, startled, then immediately drew a gun on Abigail.

Oh crap, he knows.

No — he's just scared. Back up.

Abigail stuck with her ruse, stopping about six feet from the front of the car, raising her hands to show she meant no harm. "Please," she cried, meeting his eyes. The bodyguard was muscular, with a movie star's jaw. The type of guy who likely never lost his cool. "There's a man after me!"

"What?" The guard hopped from his car. He was tall.

Abigail stayed put. She could feel his suspicion as he

looked her over, then up at the street behind her. "Who's after you?"

Larry's van surfaced from the black, high-brights blaring down on them.

"Oh, God! He found me!" Abigail started to run past the man, as if fleeing Larry.

"It's okay," he said, looking down at Abigail in reassurance. "You're okay."

The guard turned back to the approaching van, lifted his gun, and aimed. With the guard's full attention on his target, Abigail delivered a blast of energy at the back of his head and sent him to the ground.

Larry killed the van lights as he rolled up, jumped out from the driver's side door, and slipped plastic restraints around the guard's wrists. The guard moaned as he tried to open his eyes.

Larry shoved a rag in his mouth, then sprayed his face with something magickal which Larry called moon dust, though it also had another name Abigail didn't remember. The man looked up at Larry, his eyes rolled into the back of his head, and he fell back, passed out. Larry grabbed his cell phone, dropped it in his pocket, then slipped his hands under the man's armpits, hefted him up, pushed him back into his car and closed the door.

"You ready?" Larry asked Abigail.

"Yes," she said, even though she wasn't.

～

KAREN MCKENNA SPOTTED LARRY FIRST, his black ski mask pulled tight over his face, as she came from her bathroom holding a glass of wine.

The glass fell to the floor, spraying shards of glass

across the room. She turned to run toward her bedroom at the end of the hall.

Abigail, also wearing a mask, was waiting, aiming a pistol at the murderer.

"Stop!" Abigail shouted.

Karen did exactly that, her eyes wide and nervous.

"W-What do you want?" She fell a step back, looking between Larry and Abigail.

"The truth," Larry said, closing the distance between himself and the woman, then pressing his barrel of his gun into her temple.

"Don't! Please … I—I don't know what you want."

"He just told you," Abigail said, her voice muffled, though she imagined Karen must've already figured out she was young based on her size.

"Truth about what?" Karen stared at Larry, her whole body trembling.

Larry answered, "What happened to your son?"

Something in Karen's expression changed, fear twisting into something, which for a moment looked like the cousin of defiance. She buried it immediately, but not so fast that Abigail hadn't noticed.

Karen started to cry. "Is *that* what this is about? Why can't you people leave me alone? Someone killed him. I didn't do it."

"Bullshit," Larry said. "You have five seconds to start getting honest."

"Who are you people?" Karen yelled, looking from Larry to Abigail, then back to Larry.

Larry smiled, "Inquiring minds that wanna know. Five, four, three … "

Karen wiped tears from her cheeks. "I'm telling you the truth!"

"We'll find out soon enough," Larry said.

Karen was facing Larry when Abigail pulled her hands from her pockets and moved in for the kill. Abigail had been worried that she'd have second thoughts about Karen's guilt, but her hunger was consuming enough to drive rational thought far from her brain. It had been too long since she'd fed. The young, vibrant woman, supple and thrumming with energy, was waiting to be feasted upon — guilty or not.

Abigail's hands found Karen's shoulders, exposed by the gauzy scoop of her low cut dress, and connected.

Karen fell to the ground with a rattle, shaking as a scream lost its life inside her throat. Abigail closed her eyes, surrendering to the currents of energy coursing from the woman's body into hers, fleeing as if born to feed.

The feeding was bliss …

… until memories poured into Abigail's mind.

Having to see, experience, and worst of all, *feel*, her victims' memories were always the hardest parts of feeding for Abigail. Because she fed on the worst sorts of people, their memories were usually filled with something Abigail was already too familiar with, abuse — *upon* victim first, and then *from* perpetrator later — an endless cycle of misery.

Karen McKenna's memories were no different.

Flooded with horrible recall of her father's violent verbal abuse, a million images hatched from their shells in the depths of Karen's earliest memories; the horrible names, telling her she was a worthless accident, a disappointment compared to her brother.

Jesus. Stop it!

The flow of memories, once started, could rarely be stopped. While John had said they could be controlled with practice, Abigail had yet to master the flow, and it wasn't as if John was around to instruct her. Abigail was forced to

23

bear witness to all the misery of Karen's life as it unspooled in her mind like an open pit filled with rotting bodies.

Abigail let go of Karen, sending her burnt, and now empty, body falling back to the floor. Abigail stumbled backward, barely aware of her surroundings, a prisoner of memories spilling in front of her.

Just a few more minutes. It'll be over soon, she told herself.

The knot at the back of Abigail's neck eased in a rare moment of happiness — a light in the darkness, as memory turned to the birth of Karen's son, Kyle.

Sure, he was an accident with her scumbag boyfriend Marcus but her heart melted the moment she saw him, and was a puddle as she held his eight pounds and two ounces in her arm's cradle. Karen fell ... in love; felt true love for the first time ever. The unfeigned, unmitigated love of parent for child. A pure love, unlike anything her parents had ever given to her.

Karen was, for the first time in her life, happy.

In that moment, Abigail felt the woman's happiness, and wanted to slow the memories of Karen and her baby boy so she could live in them longer. But the sun was quick to set on Karen McKenna's flickering joy.

It started with Marcus. Karen thought she could make something of a "normal" life with him, scumbag or no. But other than her beautiful baby boy, Marcus only brought misery, mostly through drugs — painkillers first, meth later — and too many lies. Marcus wanted nothing to do with Kyle, seeing his son only as a burden, no different from how her own father saw her.

One day, a full darkness eclipsed her sun, then held it forever in place. Karen was passed out from a night of too much partying with Marcus. When she woke, Kyle was in his bed, blue and dead.

She had no idea what happened. Her father sent some

men in suits over, said they'd take care of everything. They took Kyle away, reassuring her that everything would be okay. *How the hell can it ever be okay?* Kyle, the only good thing in her life, the only good thing she'd ever done, was dead.

Her father suspected Marcus — who had left early that morning, a rarity for him to be awake, let alone gone before noon — had killed Kyle. Marcus disappeared, and the police immediately turned their attention to Karen.

She spun into the deepest depression, sick with the knowledge that she was responsible for her son's death. Once arrested, Karen hoped for death. But her father would never allow it. He bought off everyone to ensure his daughter would never see the inside a prison.

But Daddy hadn't been able to keep her from the prison of her making, and she descended into drugs, partying, and bad relationships, all trying to fill a void which could never be filled.

Now, her pain was finally over.

Memory crashed into the present and left Abigail shaking in brutal sobs on the floor. She was fed, and her body whole. But everything else felt wrong.

Larry moved toward her, his hands landing softly on her shoulders as he scooped her up from the floor. "Come on, Abi, I'll take you home."

He carried her from the house like a rag doll.

"We were wrong, Larry," Abigail wept, "We were wrong."

~

ABIGAIL SAID nothing on the long ride back to Washington, sitting in the front seat, trying not to see the occasional flash of memories she'd stolen along with Karen's life.

Larry tried talking to her, tried to apologize, tried to comfort her, but every time he opened his mouth, it felt like an icy blade beneath her overheated skin.

"Please," she said, retreating into a fetal ball in the front seat.

Abigail wished she could sit in the back, but that's where "the body" was, and Larry had yet to dump it. Karen's life had been mostly pain, with a rare spark of joy. Now she was a battery of memory in a thief's head, with nothing left of who she was, save the charred remains that would soon be buried in the woods.

Abigail let tears wash her cheeks, believing at first she was crying for Karen. And though she was, there was something else there, too. The little girl who could never grow older was also crying for yet one more piece of herself — forever lost to the creeping darkness.

THREE

Larry

LARRY WOKE an hour before the sun was due to set.

Being on Abigail's schedule meant he only had a few hours in the morning and another few in the early evening to himself. He'd always been a night person, so the adjustment to sleeping through daylight wasn't too difficult. While their house was large enough — three bedrooms, one for each of them plus space for his office — living with a perpetual preteen girl, and the frequent moodiness that came with it, made his alone time all the more precious.

He grabbed an ice-cold Mountain Dew from the fridge and sat in the middle of his three monitors, scrolling through his many alerts to see if anything worthwhile had surfaced while he'd slept.

Abigail was good for at least two weeks, without feeding, but Larry liked to search ahead of time for someone who met their criteria so they had enough time for all the requisite research, thereby ensuring they had someone truly deserving of death. He'd blown it last night with Karen McKenna, and Abigail gave him the silent treatment the entire trip home, then added to the onslaught

27

upon their return. She went to bed without a word, so she'd probably be extra annoying today.

Seeing nobody even close to local that they should or could pursue, Larry sifted through his email looking for word from John.

Nothing.

It had been a few months since he'd last heard from his old friend, and more than a year since he'd seen him.

Communication was limited to the rare email from one of John's many aliases. Emails were always the same — photos with encrypted data buried inside. John's last message was asking Larry if he had found Hope.

"No, nothing yet," Larry sent back in an encrypted message.

As far as anyone in Larry's network could confirm, Hope was a ghost. He'd considered hiring a Tracker to find her, but John insisted that he involve only his most trusted sources. There were scant few people Larry or John fully trusted, particularly since John was working on behalf of the Guardians and Omega, kidnapping or killing a steady stream of Otherworlders, depending on which rumors you believed. It would've been one thing, rounding up Harbinger, the group which had been helping Jacob, but innocents were being targeted: Otherworlders, hybrids and humans alike, none of whom had taken a side in the war.

Larry still had friends in the community of aliens along with those humans, like himself, who'd come to learn from the aliens, but no one he trusted to track Hope. Adam would have been able to help, but Larry burned that bridge when he killed him.

On a daily basis, Larry and Abigail had only each other.

Larry didn't mind so much — he'd always been a loner. But he could tell the loneliness was weighing on Abigail.

She didn't have John, the man who turned her and thus forged her soul's deepest bond, but she also had no friends or family, things most girls her age desperately needed. She and Larry got along reasonably well, but Larry felt that she needed someone either closer in age, or without twig and berries between their legs to rain a more positive — and decidedly more female — influence onto her life.

Larry turned his attention to the usual stream of news feeds and saw a mention of Karen McKenna's disappearance at the top. Her bodyguard was facing all sorts of questions, and "experts" were already wondering if Ms. McKenna had fled the country.

Yeah, keep thinking that.

A minute later Larry was checking for updates on the newly opened portal. Of course, there was no *real* news. Nor was anyone calling it a portal, since few knew what they were looking at, and those who did weren't saying shit. Larry had known what he was looking at the second he saw the footage on a video leak website.

The portal was exactly like the one Jacob forced his brothers to help him open a year earlier.

Hearing nothing from John made Larry nervous. Surely he'd be working on this case — unless he had somehow gone over. Larry certainly hoped he hadn't, though it was impossible to be sure. While he'd once been able to connect with John telepathically, their connection hadn't been the same since John insisted on getting wiped and buried. There was a time he would've felt his best friend nearby. Now, proximity meant nothing. John could be near, far or possibly dead, though Larry believed he would've sensed *something* if his old buddy had died.

He wondered if Abigail had sensed anything. If so, she hadn't said. Then again, her psychic link to John had been broken for a year. Larry wasn't sure, but suspected John had blocked her from his mind to make the separation easier on the child.

Things weren't easy for Abigail, and though Larry was supposed to be a father figure, he felt like a worse father than Homer Simpson, and not much better than that dipshit on the news who left his kid in the hot car while he went into a strip club to get shit-faced while watching titties bounce.

A girl Abigail's age needed structure, but what sort of structure or normal life could a child vampire ever hope to have? It wasn't like she could go to school or make friends.

A sudden idea swelled Larry's mood.

Friends. School.

He thought of Katya, the cute, young au pair who worked for the Radley family across the street. He'd spoken with her briefly a few months back when she accidentally locked herself out of the house and needed help getting back inside before the family's 2-year-old girl started crying. Larry helped her inside, and was impressed by how well she handled the sobbing child once back behind the unlocked door. She seemed like a genuinely pleasant, honest person, and someone who loved kids.

And as luck would have it, the Radleys were moving to Connecticut soon.

Larry rose from his seat, about to race out the door when he caught his reflection in the living room mirror. He looked like a slob.

Larry raced upstairs and found a decent button down white shirt — wrinkled, but acceptable. He wasn't getting the iron. He threw on a pair of jeans to replace his sweatpants, ran a brush through his thick mop of hair, wiped his thick black-framed glasses clean, then raced outside and across the street. He rang the doorbell of the beautifully landscaped two-story house, while stealing a glance back at his rental. Though Larry's house was large, and perfectly nice, it was nowhere near as well-kept as the Radley Residence. You could tell they cared about their home, whereas Larry did just enough to keep the assholes in the Rosewood Homeowners Association from kicking him out of the gated community.

Katya appeared in the window beside the door, smiling as she recognized him.

Katya opened the door and said "Hi," in a barely-there Russian accent. Her long blonde hair and blue eyes reminded Larry of a Swedish model he once knew, and he made sure to mute his natural inclination to flirt. First, she was too young — in her early 20s, while Larry was 37, and lately feeling 47. Second, he wanted to hire her, not date her. Plus, she seemed like a good girl, not at all the sort to tolerate his shit.

"Hi, Katya, how's it going?"

"Good, and you?"

"Good, good," Larry said, "Listen, I'm wondering if you've got a job lined up after the Radleys move."

"Why? Do you have a child?"

"Not exactly," Larry said, suddenly realizing that Katya had never seen Abigail. Worse, he hadn't thought of a way to explain Abigail's relation to him. It wasn't like he could tell the truth — that she was sold by her uncle to a pedophile monster who kept her in a closet until John came along and killed the fucker, saved the girl then turned her into a vampire after she'd been shot, accidentally by Larry, during a shootout with a squad of soldiers, all of them working for an alien. He imagined the door slamming in his face 10 words in.

Yet, he couldn't call Abi his adopted daughter.

Can I?

He wasn't sure, and in that moment of uncertainty that

inflated the pause for too long, Larry was afraid Katya would grow suspicious.

"Well, it's sort of complicated," he shrugged. "I'm taking care of her, for a relative who can't. But she's a super sweet kid. She's 11, and I just need someone who can maybe look after her when I work at night, maybe tutor her? Do you tutor?"

"Well, I'm not a tutor, no, but I could help her study if you have coursework or something. Wait a second," she raised her eyebrows. "You said look after her *at night?* How late?"

Larry gave Katya his widest smile, "Yeah, about that … she's got a rare medical condition where she sleeps during the day and is up all night."

Katya stared at Larry as if standing inches from bull-shit. He held his smile, frozen on his feet, waiting for the door to close on him. "I don't need you to stay up all night, just a few hours, maybe, from like seven to eleven or so. Just to keep her company, and let me finish a few extra hours of work."

"What kind of work do you do at that hour?"

"I'm a private eye, but I mostly handle one client, a super wealthy guy, who pays me well to run his security, do background checks on employees, stuff like that. Most of the work I can do from home during the day, but some things need me to leave the house, but I can't leave an 11-year-old girl at home alone, ya know. Too many creepy people out there."

Katya held his eyes, peering deeper as if trying to figure out exactly how full of shit Larry actually was. She seemed like a smart girl who could smell his bullshit. Just when he thought Katya was going to turn him away, she said, "What's her condition?"

"Um, I forget what they call it. But between you and

me, I think most of it's in her head, a psychological thing. She's been through a lot, and I don't want to make her feel bad about it, so I try not to pry or bring it up. I just deal with her as she is."

Katya smiled. "It's later than I'm used to working. How many nights do you think you would need me?"

"You give me five nights, a few hours a night, or at least four, and I'll match whatever the Radleys are paying."

"Match? For less hours?" Katya said, her eyebrows raised.

"Yes," Larry nodded. "I'm desperate to find someone soon, and I can tell you're a good person — I can trust you. I *can* trust you, right? You're not a serial killer, or worse, an actress from some MTV show?"

Katya laughed, a sweet chirp of genuine mirth. Larry couldn't help but love it, mostly because it sounded both pure and true, and given how many fake laughs he'd heard from girls, Katya's sounded like a promise.

Try not to flirt. Try not to flirt.

"No," Katya said with mock shock. "I could never be an actress."

Larry laughed. "I dunno, you've got the looks."

Dumb ass! Dumb ass! Stop it!

Larry quickly changed the subject before awkward silence yawned too far. "When could you start?"

"Tomorrow is my last day here, so I could start tomorrow night if you like, but first, I have to meet, um, what's her name?"

"Abi, short for Abigail."

"That's a pretty name," Katya said, again sounding like she meant it. "I'd like to meet Abi first. I'd hate to say yes and have us not mesh. Girls at that age can be ... "

She trailed off as if trying to think of the least offensive word.

Larry added, "Bitchy?"

Katya laughed, "I was thinking *sensitive*."

"Yeah," Larry said. "That's what I meant, too. She's a great kid, really. So, would you like to swing by tonight some time and meet Abi?"

"I'd love that," Katya nodded.

The Radleys' small daughter suddenly appeared behind Katya, looking up at Larry while sucking on a purple pacifier.

"Hi," Larry said, waving from behind with a giant grin.

The little girl's eyes doubled their size, then she spun around and ran off into another room.

"Gabi," Katya called after the girl, laughing. She turned from the girl's back to Larry. "I'm sorry. She's shy."

"No, it's okay. I have that effect on most women, no matter their age. Hey, Gabi and Abi, what a coincidence."

Katya laughed again, and Larry resisted the urge to pile the charm any more than he already had, but the only way he could manage was to force himself from the Radleys' porch and head back home.

"Okay," Larry said. "Swing by any time tonight after sundown."

Katya's nose wrinkled, maybe curious about his use of the word, "sundown," but he didn't stick around to pull the foot from his mouth. He simply said goodbye and headed home.

FOUR

Abigail

ABIGAIL COULDN'T WAKE SLOWLY because she smelled someone else in the house.

Her first instinct was to jump from bed and run downstairs, hoping it was John. But she could immediately sense it wasn't him. It wasn't even a man. It was a girl, or woman, with a light scent of flowery shampoo or body wash.

Did Larry bring a date back to the house?

Abigail wondered if she should stay put. She'd hate to ruin his date. Then again, Larry should've told her if he was planning to bring someone home, given her notice so she could've made plans for a night of movies and games in her bedroom or something.

No, he wouldn't bring a date here.

Besides, Larry hasn't dated anyone since I've known him.

Someone is here. But who?

Abigail was sleeping in a T-shirt and shorts. She changed clothes, pulling on a striped black and purple long-sleeved tee with a skull on the front and her long black skirt, then slipped into her knee-high matching purple and black socks. She looked in the mirror, admiring her gothiness.

She wasn't sure why, but Abigail took tremendous delight in sour looks earned from passerby on the streets when she went out with Larry at night. Quiet judgment burned in their sockets, as if they had any right to appraise her — as if they knew anything about her at all.

Abigail was about to open her bedroom door when she saw a note from Larry taped to the inside. She tore it from the white wood and read it.

HEY ABI,

I've got someone coming over whom I'd like to hire, so you have someone at home to watch you when I have to run out for business. Just a few hours a night.

I told her you have some condition where you sleep all day, but she doesn't know anything more than that. She used to be the au pair for a family across the street, and she seems really great. So, please, let me do all the talking, and please ... be nice.

BE NICE? What does he think I am?

Abigail crumpled the note and tossed it in the trashcan beside her desk, annoyed, then pushed open her bedroom door. Larry's voice drifting up from the stairs. His most charming version talking to the girl.

She must be pretty. I wonder if he's hiring her for me, or himself?

Abigail heard laughter: an annoying giggle, far too happy.

I can just tell I'm gonna hate her.

Abigail threw an exaggerated cough into her closed fist, announcing herself as she descended the stairs to see Larry and a pretty blonde standing, not sitting, side-by-side in the living room.

"Oh good, she's up," Larry said. "Hey, Abi, this is Katya."

"Hi." Katya smiled and reached out her hand to shake Abigail's.

Abigail met Katya's eyes but kept her hands tucked into her long sleeves. She looked at Larry, quietly asking him to take the ball.

"She's got this OCD thing. Doesn't touch anyone."

Katya smiled again, a fake smile which annoyed Abigail even more than she already was — quite a lot considering she was barely awake.

"It's good to meet you," Katya said, seemingly unsure what to do with her hand now that she wasn't using it to shake. Abigail caught herself drawing pleasure from the girl's awkwardness, and wondered why she was feeling so catty.

Her mind flashed to a stolen memory from Larry's ex-girlfriend, Abigail's first victim. She realized where her feelings were coming from — she was feeling Lydia's jealousy.

Weird. And gross!

Abigail felt awkward, as if Larry had somehow read her thoughts. She shook off the feeling and gave Katya her best smile. "Nice to meet you, too."

"Let's all have a seat, eh?" Larry gestured toward the couch. "Would you like a drink, Katya? Abi?"

"No, thanks," Katya said.

Abigail said, "I'll have a Pepsi, please."

"Okay," Larry said, then left the two of them in the living room while he went into the kitchen.

Abigail took a seat in one of the two overstuffed leather recliners, forcing Katya to either take the other recliner, or the sofa. She chose the sofa. Larry returned and handed

Abigail a cold Pepsi, searching her eyes for confirmation that she'd seen the note, and wouldn't say anything to contradict Larry's story. Abigail nodded, though she sort of wanted to leave him hanging, since she was still annoyed that he'd led her to murder an innocent woman.

Larry took the other recliner so the three of them sat in a triangle, though Abigail felt like the definite center of attention. She was sure if Larry weren't there to move things along, she and Katya would've stared at one another for a half hour before either found a word between them.

"So, Katya, where are you from originally?"

"Ukraine, though we moved here when I was 7. Well, to New York first, and then here, five years ago. Where are you from?"

"I'm from California," Larry lied. "Abi here is from Florida."

Florida? I don't know anything about Florida. What if she asks me something about Florida? Hopefully, she's never been there either.

"How do you like it out here?" Katya asked.

"It's okay, I guess," Abigail said, quietly.

"What do you like to do for fun?"

"Read, watch TV, play games. Sometimes I draw stuff. But I'm not that good."

Larry said, "Don't let her kid you, she's a great artist!"

"I've never been good at art," Katya said. "Though I do love to read. I loved *Harry Potter*, but I guess everyone else did, too. Have you ever read the *Paratime* series?"

Abigail leaned forward. "Yeah, I loved it!"

Katya's eyes brightened. "I've never met anyone else who read them before," she practically squealed. "Or at least not that we talked about. Do you have a favorite one?"

"I only had one book," Abigail said. "It had a bunch of stories in it. How about you?"

Katya laughed. "Same. I just had one collection, but I read it like a thousand times. I'd never read anything like that before, with all the parallel worlds and histories. I loved it, and I liked *Lord Kalvan of Otherwhen* best.

Abigail felt genuinely and quite suddenly happy. "That one was in the book I had! The story I liked most was *He Walked Around the Horses*. It should've been boring, but wasn't."

Paratime small talk turned into other topics and scraped two hours from the evening, conversation drifting from books and stories to Katya's early childhood in Ukraine, to a nightmare family she briefly worked for right before the Radleys. Katya held her tongue, not trashing them too bad, probably thinking Larry might not hire her if she spoke poorly of previous clients. But it was Larry who coaxed the stories, one by one from her mouth, slowly at first, then relentlessly after he practically split his middle laughing about a time the spoiled rotten mother of a horrible brat refused to change a single diaper. Her kid would sit in poop all day if the nanny wasn't around to change her. Her husband, a nice guy and ugly enough to put up with her crap, challenged his wife to change one. She did, but not without puking all over the place.

By the conversation's end they were gobbling pizza and sitting together at the dining room table. Abigail felt herself relax, a little, and actually start to maybe like Katya, the first woman she'd known in years, besides Stacy. While Stacy was nice enough, she was still Abigail's captor, along with Randy the monster who kept her in his closet, so Abigail never felt completely at ease.

"So," Larry said as he swallowed a pepperoni Abigail plucked from her slice and put on his plate — she hated the thought of eating pigs, who she felt were too cute to

39

SEAN PLATT & DAVID W. WRIGHT

eat. "You want a job? Abi is really sweet, and I promise you'll never have to change a diaper."

Katya laughed. "Yes, I'd love to watch Abi. Do you prefer Abi or Abigail?"

Nobody had *ever* asked Abigail her preferred name. She loved that Katya had . While she didn't mind Larry calling her Abi, because he'd been doing it for so long, she preferred Abigail, and told Katya.

Larry looked stunned, "You mean you don't like Abi? Wow, I feel like an idiot!"

"It's okay," Abigail said. "I don't mind either name, really. Besides, you talk fast, and Abigail probably takes too long to say."

Larry acted wounded. "Ouch. Burn."

They all laughed. It had been too long since Abigail had laughed. She watched Katya's infectious smile, and felt like the dark cloud that had been hovering over her life for so long might finally be lifting.

FIVE

John
_____

ANCHOR HARBOR, Washington

JOHN SAT at the back of The Hideaway Bar, named appropriately enough given the circumstances, waiting for what seemed an eternity.

The waitress, a redhead with green eyes and ample cleavage spilling from her tight black tee, eyed him from behind the bar. John returned her smile, nursing flirtation as much as his whiskey. Something about her, beyond the obvious, had worked its way under his skin, making John wish he could have sex without draining a life.

It was funny how quickly lust turned his words into innuendo and his thoughts naughty, considering how long it had been since he'd even entertained the idea of sex. Of course, he rarely put himself in situations where he'd run into nubile women.

She sauntered over to his table for the third time in 15 minutes.

"Your friend usually this late?" She grinned and sat across from John at the table.

He tried to avoid looking down her shirt, but failed miserably. "Yeah, he'd be late to his own funeral."

"That's okay. I'll keep you company." She met his eyes with a smile. "I'm Amanda."

"Rick."

"Ooh, I like that name. It's strong."

John laughed, knowing she would have said that for any name in the world, except maybe for Adolf.

Her laughter made music. She set her palm atop his gloved hand. "Cold?"

John flinched, pulling his hand back and spilling whiskey onto the table.

Amanda's widened in alarm. She said, "I'm sorry," reached into her apron for a handful of napkins, and swiped them across the spill, soaking a fair mess into the napkin before moving the flickering candle to the wall, avoiding John's eyes as she mopped the tiny flood, embarrassed, or maybe feeling rejected.

John felt like even more of a freak than usual. "It's okay," he said, trying to think of anything that might dim the awkward moment. He thought of three possible comments to smooth things over, but none made it to speech before Amanda slipped away from the table. She returned to the bar, asked the bartender for another shot of whiskey, then came back to the table and gently set it in front of John, still avoiding his eyes.

"Thank you."

"You're welcome." She paused, as if trying to decide whether to sit back down or switch tables and flee discomfort.

"This asshole bothering you?" a voice shot out from behind Amanda. The waitress turned, startled, and saw

Larry standing behind her with a giant grin. He was wearing jeans, a black tee and his faded green military jacket, looking every bit the slacker. "It's okay, he's no trouble. Just not used to being around such beautiful women. A bit shy, and a little on the gay side, I'm afraid."

Amanda smiled, seemingly unsure if Larry was kidding, until he laughed and reached out to shake John's hand. "How's it hangin'?"

John shook Larry's hand as he took Amanda's too-briefly occupied spot.

"Can I get you something?" she asked Larry.

"You all got Mountain Dew?"

"Um, no, we have Sprite, Coke, Diet Coke, and—"

"I'll just have whatever he's having then," Larry said.

The waitress walked off and Larry sighed. "Damn, man, she is fine. I really need to get out more, and *really* need to get laid. This babysitting stuff isn't for me."

"You're not babysitting Abigail, you're looking after her, like a father."

Larry laughed. "Dude, I am not daddy material. Look at me."

"You're doing fine," John said, then after a long pause added, "You are doing fine, right? Abigail's okay?"

"Yeah, yeah, we're doing all right. Though, you could call her yourself, you know?"

John shook his head and took a deep swig of whiskey. "No, it's a lot easier if she doesn't hear from me until I'm done working for Omega. Trust me."

"For her, or you?"

Amanda returned to the table and saved John from his answer. She placed the whiskey on a black cardboard coaster in front of Larry, then handed them each a one-page laminated menu, full of fried vegetables, chicken strips, fries and the sort. John had told Amanda he'd wait to order until Larry arrived.

"I'll give you all a few minutes." She smiled, tapped the tabletop with her fingertips, then made her way to another table to clear a young drunk couple's tempting basket of wings, along with their growing collection of empty bottles.

Larry took a swig of whiskey and swallowed with a wince. "Wow, been a while since I touched the hard stuff. So, what made you reach out for a meeting? I was starting to think you forgot about me," Larry said, pretending his feelings were hurt.

"I need to find someone, an Other."

"Who?"

"Shadow."

"You want me to find fucking Shadow?" Larry asked. "You trying to get me killed?"

"I wouldn't ask if I thought anyone else could help. Jacob's back, and if anyone can find him, it's Shadow."

"Jacob is back? From the portal I saw on the Web?"

"A new one opened in Anchor Harbor. We need to figure out how he created a new portal, why he's back, and what happened to Caleb. That means finding Jacob."

"Can't you just tune in on your alien radar and find Jacob?" Larry asked.

"No, that's the thing. I can't feel him out there. He's blocking me. Either that or something's changed, I don't know. Nothing this big happens in the underground without Shadow knowing something. Or being part of it. Shadow is the only one I can think of who would know if Jacob's reached out to his old Harbinger contacts."

"You mean whoever's left in Harbinger you've not yet killed." Larry's words fell out fine, but the wink was clearly a veiled accusation.

"No reason not to say what you mean to say." John

pointed at Larry's glass. "Take another few sips and you can blame it on the whiskey."

"I don't have to sip whiskey to say shit that *needs* saying," Larry snapped, ironically taking a sip. He swallowed, then set his glass on the table. "You've got the Others pretty damned scared, John."

"I do my job. We protect the world from the Harbinger threat."

"Yeah, but it's not just Harbinger you're after."

"Sometimes there are obstacles on the way to the bad guys. Sometimes we have to question innocents caught up in the whole mess."

Amanda was approaching their table, but froze five feet away after crashing into the frosted conversation. She turned and made herself busy two tables over.

Larry measured his words then opened his mouth. "So, they've got you parroting the company line, eh? *Question* innocents? What happens when you're done questioning them? They getting returned to their lives?"

"I don't know, I help find and bring them in. After that, I'm done. I don't do the questioning."

"Word on the street is, *nobody's* coming back, John. Omega sweeps in and takes everyone, entire families in the night, and they're never seen again. Everyone thinks you've turned on your kind and are into extermination; Harbingers, Others and the Halfworlders — anyone who knows anything, gone." Larry leaned down and blew out the candle. "POOF! Like that. So I gotta ask you, John, is this some sort of Guantanamo thing where you're keeping them all tucked in secret prisons, or are you blowing out candles, one at a time?"

John finished his whiskey and met Larry's eyes. "We're not murdering innocent people." He thought of Mathews shooting Emilia as the words *not murdering* burned from his tongue. "From what I'm told, they're putting people in a detention camp until this whole thing blows over. I don't know where it is, nor do I think they trust me enough to tell me."

"You really believe that? Or is that the lie you tell yourself to make it easier to step in their footprints?"

Where the hell is this animosity coming from? How long had Larry been holding this in?

John reached out, tightly grabbed Larry's wrist, and squeezed.

"You think I *want* to hunt my own people? You think I *like* that they're using Hope as a chip to play me? I wouldn't even be here if *you* hadn't betrayed me, Larry. None of this would be happening if not for you. I'd be dead like I wanted, Abigail would never have been turned, the portal would never have been opened and Caleb would still be here. This is all because of you, and all I'm doing is cleaning your mess. No, I don't like it, but I don't have a choice. *You* put me in this position — so sit there and judge me from Olympus, fine, but remember, it was *you* who set this into motion. *Your* greed."

I guess I've been holding shit in, too.

John stood. "Screw it, I'll find Shadow on my own."

"Wait," Larry said. "You're right."

John turned, waiting for Larry to finish.

"I'm kinda freaking out now. Feeling like shit for something that happened with Abigail. And all I keep thinking is this shit wouldn't be happening if you weren't out there in the field. You are so much better with her than me. This shit wouldn't have happened if you'd been with her, instead of me. I fucked up."

John sat back at the table, his heart frozen in fear, thinking that Larry was about to say something awful.

"What happened?"

Larry told him about a woman they'd killed — a woman he was certain had murdered her own child, but hadn't, which Abigail discovered while feeding. The girl was feeling horrible, and Larry responsible, thinking maybe he let emotions cloud judgment, and that he should've done a better job making certain the woman was guilty, or switched their target to someone else, for whose culpability wasn't in doubt. Finding truly guilty people wasn't hard, but something about the woman had worked under Larry's skin, and he might not have been as thorough as he usually was.

John shook his head, thumbs on his temples, wishing he could have been there to spare Abigail the torment. Larry was right — John probably wouldn't have made such a mistake, though there was no way to be certain. It was one thing feeding yourself, another to help feed another. Perhaps the constant pressure to provide people for Abigail made the mistakes easier to come by.

"How is she doing now?"

"I think I found someone who can help," Larry said, explaining that he'd just hired an au pair to watch Abigail, a nice young woman he felt would be great to have around, especially since Abigail had no other females in her life.

Larry joked, "It's not like I know shit about preteen girls, what they're into, or anything about periods or shit like that. Hell, I know Abigail stopped aging, but what if she goes through puberty? I am *so* not prepared for periods and training bras!"

John didn't like the idea of someone else, someone he hadn't vetted, being around Abigail. "How did you find the au pair? How do you know you can trust her?"

"Relax. She used to work for our neighbors across the street. They're moving and she needed a job. It's a few hours a night, and half the time, I'll probably be home, anyway. But she'll be there for Abi. I'm basically hiring a friend for her."

John remembered what happened with Lydia. "What if they accidentally touch?"

"Abi and I had a long talk. She's wearing long sleeves, pants, and gloves. I told Katya she's a bit OCD, and not to touch her."

"She bought that?"

"Yeah," Larry nodded. "There's tons of people out there with weird disorders and shit. Hell, hit cable and you'll see a TV show devoted to one disorder or another. They got one now with people who eat plastic, cat fur and other funky shit. Weird shit. People don't even blink twice when you're wearing gloves. Hell, you could wear a painter's mask, and half the people wouldn't even notice. Dude in Guns & Roses wore a bucket of chicken on his head."

John thought Larry was making light of the subject, but had to trust that he was making the right choice. John hadn't thought much about the lack of a woman, or other girls, in Abigail's life, but it made sense that she'd need a maternal figure, or at least a big sister.

Reluctantly, John said, "Do you think I should stop by and see her?"

"I know she'd love that. But maybe if she bonds with Katya, she'll feel better."

John was torn. On one hand, he desperately wanted to see Abigail. He missed her more than anyone other than Hope. But at the same time, she had to grow strong and independent of him. The agency could decide to kill him any day, and then he'd be gone forever. It would hurt Abigail far less if he was mostly a memory.

John said, "I don't know what's gonna happen with the Agency once I'm done. I mean, they say I'll be free, but you and I both know we can't fully trust them. And if they decide to get rid of me, it would hurt Abigail a hell of a lot less if I was already a memory."

"You think they'd do that?"

"I don't know what to think," John said. Seeing Mathews shoot an innocent woman, a mother, no less, shredded whatever safety he was feeling in his future. "But you guys are set. Right? You've still got money and places that they won't find you?"

"Yeah, yeah, we're good. Don't worry about it. Besides, maybe she wouldn't bond as well with Katya if you came back right now. Maybe this is the best thing for Abi."

After several silent seconds, John said, "I think so. But you have to let me know if she's not improving."

"Will do. And as for the other thing — Shadow. I'll find him."

"Thank you."

"What do you want me to do afterwards? Do I let you know where he is, or set up a meeting?"

"Depends where he's at," John shrugged. "If he's surrounded by Others or Harbingers, it's probably better that you set something up. If I walk in there, it's gonna get ugly. Set up a meeting on neutral ground if you can. If he's isolated somewhere else, don't make contact. Let me know and I'll come right away."

John handed Larry a cell phone with his number pre-programmed. "Call me, anytime. Day or night."

"Day?" Larry said, eyebrows furrowed.

"Yeah, they made this special suit for me with a helmet that blocks out the light. It looks stupid, but I can travel in daylight when I need to. And I can't feed or anything with gloves on, so it's semi-useless, but I do have more freedom."

"Cool, is it like a super hero outfit? Like Batman or

some cool shit?" Larry asked, giddy like a kid. It looked like he might start clapping.

"No," John couldn't help but smile. "Nothing that cool. It looks military, kinda like that Harbinger squad we took out at the hotel, actually."

Larry wrinkled his nose. "Lame. If I was designing your outfit, I'd make it bad ass, black with flames and shit. Maybe a big fucking *Captain America* star on the chest. People would know to back the fuck up when you hit a room. Of course, we'd have to come up with a cool name."

"Like what?" John asked, playing along.

"I don't know, something cool, though. No pussy shit like Flash or Ant-Man. It should probably at least have one obscenity in it. I dunno — if it were up to me, I'd call you Captain Fuck Yeah!"

"Captain Fuck Yeah?" John laughed.

"Yeah, though it would probably limit your marketing potential with toys and shit. Imagine kids asking their parents for the new Captain Fuck Yeah action figure? Your movie would have to be R. A hard R, not that weak shit in theaters nowadays. We're definitely looking at a far smaller potential for dollars."

John laughed, eyeing his empty glass, thirsty for more — drink, laughs, and maybe another ogle at Amanda.

SIX

Hannah (Hope)

HANNAH QUINN WAS RUNNING LATE, again. So, of course, traffic and weather were both horrible, conspiring against Hannah and her Honda Element, packed corner to corner with flowers.

Every bloom had to be at His Father's Holy Grace Church by five to noon, or Hannah would surely get screamed at by Cori Truman, the city's biggest, flashiest and most grand standing wedding coordinator.

This wasn't just a wedding — bread and butter for any florist who knew how to build and bill them — it was the biggest wedding gig Hanna's Bucket Boutique had ever done. The bride belonged to Mr. And Mrs. William Graham, Las Orilla's closest cousin to power brokers.

Judy Graham, mother of the bride, clicked with Hannah moments after first setting her Manolos inside Hannah's small shop a year before. Hannah had a front fridge stuffed with blown open Leonidas roses; big and brown, in many shades of copper, all about to die. Judy oohed and aahed as Hannah handed her the bundle, wrapped in brown paper with a drop of blood, fresh from a small cut on Hannah's pinkie.

Judy spent $1,200 in candles and orchid plants to say thank you.

While there were a half dozen flower carts dotting the coast for 10 minutes in either direction, cheap chain grocery stores and at least six other quality shops within driving distance, with far more experience and staff, all who could have conceivably done the wedding as well as Hannah, and most of them better, Judy insisted that she do the job.

And so here she was, battling traffic and rain to recover lost time from her morning disaster. Hannah was either too stupid or too inexperienced to know about the effect that ripening fruit had on flowers. She'd never filled her cooler to spilling before and had to ask Mr. Fanaroff from the Taco Beach next door if she could use his fridge. Of course, Mr. Fanaroff would do anything for Hannah, including allowing the use of his cooler, filled with avocados and tomatoes and everything else that makes Mexican food delicious.

Thank the Good Lord above, Hannah had only loaded the bridal party's flowers into Fanaroff's fridge, wanting to keep them separate after packing everything else into her cooler. By morning, the fruit had turned her flowers translucent. Hanna had been smart, or at least scared enough to over-order, so she had plenty of flowers, though not enough time to arrange them all. She raced through the morning, and rushed to finish the same bouquets she'd spent half the previous day making in less than an hour.

It wasn't Hannah's fault, *exactly*, but she wasn't paid to deliver excuses. Her rather substantial check was in exchange for a promise that she'd deliver flowers beautiful enough to make Becca Graham weep from memory when telling her granddaughter about the best day of her life four decades later.

The job could make or break Hannah's Bucket Boutique.

Her dashboard clock read 11:51 a.m., still 20 minutes away.

Hannah's phone buzzed with a text — Jenny her assistant calling from the church, where she was waiting with the wedding coordinator Cori Truman who had strongly advised Mrs. Graham to use a different florist. Anyone, other than Hannah, would do, according to Cori.

WHERE ARE YOU?

Hannah reached down and texted back:

15 minutes out, I hope. Be there soon. Sorry!

Hannah stared out the window through the ragged smears left by her fraying wipers, cursing herself for forgetting to swap the blades, again, after having her oil changed at Bud's the week before.

Aren't they supposed to check stuff like that?

She thought they were, but maybe it was one of those things you were supposed to specify, no matter how obvious you figured it was. Hannah imagined calling the garage, complaining, and being told, "Sorry, ma'am, we saw that your wipers were hanging by strips like noodles, but if you didn't ask, we didn't fix!"

Because of her rotted wipers, Hannah was forced to drive even slower than the already slower-than-molasses traffic, and focus on the blurring lights ahead as she navigated the street.

The light went yellow and the car ahead of Hannah stopped short, even though they both had plenty of time to make it. She hit the brakes, shouted, "Come on!" and slapped her open palms hard on the wheel.

Hannah tried telling herself to relax.

She had time. Weddings were planned with plenty of cushions in case someone was running late, like the cakes she always had to wait on. Hannah was still well within her cushion. The worst that would happen was that an impatient photographer couldn't start his battery of photos at the precise moment he wanted to. But there was no doubt Cori would overplay her tardiness to Mrs. Graham, hoping to poison Judy's opinion of Hannah and her shop.

The light went green and traffic crawled. Rain fell harder, as if refusing to aid Hannah, despite her pleas.

Relax. Focus on the road. Think of Greg and you'll be there before you know it.

Greg was Hannah's longtime boyfriend. Their trip to Arbor Falls, California for a long overdue vacation — a week at a cabin passed down to Greg from his parents — was the coming Tuesday, and Hannah couldn't wait. Though she and Greg had been dating for two years, this was their first real romantic trip. Time had never allowed such an indulgence. Greg was an analyst, and Hannah had her shop. Between them, available minutes were few. Six months earlier, they carved a date in stone marking their calendar with a promised week off. They owed it to themselves, and each other. Now, with the trip two days away, Hannah started thinking of the many things she needed to do before then, and hoping her shop would survive for a week without her.

Anxiety found its familiar home inside her, nesting deeper as she hit her millionth red light.

You were supposed to think about the trip to calm down, not worry more …

Hannah closed her eyes, listening to her thumping wipers and rain drumming on metal. She hoped the sound would soothe her, even if traffic couldn't.

Everything will be okay.

The wedding will go off without a hitch.
Jenny will handle the shop just fine.
We'll leave with everything we need.
Everything will work out.

A horn blurted behind her. The light was green, and cars were already moving through the intersection. "Sorry," she mouthed, waving to the driver behind her, though they couldn't hear her words or read her lips.

Hannah stepped on the gas, crossed the light, and flew onto the on ramp, relieved to see the highway traffic buzzing at a reasonable clip. She sped into a two-lane change, hoping to recover lost time. She looked in her mirror, then over her shoulder, and crossed another pair of lanes, nudging the Element 10 miles over the limit, the fastest she'd let herself go, especially in the rain, and within what she believed would be an acceptable speed to still slip from a ticket with a smile if needed. She kept her eyes on the road, and the rearview, hoping she wouldn't see flashing lights behind her.

Even at 10 miles over the limit in the rain, Hannah was still slower than half the cars on the highway. She smiled as the sign announcing her exit in another four miles.

Almost there.

She was flying along in the left lane, and needed to cross to the right, but a quick glance in her rearview told her to wait. Hannah's cell phone rang, instead of buzzing. Her stomach churned at the screen: Cori Truman.

Shit.

Hannah reached down and grabbed the phone. "Hello?"

"Where are you?" Cori screamed.

Hannah hoped Cori wasn't in front of Mrs. Graham, putting on a show, though she more than probably was. "I'm on my way. I'll be there in five minutes."

"You do realize you're ruining this wedding, don't you?"

Hannah swallowed to control her emotions. "I'm sorry, it's not my fault."

Hannah wished she hadn't said, "not my fault" before she even finished. The excuse marked her as an amateur, and poured unnecessary cement in Cori's crappy attitude.

Hannah checked her rearview, saw the coast was clear, and merged. "I had a situation with the cooler. It *was* my fault. But it's handled now. Everything is fine, I took care of it, and will be there in less than —"

Hannah's world exploded.

Her Element spun, then slid out of control in a violent twirl toward the railing.

The flowers!

She could hear the arrangements sliding along with the truck.

The phone flew from her hand as she grabbed the steering wheel, clutching it tight while pumping her brakes and praying for control. Moving too fast along a too-slick road, she slammed into the railing. The Element crashed against it then tumbled over the side with a horrible screeching of metal. Screams filled Hannah's cabin as she roared down the incline into nothing but darkness.

HANNAH WOKE in an oddly familiar room, though it held no specific memories, and she couldn't recall actually being inside it before.

It was an art studio in an old house. A cool breeze blew in from a warm summer night outside, just past the perfectly square window overlooking a placid lake. Paintings on easels in various stages of completion surrounded her, all equally familiar. One of the easels was turned away from her, facing the window.

Hannah moved forward in a floating dream's half-walk.

First, Hannah was drawn to the window, looking out at the moon hanging fat and full in the sky. "Goodnight, moon," she said, recalling the children's book she once read to her cousin for most of a summer.

Wait, I don't have a cousin; do I?

She turned from the window, her eyes drawn to a painting draped beneath a long piece of thick plastic. She reached out, peeled the plastic sheet away and letting it fall to the ground. It took forever to hit the floor, as if the fall were as endless as the night outside.

There was no canvas behind the sheet, only a man.

Hannah stumbled back, startled by the sight of the naked man with long dark hair and angel wings.

His eyes were closed as if he were sleeping. *Or dead.*

Like the room, and the paintings, he seemed *so familiar.*

Or more than that.

Without thinking, Hannah reached her hand out to touch him, as if to see if he were real, *or alive.*

A name bled through her lips without her thinking it.

"John?" she whispered.

No response.

Her fingers touched his chest.

He opened his eyes.

Hannah opened hers, and the dream was gone.

SHE WOKE DISORIENTED in a brightly lit but unfamiliar room.

She squinted through fuzzy eyes, trying to focus on the blur slowly taking shape, a man sitting beside her.

Her eyes finally adjusted, and settled on a stranger — a man with short blond hair and a big smile.

"How are you feeling, Hannah?"

She looked at him, confused.

"Who is Hannah?" she spoke through a burning throat. "And where is John?"

SEVEN

John

IT TOOK Larry just six hours to find Shadow, a pleasant surprise that gave John hope he might manage to find Jacob and finally be done with Omega's bidding.

According to Larry's source, Shadow was holed up in Room 213 in the Channel Hotel, an expensive spread over by the Riverfront. John had driven by the hotel plenty of times, but never had reason to set foot inside.

Just before dawn, Mike Mathews sat with John in the back of an Agency van in the hotel's parking garage, waiting for the agents to settle in place. Six plainclothes were waiting inside the hotel — one in the lobby, and the rest scattered across the hotel's dozen floors. Another three Agency vans were on standby outside in case things turned ugly. John thought the number was overkill, especially since he hoped not a single one would be needed.

He wished he'd come to the hotel alone, but knew if he did, and Mathews found out, he'd be risking treason. Omega had a specific set of rules, and they expected John to play by them, just like everyone else. If not, he risked

Hope's life. So, John played ball and hoped he could talk with Shadow one-on-one without the need for the macho Mathews calling in his men.

Mathews' eyes were eager, and did nothing to buoy John's hope for a peaceful meeting.

"You're going to give me time to talk to him, right? Before calling in the dogs?"

Mathews looked offended, "Of course. But you know as well as I do that Shadow is one slippery fuck, and the moment shit goes south, we're going in."

John nodded. "Just checking that we're on the same page. I'm sure we can turn Shadow into an asset if we leave him on the streets. But you have to trust me on this one, Mike."

Mathews nodded. "I get it, John. You do your job, I'll do mine."

John had a sick feeling that he knew exactly what Mathews meant — he'd get what he could get from Shadow, then the squad would move in and try taking him into custody. Maybe even kill him.

Shadow was one of the most well-respected Half-worlders — a son of an Otherworlder — someone who had got along well enough with both Guardians and Harbingers before Jacob activated the portal and brought civil war among the Guardians.

Shadow had run a magick shop in the underground, catering to Otherworlders, Halfworlders and the few humans who knew how to find him, specializing in artifacts and information for collectors willing to recognize, and pay, for their value. Omega started purging Otherworlders, and Shadow went deeper underground. John thought he would have fled the area, but for some reason stayed. He was either the smartest of Otherworlders, or the dumbest.

Mathews checked with the other teams on the radio, making sure everyone was in place, then looked at John, "You ready?"

"Yes," John said, climbing from the van's rear.

John was wearing his street clothes; jeans, a black shirt, black trench coast, boots and shades. He checked the tiny receiver pinned inside his coat's collar and whispered, "You hear me?"

"Yes," Mathews' voice came across the ear piece hidden under John's long dark hair. "You copy?"

"Yes," John said, making his way inside the lobby. He crossed the empty hallway, then stepped inside the elevator and took it to the second floor. The doors parted and John saw a man standing in front of a door halfway down the hall. John got out and started walking the hall, figuring Shadow's room was roughly three doors down from where the man was standing.

What the hell is he doing?

John got closer and heard the man's slurred speech, "Please, baby, let me in. I'm sorry."

Great, a lovers' quarrel.

The man turned, red-eyed, and glared at John, looking him up and down. "What the fuck you lookin' at?"

John looked down, ignoring the man. The last thing he wanted to do was alert Shadow by getting into a fight with a drunken man down the hall. John kept walking, head down, stopping in front of Shadow's room. He could feel the drunk's eyes all over him, waiting to see what John would do, as if trying to decide between picking a fight and resuming his plea, begging "baby" to let him back inside.

Maybe he was waiting for John to leave before he finished humiliating himself.

John planned to take his time, see if he could sense

whether Shadow was awake, but given the drunk in the hall, he had to keep moving, as if it were his room. He retrieved a key card from his coat pocket, one Omega created to open any door in the hotel, and slid it into the reader.

The door unlocked. John turned the knob and gently pushed.

The door caught immediately on a latch, which John half-expected. He stepped back and kicked the door hard above the knob.

The door burst open, snapping the lock as the drunk screamed, "Hey!"

John stormed into Shadow's room, hands ready to deliver a deadly blast of energy, but Shadow's bed was empty. So was the room.

John turned, about to check the closed bathroom door when the shape appeared in front of him — something barely there against the wall in the darkness, then fully formed — a skinny, young Asian man in a black robe.

John raised his hands at Shadow. "I just want to talk."

Before John could send a blast to knock him out, Shadow's hands dropped something to the ground and blinded John with a blast of smoke.

Shadow knocked him back with a kick to the chest. John tried calling for backup, but could only cough on his way to the carpet. To John's horror, he couldn't move his arms or legs.

Oh, God, he poisoned me.

Suddenly, they weren't alone. The drunk was standing in the door, yelling, "What the fuck is going on in here?"

Shadow swung his arm up, sending a long wire flying from und his sleeves into a coil around the drunk's neck. The drunk started screaming, but only screeched a syllable before Shadow pulled the wire and sliced the man's head clean from his already-sagging shoulders. He dropped his end of the wire and looked down at John, eyes blazing orange.

"Why are you here?"

John tried to speak, but could barely suck air through his cough.

Shadow's hand unfolded, drawing John's eyes to a swirl of dark and light spiraling from the center of his palm, before filling the room with a brilliant blue radiance. The light spread into a perfect circle hovering in the air above them.

John stared, unable to believe the small portal appearing before him.

How is he doing this?

Shadow reached down, grabbed John, yanked his body up with seemingly no effort, and slung him over his shoulder.

John tried screaming, but couldn't even cough. The world was spinning around him as Shadow leaped up and into the portal with John.

JOHN FELT PULLED from his body.

He was being moved but was too numb to truly feel it, as if it were happening through several layers or reality, too thick to reach him.

The world was darkness, but at least he was still alive.

Where am I?

John remembered Shadow creating the portal and carrying him through it, but he had no idea where the portal led.

Am I in Otherworld?

He closed his eyes, trying to forge a connection with

either Larry or Abigail, but he felt nothing, especially them.

Then, he heard a woman's voice as clear as if in the Darkness with him.

"John?"

"Hope?"

EIGHT

Duncan

DUNCAN ALDERMAN SAT, phone to his ear, wondering if he'd made the biggest mistake of his life by letting John live. He'd had the chance to kill John many times throughout the years. But John was Caleb's brother, and Caleb was the closest thing to a son that Duncan would ever have. So, each time, he'd surrendered to his better angels, figuring that the Guardians could manage the situation before it got out of hand. Yet, each time he was proven wrong.

"What do you mean *they* have John?" Duncan asked Bob Cromwell. "*Who* has him?"

"We're not sure. Harbinger, or maybe Outsiders."

"Outsiders?" Duncan tapped his pen against the glossy surface of his large desk.

"Aliens, freaks, and the humans who mingle among them. Our operations have made us some new enemies. More than expected. People who might not have been a threat before are starting to organize against us. They're calling themselves Outsiders."

"Great," Duncan said. "So we have no idea who took John?"

"No. John went to meet a Halfworlder called Shadow at the Channel Hotel. He's an Outsider and information broker. We believe he has a lead on Jacob. John insisted on going in solo, though we had teams in place waiting to move. Something happened inside, we're not sure what. Both John and Shadow vanished."

"*Vanished?* How the hell did they disappear if you had teams working this?"

"I don't know, sir."

Duncan closed his eyes, taking a deep breath and trying to keep calm. Cromwell was paid too much for ignorance. This was pathetic. He wanted to cut the man to nothing with his tongue, but could sense the remorse in his voice. Besides, Cromwell was so fueled by his need for approval, Duncan's silence was already a sentence served.

Duncan remained quiet, gazing at the long rows of books lining the many shelves inside his private library. He noticed, with some annoyance, that one of his leather-bound first- edition encyclopedias along the top shelf, 15 feet from the ground, had a slightly jutting spine, as if someone had recently drawn the volume and hadn't pushed it all the way back into its slot.

Who's been in my library?

Duncan wondered if one of the housekeepers had been dusting and left the book out of line, then made a mental note to talk with Helga, head of housekeeping.

"I've my best men on this now," Cromwell said. "We'll keep you apprised of the situation."

Duncan said, "I expect you will."

"Yes, sir."

A pause, then, "You *will* find John. You will get him back. Right, Bob?"

"Yes, sir. I promise. We *will* find John."

Duncan hung up and found his eyes drifting back to the errant volume.

He glanced at the time on his laptop, 7:12 p.m., and wondered if Helga had left for the evening. He clicked on his computer's intercom program, then on Helga's name, and waited for an answer.

No response.

He looked up and down the list of his other house help, most likely gone for the day. Security would be the only staff left. One could come fix the book.

He clicked on "Otis" his head of security and awaited a response.

He heard nothing but silence, even after a minute.

That's odd. If Otis is unavailable, the system should patch me through to someone else.

Duncan clicked on his name again, waiting.

An uneasy creep stirred inside him, staring at the unresponsive screen, waiting for some sort of answer. The feeling was familiar, but because he'd not felt it in a reasonable forever and it took a moment before recognition hit him.

Something was wrong.

Duncan yanked open his desk drawer, reached inside, pulled a loaded pistol out from inside and wrapped it tight in his palm, a half second before the door burst open to the last person in the world he wanted to see. The gun stayed in his hand, but fell beneath the desk.

"Well, hello, Mr. Alderman!" Jacob stepped inside Duncan's office with the giddy voice of a carnival barker and a salesman's faux smile. He was dressed in an ink-black robe, like a fairytale's evil magician, hands buried in the folds. Behind him stood a pair of tall, spindly wraiths he'd either created here or brought from the In Between.

The dark, naked creatures were mostly legs and arms, with oversized hands and feet ending in blunt nubs, curled into sharp talons. Clawed hands were caked in blood and flesh, likely from Duncan's security team. The wraiths' emaciated faces and hollowed sockets stared out at Duncan, likely seeing him through Jacob's sight, since he was surely connected to and controlling the hellish creatures.

"What are you doing here?" Duncan shouted, keeping his gun hidden, wondering if his weapon was any good against Jacob and his swiftly-moving wraiths.

Jacob pulled something from his robe, tossed it to the ground, then smiled while it rolled to the edge of the bookcase on Duncan's right, stopping three feet from his ankles.

Duncan looked down, swallowing bile as the dead eyes from Otis' severed head stared back up at him from their glassy hell.

"I've come for the vessels' names," Jacob said, stepping from the threshold into Duncan's office, glancing up and down the walls of books as if admiring the collection, or perhaps searching for the hidden room behind.

"What vessels?" Duncan tried not to look at the bloody remains of his head of security, but was unable to keep his eyes from the frayed skin at what was once Otis's neck, like fabric sheared with dull scissors.

Are they all dead? If they got Otis, they probably got everyone.

Jacob smiled, "Tisk, tisk, Mr. Alderman. Do you think I'd return home and *not* hear of the vessels? All this time I'd been wondering what had happened to the wizard after he helped my mother come here. All this time we thought him dead." He hissed through his smile. "But you knew better, didn't you?"

Duncan shook his head. He had no idea what the

vessels were, but anything on Jacob's wish list was certainly bad for Earth.

"Oh, my, you *don't* know, do you?" Jacob smiled, like an evil child chewing a secret.

Duncan said nothing, his hand wrapped tightly around the grip and his finger on the trigger, holding his weapon under the desk, ready to fire. If he could kill Jacob fast enough, the wraiths would be blinded, if not incapacitated entirely. It had been many years since he'd seen a dark magick user controlling such creatures, but he was reasonably certain with the master dead the monsters would fall or return to the In Between.

Jacob paused five feet in front of Duncan's desk, finally meeting his eyes. "Tell me, Mr. Alderman, how many Pioneers are left?"

"I don't know. Why?"

Jacob smiled, "Because I'm going to give them a choice. A choice to be on history's right side. The same choice I'm about to give you."

Duncan's finger tightened on the trigger. Jacob took a step closer.

"What choice is that?"

"I'm going to find the vessels, Mr. Alderman, and you will definitely *not* want to be in my way once I do." He smiled, then looked from left to right, grazing his eyes against the two wraiths and teasing the rest of his insanity. "There are only two sides in a war, Mr. Alderman. You must decide, right now in this room, are you with us or against us?"

"That depends on what exactly you have planned."

"I think you know what we have planned," Jacob smiled, as if Duncan were silly. "We're going to finish the job you and your Pioneers were sent here to do. We're going to take this world."

SEAN PLATT & DAVID W. WRIGHT

Duncan narrowed his eyes. "And what gives you the right?"

"Right?" Jacob snapped. "What gives me the *right?* Nobody *gives* me the right, Mr. Alderman! I *take* it! *I* should be asking what gives you and *your* kind the right? The right to imprison and murder ours? To force us into ghettos? To keep an entire race banished to one sector of a world like caged animals? Oh, yes, I've seen what your kind has done to mine in Otherworld. You're no different from the humans here — a few controlling the many; strong devouring weak. Well, Mr. Alderman, you can't fight evolution. Our species will shatter your shackles. We will take this world as we should, then do to you and yours what you've done to us for millennia."

Jacob finally moved, almost drifting from the doorway to Duncan's desk, whispering death and promises on his way.

"I'm giving you a chance, Mr. Alderman, an opportunity to find yourself on the winning side. A chance to be one of us."

"Never!" Duncan raised his pistol, aimed it at Jacob, and pulled the trigger.

Duncan was too late.

One of the wraiths jumped between the men, took the bullet in its blackened chest, and screeched like a cat torn in half as it stained the carpet.

Before Duncan could fire again, Jacob was in front of him, a hand at his throat, bony gloved fingers squeezing tight, while the other wrested the gun from his twisted digits and sent it to the floor.

"Wrong choice." Jacob yanked Duncan up from behind his desk in his curled fist and shoved him to the ground.

Pain flared through Duncan's body. Jacob hopped atop

and straddled him. His weight, combined with his powerful grip on Duncan's neck, rendered the old man into a helpless glob of jelly.

He cried out for help, but there was no one left.

Jacob's eyes met Duncan's, and the intruder smiled like a snake.

"Tell you what, Mr. Alderman," Jacob leaned in toward Duncan. "I do appreciate your spirit! You've admirable fight, especially for a withered old man. I hate the thought of you winding up on the wrong side of history, simply because you were too hasty to make the right decision. So to save us both from the trouble — you the agony and me the disappointment — I'll decide for you. You will be with, and not against us. Does that sound right?"

Jacob lowered his weight onto Duncan, as if trying to push words from his body.

The old man struggled to speak, but Jacob's grip was too tight, choking his air and killing his words. He squirmed beneath the weight, shaking his head *NO* as best he could.

Jacob's smile spread wider, moving his fingers from Duncan's neck to the corners of his mouth where he pried his lips open against his thrashing.

Oh God, what is he doing?

Jacob's right hand held Duncan's head firmly in place as he lifted his left, and showed the old man his now ungloved palm along with the parasite slithering under his skin.

Oh God.

The flesh on Jacob's hand split then broke open as drops of dark blood started to fall, first in a trickle and then in a gush, pouring from the widening wound as the terrible something under his skin burrowed out.

Duncan choked on his scream as the creature surfaced; an inch in width, a bulbous, dark, segmented body, with hundreds of tiny legs skittering from the open wound of Jacob's hand, and snaking its entire length — nearly a foot long — around Jacob's left hand like a pet millipede from a world of monsters.

"Open wide," Jacob said, his right hand prying Duncan's mouth open further.

The old man struggled, but the pain in his back made movement impossible. He tried closing his mouth, moving his head, everything and anything, but Jacob's grip was too strong. Duncan could only watch in wide-eyed horror as Jacob moved his left hand, and the terrible creature in it, towards his mouth.

"No!" Duncan screamed in a muffled, gagging cry.

Jacob forced his jaw even wider, pressing his tongue into the bottom of his mouth to prevent it from moving as he brought the parasite closer. The insect-like creature unspooled from Jacob's hand, descending slowly like a rope with its thousands of moving legs, wiggling and eager to burrow.

Oh God, help me!

Jacob's parasite dropped into his mouth.

Duncan lay helpless as the monster burrowed into his throat, then down on its way to God knows where.

Duncan cried for Jacob to let go, but he kept smiling like a maniac, holding the old man in place.

"Relax, Mr. Alderman. I gave you a choice, and you chose wrong. Fortunately for you, I care too much to let that happen. So, I'm deciding for you. Only now, Mr. Alderman, are you are one of us. One of the winners."

NINE

John

HOPE'S VOICE faded to a barely-there wisp almost as soon as John heard it, just fleeting enough to make him wonder if it was only cruelty of loneliness and memory blending to taunt him with a lie.

He was again alone, lost in the darkness.

Where am I? How long have I been out?

Only after his eyes adjusted to the gloom did John finally realize he wasn't in complete darkness. Thin slits of moonlight illuminated the brick circular wall spiraling upward above him. A pair of charred bodies and the scattered remnants of who-knew-how-many skeletons lay beside him. He was, he realized, at the bottom of an old well transformed into something else — a tomb for his kind. Once the sun devoured the moon, John would be charred, just like his wellmates.

He scanned the darkness, searching for any weaknesses, or something he could use to climb out from the well. It took him less than five minutes of squinting and running his hands along the wall before John found the outline of a door, like a grin in the brick.

He pressed his fingers against the cold metal, feeling for anything — a slot, a knob, anything to help him pull or push the door open. Finding nothing, he used his shoulder instead, ramming at a door that refused to budge.

He banged on the door with the full brunt of his folded knuckles, alternating fist with shoulders. Though both pounded hard enough to knock the door from its hinges, John couldn't manage to rattle the door in its frame.

Something was wrong. John was weakened, with everything in him ebbing.

He tried to focus, send a blast of energy at the door, but nothing left his hands.

What did Shadow do to me? Have I been out so long that I need to feed?

He didn't feel the hunger, but John had grown so used to going longer between feedings that he wasn't even sure he would recognize his energy dropping too far. The few times he'd been depleted on the job, he had enemies to feed from. Now, there was no one nearby.

"Hello?" he shouted, hoping someone was on the other side of the door. He banged hard on the metal, shouting louder and getting no response. "Why are you doing this?"

John wondered if his captors, assuming Shadow wasn't working alone, were on the other side of the door, or if they'd simply left him alone to burn in the sunrise. He closed his eyes to gain a clearer sense of his surroundings, to see if he could sense anyone nearby. John tuned into the world and felt life teeming around him: insects and rodents in the dirt, birds above, a fox somewhere nearby.

But not a single soul.

He had no idea of the time, unconscious long enough to feel certain of nothing. It *felt* like midnight as much as four in the morning. Unable to see the moon, John couldn't judge where it was in the sky. He had minutes or hours until death, and no way to know the difference between them.

John tried reaching Larry and Abigail telepathically, but could find neither's signal — not surprising since he'd been largely unable to tune them in with any sort of consistency for a while. The best he usually managed was the occasional fleeting thought from one or both, though they rarely came together. His attempts to communicate, or even read their thoughts from afar hadn't borne fruit for a while.

John wondered if Omega had somehow drugged him to dampen his abilities, and keep him from using his telepathy. He had no clue how they could consistently deliver a drug into his system, unless they were spiking food in his apartment, but they were capable of anything, and despite their aversion to all things magick, they had no problem using it to achieve their means.

John wanted to believe he was sharp enough to sense if someone were inside his place while he was out, but his senses tingled whenever he was in his apartment, no matter what. He'd never felt right there, partly because it wasn't really his home and never would be no matter how long he slept there, and partly because Omega routinely checked in on him. John always felt like he was being watched, and probably was.

If they were already watching, why not drug him, too?

Finally, more because he was out of choices than keen on the idea, John tried reaching the only human other than Abigail he'd ever turned — gangster turned vampire, Tiny.

Tiny? Tiny? Can you hear me?

John felt nothing.

Shit.

A deep voice suddenly echoed in his head:

"Johnny? That you?"

Tiny! Yes, it's me, John!

"*What the fuck you doin' in my head, Man. Your phone broke?*"

John laughed.

Oh, thank God I found you. I'm in trouble, Tiny. Someone's got me locked up in a well. I've no idea where I am, but I'm sure once the sun rises, I'm gone. What time is it?

"*It's about four in the morning in Seaside Heights.*"

I didn't wake you did I?

"*Hell no, I'm a creature of the night like you now, remember?*"

Of course. I need you to focus on my voice, okay Tiny? Can you feel where I am?

"*Feel where you are? How the fuck I'm supposed to feel somethin' like that?*"

I don't know. But sometimes I can feel how close someone is to me, and can find them by concentrating.

"*Well, can you feel me, then?*"

A little, and you don't feel too far. But I don't really know because I don't have any idea where I am, and I kind of need to know where I am in order for it to work.

After a quiet moment Tiny said, "*I think I feel something.*"

Yeah?

"*I don't know. I think I have an idea where you are, but I'm not sure. I'll hop in the car and see if I can find you, cool?*"

Okay. If I don't hear from you soon, I'll try reaching you again.

"*Okay,*" Tiny agreed, then a second later said, "*Hey, John?*"

Yeah?

"*You ain't always listenin' to my thoughts 'n' shit, are you?*"

John laughed.

No, that's not how it works. It's not a permanent, always-on connection.

"*Good.*"

Why's that? You thinking stuff you're ashamed to be?

"*Shit, you don't even wanna know, man. You didn't tell me I was never gonna be able to fuck again, man. My sack started boiling, and it ain't never stopped. You don't even wanna guess at some of the places I think of sticking it."*

Sorry. Again, John laughed.

"It's alright. I found a way to get off."

John was curious what the big guy was doing to take care of his needs, just not enough to ask. He could imagine Tiny getting started, then digging too deep into the sorts of details John didn't want to hear, and would regret if he did.

"Okay," Tiny said. *"Hopefully, I'll be seeing you in a half hour or so."*

Please, hurry.

"See ya, Johnny."

John sat in the darkness waiting, hoping Tiny could find him in time. If it was around four in the morning as Tiny said, then he had maybe two hours before the sun started to rise. If Tiny failed, John would be ashes in hours.

A sudden movement nearby startled John. *Is that on the other side of the door?* He leaned against the door, pressing his ear against it.

"Hello?" he said, tapping the metal.

Movement ceased.

"Hello, I know you're there!" John smacked the heavy iron door. "Hello?"

The other side stayed silent.

John sensed no one, but was certain he wasn't alone.

TEN

Abigail
_____

"WELL? DO YOU LIKE IT?" Katya asked.

Abigail tore the end from her fried mozzarella, holding it between her teeth before tasting it with the tip of her tongue. "Not bad," she said, surprised by the blend of salty and cheesy, the two flavors coated with the perfect amount of fried crunchiness.

"I can't believe you've never had these before. They're even better dipped in marinara."

Abigail looked down at the green shallow bowl with red sauce and dipped the cheese stick in, timidly at first to get a bit of sauce, then she put it in her mouth. It was maybe the best thing she'd ever had, at least besides McDonald's fries dipped in a milkshake.

"Wow! That *is* good!" Abigail said as the waiter, a tall young man with neatly gelled brown hair, set a giant pizza on a stand beside them — easily the biggest pie Abigail had ever seen.

"It came out earlier than I thought," he smiled. "Would you like your slices now, or would you rather wait?"

"We'll wait until we're finished with the appetizers, thank you," Katya said.

The waiter left their table and Abigail looked around the cozy Italian restaurant, marveling at the wooden trellises and fake vines creeping along the walls and separating each booth. Old, black iron lamp posts stood in each corner. Abigail wondered if they actually worked. The walls were painted with an ornate scene of what Abigail imagined was an Italian countryside, not that she'd ever seen an Italian countryside, pictures of an Italian countryside, or any countryside at all besides what passed outside a window while trapped in the seat of a swiftly moving car. The restaurant, with its delicious scents and lush interior, filled Abigail with a sudden longing for all the places she'd never been and might never go.

Katya caught her looking and smiled. "Do you like this place?"

"I love it! Are all restaurants this nice?"

"You've never been to a restaurant before?"

"Not in a long time, not since I was a kid," she said, realizing only after she said it that to Katya, she still was a kid. Abigail added, "Not since I was like 5 or 6, maybe, I don't remember."

"Wow. Did you grow up in a cave?"

Not a cave, a closet.

Abigail thought of the closet she'd spent too long imprisoned inside, then of Randy Webster. Again. She hated thinking of the monster. Abigail took another bite of cheese stick, buying her answer several seconds. She swallowed, then said, "My family didn't have a lot of money," hating the lie on her tongue.

Katya smiled. "Oh, I'm sorry. I didn't mean to make you feel bad."

"It's okay," Abigail shrugged, "That was a lifetime ago. Things are better now."

Abigail had only met Katya two days before, but already felt more comfortable with her than she'd felt with anyone else in a long time. She had tried not to like her, partly because she didn't want another disappointment in her life when it was time for Katya to move on, but Abigail couldn't help it. Katya was pretty, nice, and maybe the happiest person Abigail had ever met.

Katya, seeming to sense Abigail's reluctance to discuss her past, changed the subject. "So, what do you want to be when you grow up?"

"I don't know," Abigail said, realizing it had been forever since she considered such things. Now that she would never grow up, dreaming about what might be was pointless. She tried to think of something that wasn't, and wouldn't sound like a complete lie, something that shared reality with the things she and Larry did together, approximately twice a month — tracking bad people and killing them.

"Maybe I'll be a police officer."

"Really?" Katya dipped her cheese stick into the marinara and then sprinkled some pepper on top of it. "A police officer? That's cool. Why do you want to do that?"

"To help people. To protect them from the bad guys."

"That's nice," Katya nodded.

"What do you want to be … I mean when you get older?"

Abigail wondered if she'd insulted Katya. *What if watching kids is her career and what she wants to do? Crap.* She wasn't sure what to say without sticking one of her two small feet deeper in her mouth, so she waited for Katya to finish her bite of cheese stick and answer.

"I don't know. I used to want to be a realtor. My dad owns a real estate agency, and I was a big-time daddy's girl and would help out around the office and stuff. But a few years ago, I thought, 'Do I really want to do this, or am I just doing it because it's easy to follow Daddy?' So, I decided I'd wait a while and make my own money, just to see if I could. I went to school for a few semesters, took some fashion and art classes, then took time off to think about what I really wanted. That, I'm afraid," she said with an embarrassed laugh, "was two years ago."

"You haven't been to school in two years?"

"No, and I thought it was because I was confused about what I wanted to do. But then a part of me thought, 'Maybe I just don't want to limit myself. I mean, I'm young. I have my whole life ahead of me, why not explore my interests and see where they lead?'"

"So what are you doing now?" Abigail asked as Katya piled a piping hot slice of pizza onto each of their plates. Abigail took a bite of the pizza, stringing hot cheese in a stretchy line from the steaming triangle into her mouth. The pie was even better than the cheese sticks. "Yummy!" Abigail moaned, her mouth full of pizza.

"I don't know," Katya smiled. "Lately, I've been thinking a lot about traveling next year, and trying a few different things — things I'd never even considered."

Immediately, Abigail felt a sting. *She's going to leave next year to travel. Stop it. Just focus on the conversation and try to enjoy the moment.*

"Really? Like what kinds of things?"

"Oh, I don't know, maybe work on some organic farms upstate, or travel to the Northeast and work on a fishing boat. I'm not sure, I guess I just want to see what's out there, you know?"

Abigail admired Katya's adventurous spirit, and wished she was brave enough to go out and do whatever, without a care in the world. She wondered how hard it would be to talk Larry into moving, then wondered if Larry *could* leave the area, or if John needed him nearby.

"Is your dad rich?"

Katya's eyes widened from surprise. For a moment, Abigail was afraid she might have offended her.

Katya laughed, "Yeah, you could say that. And yes, that does give me freedoms that most people probably don't, and won't, ever have. Most people my age have to worry about finding a job, providing for a family, paying rent, real-life stuff like that. So, yeah, I probably seem like a spoiled brat who doesn't know what she wants to do, boo-hoo, and all that garbage."

"No, I didn't mean that at all. I think it's awesome that you want to do all these things. I wish I could get up and leave, go far away, and see what happens."

Katya smiled, but the corners of her mouth were sad. "You're still young, and smarter than most kids I've met. I'm sure you'll never let anything stop you from doing whatever you set out to do."

Abigail sipped her Coke, nodding.

She lifted her head, popped the straw from her lips, pushed her soda six inches across the table, then noticed a pair of police officers sliding into a booth, three away from them. One of the cops, an older heavyset man with glasses too large for his face, looked at Abigail with what she felt certain was a flare of recognition. Her eyes fell to the table, and her hair cascaded in a shroud around her face. She wondered if the cop recognized her from all the news reports of her "abduction" by John.

What would he do if he did? *Will he come over here and*

*ask me to come with him? Or make some calls for backup and have
the whole place surrounded? Crap, crap, crap.*

Abigail's leg bounced beneath the table, a mean sickness stirring in her belly.

Please don't recognize me. Please, please, please.

Abigail dared to peek past her curtain of dark hair, and saw that the cop was still looking at her oddly, almost owl-like as he peered out through his oversized glasses.

Cold sweat beaded Abigail's back.

God, he does recognize me!

She pictured the cop getting up and coming over, then grabbing her by the arm and saying something like, "Hey, don't I know you?" His hand would lock onto her, then burn along with the rest of his body, an inferno from the inside out as she sucked his life to nothing, even while trying not to. Katya would leap up from the table, terrified and screaming, wondering what sort of monster had been sharing her meal.

The nausea in Abigail's stomach rose into to her throat, coating it with vinegar.

Seconds from vomit, she stood from the table, silent as she walked as fast as she could without drawing attention, across the restaurant toward where painted ivy ended on the wall at the small hallway leading to the bathroom. Sickness threatened to burst from her mouth as she ran past diners nestled in their booths, focused on the restrooms ahead in the dark hallway at the restaurant's rear.

Vomit was seconds from spilling. She hoped the bathroom wasn't occupied, or worse, locked.

Please be open, please be …

She pushed the door, half expecting resistance. Finding none, Abigail fell into the bathroom, ran into a stall, and fell to the floor as vomit spewed from her mouth in a violent, painful eruption, spraying everywhere: some in the toilet, and the rest on the seat, wall, and chipped tile floor.

Abigail felt knives in her head, piercing her thoughts, until suddenly she was flashing back on memories that were not hers.

Karen's past tore through her system first, shredding Abigail's thoughts as they went — first Karen was laying in bed with her newborn baby, feeling so happy, softly pinching his squishy cheeks, singing to him. Then more memories: Karen stressed out and weeping, her son crying, sick with a fever. Karen was exhausted and didn't know how much more she could take. She felt awful for thinking of herself when her child was sick, but was running on empty.

God, why can't you help me?

Karen's memories were swallowed by another's — Hank Terault's, a man she'd killed three months ago. A monster of a man who bullied his wife, child, and senile father. He'd escaped the justice system, but not Larry and Abigail.

She suffered through the man's final moments and abuses in rewind until flashing through his memories as a child, before his doddering father was fighting dementia, and was quite the monster himself. Hank was 6, and had accidentally turned off the TV during a football game. His father shoved him aside, to the ground, grabbing the remote from Hank's hand. As the TV flickered back to life, his father screamed, "You dumb fuck! I missed the touch-down!" His dad smacked him hard in the head with the remote, repeatedly until the black plastic was sticky with red.

Hank balled up on the ground crying. His mom tried to pull his father from his body until he turned on her, and let everyone in the house feel his hellfire's unrelenting heat.

Abigail's head swirled with their memories, before a trio of others joined them, all five flashing through her mind like a blitzed-out cable box furiously switching channels. Abigail was barely aware of herself, as if she'd been banished from her body, clutching the toilet, emptying her insides until she felt a sudden but gentle hand on her back.

Abigail jumped, startled, and turned back, yelling, "Don't touch me!"

Katya withdrew her hand, eyes wide and startled; still alive, but only because she'd touched Abigail's shirt, and not anywhere on her skin.

Abigail was finally back in her own head, her victims' memories gone.

What was that?

She'd been assaulted by memories before, but only during a feeding and just after. Memories had never returned like this. Her head was swollen with a dull ache, and her body felt as if she'd thrown up half a cow. Her ribs felt ruined and her stomach spoiled. She was cold and shaking, as if stricken with flu.

"Are you okay?" Katya kneeled, and she got a better look at the girl whispered, "Oh, my God, Abigail, you're so pale."

Abigail looked away and closed her eyes as tears fell from between her shut lids.

Katya reached out to comfort her, but Abigail pulled back. "Don't touch me," she half snarled.

Their eyes met, and a sort of raw understanding seemed to light Katya's eyes, even though Abigail couldn't imagine how anyone *could* ever understand that there was a monster inside her.

Or that her monster needed to be continually fed, one life after life in a never-ending string of murders.

～

THEY RETURNED TO THEIR TABLE, and Abigail sat, not knowing what to say. She told Katya that her stomach was sick and that she wanted to go home, but they had to wait for the bill. They sat mostly in silence, the cop stealing glances.

He knows. He recognizes me.

Abigail looked down at the table, trying to ignore him.

The waiter set the bill on the table. Katya paid and they stood to leave. On their way toward the door, Katya stopped at the officer's table.

Oh God, no, what are you doing?

"I'm sorry, Jerry," she said to the cop who'd been eying their table. "I'll have to catch up another time. My friend here isn't feeling well."

Wait. He wasn't looking at me? He knows Katya?

A wave of relief washed against Abigail's shore.

"It's okay," he said. "Not feeling too good, eh? My kid's got a bug, too. It's going 'round. What's your name, sweetheart?"

"Abigail," she said, meeting his eyes with her best smile.

"You look so familiar. You go to Elmswood?"

Abigail shook her head.

"She's homeschooled," Katya said, setting a light hand on Abigail's shoulder. "OK, Jerry, see you later. I'll tell my dad you said *hi*."

"Tell him he still owes me for that Seahawks game!"

"Will do," Katya said, then waved goodbye to both officers.

"Bye," Abigail said, quick to follow Katya out the door, hoping the cop wouldn't remember where he'd seen her. Far more troubling than the officers, Abigail couldn't stop thinking about what happened in the restroom. Why had all those memories returned, and would it happen again?

It was if Abigail held a million scars inside her, each suddenly itching to be ripped open again. It was enough to have lived through the nightmares she'd endured — she prayed she wasn't now cursed to repeatedly live through her victims'. If so, she didn't know how long she could go on before she snapped.

ELEVEN

Hannah

GREG STARED at Hannah from across their kitchen table as if she were a delicate flower whose bloom might be lost to the slightest breeze.

"I'm fine," she insisted. "I just want to go."

Their trip was slated for the morning, delayed once by her accident. She wasn't willing to postpone it again. Given their schedules, if they didn't leave tomorrow, she and Greg probably wouldn't find time for another year.

"Are you sure? You're not just doing this for me?"

"I swear. They wouldn't have let me come home if I wasn't Okay. You heard the doctor, I'm fine."

Greg pushed his coffee mug aside and reached for Hannah's hand. "I'm sorry, I know what the doctor said. It's just that I can't help but think … "

"What?" she asked as he trailed off, as if afraid to voice his worst fear.

"I just can't get over the feeling of you looking at me like I was a stranger. I mean, you had *no* idea who I was. It was so, I don't know, *surreal*," he finished with a whisper.

"The doc said it was temporary. Hell, I don't even

remember waking up that first time when you said I didn't recognize you. Everything was normal when I woke up again, right?" She smiled, but didn't wait for Greg to smile back. "I'm okay, Honey. Really. We should go. Besides, after messing up the wedding, I *need* this trip! The last thing I want to do is go back to the Boutique right now."

"Mrs. Graham will get over it."

While Hannah's man always had the right things to say, he wasn't always convincing. She knew he didn't really believe Mrs. Graham would get over her daughter's wedding being ruined. Sure, it was an accident, but it was an accident that never would've happened if Hannah hadn't stored the stupid flowers in Mr. Fanaroff's cooler. The *why* didn't matter, Becca's wedding was botched. There was a good chance Hannah's shop would never recover once whispers grew to shouts that she'd shit the bed on such an important wedding. Who would entrust her with their most important of days after this?

"Maybe," she said, not wanting to argue. "But right now, I need to get away. And I think we *both* need the time together, don't you?"

"Yes, I just want to be certain you're okay."

"I have a few bruises, a wrecked van, and plenty of dead flowers, but other than that I'm fine. I swear."

Greg smiled. His smile, blue eyes, and boyish charms always had a way of disarming her frequent bouts of anxiety. He was an always-calming influence in her otherwise hectic life. How he could remain so relaxed through even the most stressful situations, Hannah had no idea, but it was one of the things she loved most about him. Even if she wasn't up to going on vacation, she still would have felt like she owed it to Greg. He was always there for her. In a sea of dipshits, he was the one man who held her heart.

"Thank you." Greg stood from the table and took their

plates to the sink. "I'm going to call the office and let them know we're going for sure."

"Tell them you'll be unreachable for the week!" Hannah said, as if there were actually a chance of *that* happening.

Greg went to his office to call his boss. Hannah stayed at the table, running through her mental inventory of stuff she had to ready by morning. She'd already packed their essentials, but wanted to make sure she thought of all the little things she might need as well — her iPad, camera, memory cards, battery charger, and of course, her new sexy lingerie. This was a romantic getaway, after all.

She wondered *how* romantic Greg was planning to make it. A small part of her wondered if this would be when he popped the question, not that she was even sure she wanted to get hitched. Greg wanted a family, and Hannah thought she probably did, though she often wavered on the thought. At first, she thought she was too selfish for a child, driven by her work. But hell, there were plenty of successful women entrepreneurs who also raised a family. Many did it without a partner's help, so there wasn't any reason she couldn't, too.

For as long as Hannah could remember, she felt something was missing from her life — a void to fill. At first, she thought it was a steady relationship she'd been missing out on. She'd had enough crappy ones to appreciate a good one when it came along. And even though Greg was great, *something* was missing. Only recently did she begin to think it might be her biological clock ticking.

It began with a feeling she got when seeing parents with their kids. While children had previously seemed like an obstacle and a time suck she couldn't afford, lately, those feelings were replaced with *awws* and wishful thinking, wondering what it would be like to carry a life in her, to see the look of unconditional love in her child's eyes. Hannah had thought she'd been above "baby fever," but it turns out she wasn't.

And she wasn't getting any younger. Still, as untraditional as she was, Hannah didn't want to have a child without being married, and wasn't enough of a nontraditionalist to ask Greg *to marry her*.

She wondered if Greg was on the phone making secret plans for something grand and romantic. That was like him. The thought of coming home from their trip engaged put a stupid, happy happy smile on her face.

THAT NIGHT, they made love for the first time in more than two weeks, though it was less like making love and more like down-and-dirty fucking. Greg was usually a slow, sensual lover, but something primal growled from inside him. He was stronger, more assertive, and willing to take charge like he had during their first weeks in bed. More animal than man.

"You're so fucking sexy," Greg whispered into her flesh, his words sending currents through her veins. He claimed every inch of her skin with his mouth, moving slowly toward Hannah's small patch of tiny curls.

"Touch me," she panted.

He did, everywhere, before groaning so deep it was nearly a growl, then spinning her around and laying a heavy hand on her back. He pushed her down, hard into the mattress, then claimed her, speeding his thrusts as he took her from behind.

Greg grabbed a handful of Hannah's hair from the nape of her neck, then went even faster. A low roar shuddered from his mouth, swelling up and out from deep within his lungs as Hannah's breath snagged in her throat and her lower muscles tightened for release.

Greg pulled out, flipped Hannah in a return to her back, and sent her into a scream.

Greg was no longer there, in his place a man with long dark hair and piercing blue eyes. The man was gone in an instant, replaced by Greg, and Hannah's scream fell into a whimper. Greg seemed to mistake her momentary shock for lust, and used it to feed his animal.

He pounded her harder.

Hannah squeezed her eyes tight, imagining the dark-haired man ravishing her from above. He'd seemed somehow familiar, yet new and unknown. But something about him, even though she'd only seen him for a moment, was incredibly sexy. She thought of his eyes, staring deep into her soul. She kept imagining him, instead of Greg, and sank into the beautiful depths of fantasy.

Time swam until they finished, and Greg had emptied the animal inside, into her — the first time they'd had sex without a condom. And in that moment, she didn't care. Maybe she'd get pregnant and engaged in the same week. They lay entwined in one another's warmth, flesh on flesh, as Greg's eyelids fluttered, and quickly collapsed. Soon, he was snoring, leaving Hannah alone with her thoughts of the dark-haired man, wondering who he was and why she could think of nothing else.

As she began to drift, finally joining Greg in slumber, a name danced at the edge of her mind.

John.

TWELVE

Larry

"SHE GOT SICK AT THE RESTAURANT," Katya said.

Abi looked down, not wanting to meet Larry's gaze. He wasn't sure if she was still mad at him — he didn't think so — or if something had happened. Whatever it was, Abi wasn't saying, and Larry was growing worried as they stood in the kitchen trading small talk that meant nothing. He wanted Katya to leave so he could talk to Abi and figure out what had gone down.

But Katya was hanging around, like she wanted to speak with Larry alone, which stoked both curiosity and fear.

What the hell happened?

He wondered if Katya had somehow discovered her secret.

Eventually, Abi decided to head up to her room, saying she wanted to rest.

"I'll be up to check on you in a minute," Larry said, listening as she trudged up the stairs, into the bathroom, then into her room.

As her door closed, he mouthed the words, "What happened?"

Katya's eyes turned glassy with tears, but they didn't fall as she moved closer to Larry. "What happened to that girl?"

"Excuse me? She was with you tonight."

"No, not tonight, I mean before now. What *happened* to her?"

Larry wasn't sure what she'd pieced together, but his mind cycled through the many possibilities, trying to figure out what Abi might have said to trigger Katya's questions.

"What do you mean what *happened* to her?"

"Someone abused that girl,. Who was it?"

Larry stepped back, raising his hands, hoping like hell that Katya didn't think *he'd* done anything to Abi. She definitely sensed something, which meant Larry had to tell Katya some sort of story. It had to be believable without touching the truth.

"Keep your voice down," Larry whispered, motioning for Katya to quiet. "Let me walk you to your car, and I'll tell you more outside."

Katya eyed him, almost suspiciously, then followed his lead out the front door.

In front of Katya's car, Larry looked up toward Abi's bedroom window, blacked out to keep the nighttime inside, without any part in the curtains. Unless she'd gone to another darkened window, Abi wasn't watching.

"What happened to her?" Katya repeated.

"She was in a bad situation before she came to stay with me, that's all I can say."

"Was it your brother?"

"Oh God, no, but you're right, she was abused. That's why she's staying with me. My brother, her father, went to jail for killing the man responsible." Larry felt bad lying to Katya, but it was the first fiction to fly from his tongue, and one he felt might help explain whatever Abi had said or done.

He studied Katya to see if his lie was doing its job.

Her eyes softened. "Oh my God, the poor thing,"

"Yeah, she blames herself. A lot," Larry added for emphasis. "So, you want to tell me what happened tonight?"

"We were eating dinner and, out of nowhere, Abigail jumped up and ran to the bathroom. I followed after a minute, and went to check on her. She'd puked all over. I asked her if she was okay, but she didn't answer. So I reached out and asked her again, putting my hand on her back. She turned on me, her eyes like some sort of scared animal, screaming at me not to touch her. I knew something was wrong, but she wouldn't say what. Oh, God," Katya shook her head, palm to her forehead. "I feel so bad."

"It's okay," Larry said. "She'll be alright. Some nights are better than others. But this is why I can't leave her alone. I know I should've told you something before you took the job, but the Radleys said you were so good, and I saw how you were with their kid, and I didn't want to scare you off."

Katya nodded, wiping the falling tears from her eyes.

Larry felt like an asshole for lying, but it wasn't like he was more than a mile from the truth. Abigail had been raped by a monster and kept in a closet for years. She had no family. In reality, her situation was worse than the picture he painted, but Larry figured there was enough truth in the brush of his lie, that good intent would outweigh his crooked karma.

Larry met Katya's eyes and said, "Thanks for being

there for Abi tonight. I'm sure it means the world to her. Right now, she's probably just embarrassed."

"It's okay," Katya said. "Wow, I just feel so bad."

Larry hemmed and hawed, trying to find the best way to ask his next question. "Did we scare you away?"

Katya shook her head, sniffling, "Oh, God no, now I want to help her more than before. I feel so awful."

"Thanks again," Larry said, putting an awkward hand to her lower shoulder. "I better get back inside."

"Okay," Katya said, opening her car door. "Tell Abigail I said goodnight."

"Will do. 'Night, Katya."

"Goodnight," she said as she climbed into her car and started the engine.

As Katya drove off, Larry returned to the house, eager to find out what really happened at the restaurant.

~

LARRY KNOCKED ON HER DOOR. "ABI?"

After a long moment, she said, "Come in."

He opened the door to her pink and purple bedroom. She was laying in bed, in a T-shirt and sweats, a pillow over her face, probably crying.

"Are you okay?"

"I don't know," Abi said, her voice muffled beneath the pillow.

"Katya is worried about you."

"Yeah, I kinda freaked out on her."

"She told me."

"And? Is she going to quit watching me?"

"No. She'll be back tomorrow. She said you can't get rid of her that easily."

"Really?" Abigail pulled the pillow away from her face. Larry was relieved to see her eyes hinting at a smile.

"Yeah, she likes you a lot, Abi. She did ask if anything had *happened* to you," Larry said, unsure how to broach the girl's abuse. It wasn't something they'd discussed much, even though they'd gone together to her uncle's house to repay the man that sold her into slavery.

"I told her someone had abused you, and that your dad, my brother, killed him and went to jail."

"Wow," Abigail said. "You're a good liar."

"Well, I had to tell her something close to the truth, without telling her, well, you know, the truth."

"Yeah," Abigail said, staring at her bedspread. "What do you think she would do, you know, if you did tell her the truth?"

"What part? What happened to you, or about you being a vampire?"

"Vampire," Abi said.

"I don't know," Larry said, hoping Abi wasn't getting any ideas of confiding to her new friend. "But we can't take the chance, you know that, right? Katya's a great girl, but we don't know her that well, and we have to fly under the radar here."

"Yeah," she nodded. "I know."

Abi squeezed her largest, softest pillow, tightly to her chest.

"What?" Larry sensed that Abigail wanted to say more.

"I think there's something wrong with me."

Larry sat at the end of the bed. "What do you mean?"

"The people I killed," Abigail said, pausing with a swallow before she continued. "When I was getting sick at the restaurant tonight, I kept seeing their memories in my head. I was remembering things like they happened to me, but all of the memories were *theirs*. None of them were mine. It's like what happens when I feed, but this was the first time it's happened while I wasn't feeding."

"Whose memories were you seeing? Karen's?"

"Hers and others. A bunch."

"How bad was it?" Larry said, suddenly and almost painfully nervous. "And how long did it last?"

"Terrible. I felt like I wasn't even in my body. Not sure how long it lasted, but I don't think it was long."

"And that's the first time it's ever happened when you weren't feeding?"

"Yeah," Abi nodded. "Do you think you can get John to come visit? I want to ask him if this is normal."

"I think so." Larry nodded.

"How do you feel now?"

"Fine, I guess. Just tired. And sad."

"Why are you sad?" Larry said, knowing the girl could reel off any number of reasons, and each one legitimate. She'd had a shitty life, and was now living mostly alone, except for his lousy self, and now a few hours of company with Katya per day. Far from a normal life for a girl her age, or any age.

"I don't know. I'm just so tired of killing."

Larry sighed. "But you have to feed, or you'll die. I thought you were fine with it, so long as we were killing bad people."

"But they're not all bad."

Larry swallowed. "Listen, I know Karen was a mistake. And I'm sorry. I should've done a better job with my research. It won't happen again. I promise."

"It's not just her," Abigail said, meeting Larry's eyes.

"What do you mean? There are other innocents?"

"No, not that. But they aren't *all* bad. A lot of them were good as kids, then their parents, or other people, hurt them. Abused them like Randy did to me. For some of them, stuff was even worse. They were turned into monsters."

Larry paused, not wanting to say the wrong thing. "Are you saying we should feel bad for them?"

"Well, yeah, we should, but that's not what I'm saying. What I'm trying to say is that every time we kill another one, I feel their pain. *All* their pain. Their sadness gets added to mine, as if all the bad things that ever happened to them have happened to me too. I don't know how many more times I can feed on that, especially if the memories are going to keep coming back.

Larry swallowed. He'd never considered the consequences of feeding from evil, or how it might affect someone so young. "I don't know what to say."

"How does John do it?" Abigail asked. "He only kills bad guys, too, right?"

"Yeah, but he's been doing it a lot longer. Plus, he's not human, so I'm thinking it's probably different for him. He might be able to compartmentalize things better." Larry smiled. "Maybe he can teach you to do it, too."

"You think?"

"Yes," Larry nodded, still smiling while hoping he wasn't telling yet another lie.

Abi smiled, then reached out and circled her sleeved arms around Larry's gut, leaning into him with a giant hug.

"Thank you, Larry."

He hugged her back, swearing she felt more fragile than ever.

THIRTEEN

John

IT HAD BEEN MORE than an hour since John heard from Tiny, and, adding another layer of dread to his worry, the big man wasn't answering any telepathic attempts to reach him.

Has our connection dropped?

Has something happened to him?

John didn't know the man well, but Tiny had sacrificed his mortality to become a vampire and help John battle Jacob's Harbingers. In turning Tiny, John had seen inside the man enough to know he was nothing if not loyal. If Tiny said he'd try to find him, he would.

But will he in time?

John sank to the ground, leaning against the iron door where he felt certain someone was either standing or sitting on the other side. He would have thought it was Shadow, waiting for him to die, except that didn't make sense. If they wanted him dead, why not just kill him while unconscious? Surely, someone like Shadow had a magickal onyx blade at his disposal that could easily kill John.

But they hadn't killed him, which meant something

else. John wondered if they were trying to scare him, or maybe waiting to question him. He supposed that made more sense. They saw him as the enemy, and rightly so, which gave them plenty of reason to interrogate him.

Or maybe they're holding you hostage, trying to trade money for your life.

That was a possibility John had yet to consider, but it didn't seem like something Harbinger, or even Shadow, if he was working alone, would do. While he supposed they *could* extract money from Omega, John didn't think it was likely that Shadow would hand him, a powerful enemy, back. They *had* to be looking for information.

"Why are you holding me here?"

Still, no answer. After another minute of horrible silence, someone finally spoke.

"Why did you find me?"

"Shadow?"

"Yes. Why did you find me, John?"

He knows who I am. Of course, it's his job to know shit.

"I'm trying to find Jacob. He's back."

"Yes, I know."

"That's all I wanted. Can you help?"

Shadow laughed, long and hard until the laugh collapsed into a rattling cough. "You want help from *me*? After what you've done to my people?"

"I've done nothing to your people."

"Don't insult me with lies, John. I have no patience for the profanity of truth. What's it like working with the Gestapo? How do you sleep through your daylight without torment from what you've done?"

John said nothing. What could he say to defend the past year? Shadow was right, and right to condemn him.

"What do they pay you, John, to betray your people? How much are our lives worth?"

"They don't pay me," John said.

"So, you volunteer?"

"They're forcing me. They have someone close to me, and they said if I didn't help them find Harbingers, and eradicate their threat, they would kill this person."

Shadow coughed again. "That's a touching story, John. It's good to know there's at least a reason for your betrayal."

"I didn't betray anyone!" John growled. "It's not my fault if some innocents were swept in the raids."

"No, they're just collateral damage, right, John?"

"If you consort with the enemy, you *are* the enemy, at least in Omega's eyes."

"In mine, too, John. If *you* consort with the enemy, then *you* are the enemy. So, tell me, how many lives have you taken for the enemy?"

John shook his head. "I don't know."

"How many?" Shadow screamed from the other side of the door, pounding on the metal before falling into another fit of coughs.

He was angry, but why, John wondered — had he, or Omega, killed someone close to Shadow?

Shadow, quieter this time, repeated his question. "How many?"

"Seventy-one."

Silence from the other side. Then, "Do you see their faces when you sleep?"

John nodded, then said, "Yes."

"And among these faces, do you see this one?"

John was confused. "Which one?"

His brain was suddenly invaded by Shadow, forcing his way inside John's mind swiftly enough to break through every defense. Before John could fight him off, or push him back, Shadow was in full control, forcing John to flash through memories from all the people he'd either helped kidnap or murder through the year. Faces, eyes, and terrified screams rang through John's mind and memory as Omega raided houses, squatter's pads, apartments, and even hidden camps in the mountains.

Memories flashed like lighting, striking at his psyche, but not enough to make him feel the pain he'd inflicted. He'd killed no innocents, at least none he knew of. John's targets were all Harbinger. Yet, Omega's agents had, and the flooding memories paused as Shadow found the one which interested him most.

He tapped into the memory and forced John to watch.

It was a house in the Cherry Grove suburbs. They were acting on a tip that a known Harbinger magick user was hiding in one of the homes. They stormed the three-story lookalike house at three in the morning, with John leading the charge through the living room, then up the stairs to a family waking in chaos.

A father, mother, and a 6-year old girl.

John didn't need the memory played further, he knew what was coming. Shadow forced him to watch anyway.

John was led to the basement where they found the man they were looking for, despite the homeowner's pleas that they knew nothing. John helped the agents subdue the magick user, shoving a hood over his head while ignoring the gunshots erupting upstairs.

Mike Mathews had control of the hostage, so John, along with three other agents, ran up to the second floor where all three family members lay sprawled on the carpet, shot dead.

"The man pulled a gun on me," Agent Broslin said, though no weapon lay on the ground.

John stared at the trio of bodies, horrified as the little girl looked up, not yet dead — a glimmer of life barely lighting her dying eyes. He kneeled beside her, remembering staring into Abigail's dead eyes.

The girl looked confused more than anything. John wanted to save her — to turn her — but was afraid of what the agents would do. Even if they let him save her, there was no way they'd let her go. If turned, they'd either imprison her, or use her, same as him.

"I'm sorry," he whispered.

The light in her eyes faded then died.

As the memory collapsed, Shadow fled from John's mind as suddenly as he'd invaded.

"Who was she?" John whispered.

"My daughter. Her mother died giving birth. I couldn't take care of her, so I found someone who could. An old friend. An ally to our people."

"I'm so sorry," John said, knowing there was nothing he could say to soothe the man's pain, or earn his forgiveness.

"Yes, I see that. But as you say, those who consort with the enemy are the enemy. Goodbye, John."

John heard Shadow moving away from the door.

"Please," John cried out, pounding iron. "If Jacob returns, many more innocents will die! You know it, Shadow!"

Shadow said nothing.

John kept screaming until he finally surrendered, knowing that Shadow was either gone, or sitting with his back to the door, enjoying John's torment.

All John could do was focus on the space above, feeling the earliest hints of the morning sun, no more than forty minutes from bleeding over the horizon. John had another hour, two at most, before the light was strong enough to reach the well's bottom.

"Hello?" John called out on the off chance someone

was above ground, or that maybe Tiny was close by. He heard nothing.

Several minutes later a car pulled up and stopped at the top of the well.

Tiny?

"Hey, John, can you hear me?"

Yes!

"Yes! I'm down here! In the well!"

"I'll be right there!"

Wait, Tiny. Watch out for Shadow! He's close by, though I don't know where!

"Who?"

John felt an explosion of excruciating pain in his head — shared by Tiny.

John shouted through his torment. "Tiny!"

Moments later, a dark shape appeared, blotting the purple sky. John squinted, trying to see who it was. Two seconds into his squint, the shape plummeted toward him. John jumped out of the way as the shape hit the ground.

Tiny lay on the ground, gushing blood.

FOURTEEN

Greg

GREG WOKE TO MURMURING.

He slowly opened his eyes and turned to see Hannah's beautiful face, barely lit by the blue light softly glowing from their bathroom.

Greg couldn't wait to get to the cabin. His cock throbbed at the thought of another night like the one they'd just shared. He wasn't sure what had got into Hannah, but *damn* if he couldn't do that on repeat.

She murmured again, as she sometimes did in her sleep, just one of the many cute things he loved so much about her. Hannah's brow furrowed, her eyes moving rapidly move under their lids.

"No," she cried, kicking her leg hard into his shin.

Greg pulled back, surprised, expecting her to wake after kicking him. But she didn't, still in the depths of her nightmare.

"Stop it," she cried out, loud enough that Greg would have thought her in danger had he heard her from across the house.

He thought about waking her, but something inside him said to wait it out.

Her face relaxed, then she giggled.

He smiled, relieved to see her self-soothing.

Her giggles turned to moans, and Greg's cock grew hard again.

Is she having a sex dream? I wonder if I'm the star?

He was pleasantly shocked as her hands drifted down to her crotch, moaning louder as she churned herself into a sticky mess beneath the sheets.

No way she's sleeping. She's messing with me. I know it. I should crawl on top of her so we can start round two.

He glanced at the clock. Only four in the morning. They could go another round and he'd still be able to get a few more hours of sleep before hitting the road in the morning.

He slid off his boxers, but before he could mount her, Hannah moaned again.

"Oh, John," she said, her voice sounding somehow different.

Greg's eyes widened.

John?

"Stop, John," she said playfully, giggling, her hands still stewing beneath the sheets.

Greg stood, heart racing and erection dead.

He slipped quietly from their room, then went down the hall and into his office, clicking on the small lamp beside his desk.

He opened his laptop. Its glow lit his face as he clicked on email and started typing a message to Bob Cromwell.

We have a problem. Hope is remembering.

FIFTEEN

John

"YOU OKAY?" John asked.

Tiny stared up at him, confused, blood gushing from a six-inch gash, slashed in a lazy river across the big man's stomach.

"Yeah, I think so." Tiny sat up, pulled his black tee up the length of his torso, and lightly pressed his fingers into the depths of his wound through the pouring blood. His flesh was already stitching itself healed. "Shit, I had worse than this before I was near invincible."

"What happened?"

"Little fucker snuck up on me, stabbed me before I even saw him. Confused the sense out of me before I knew what was happening. I couldn't think straight, or defend myself. He picked me up and threw me in here, even though he was a buck thirty tops."

"That's Shadow; he's a Halfworlder," John said. "With all sorts of magick weapons, powders, and spells. No telling what he did for sure, but I'd guess he only stunned you. Think you can get up?"

Tiny stood, wobbly at first, then looked back to his

wound, completely healed and nearly invisible except for the fresh pink scar painted across his dark skin, where it would stay for at least a day until it turned invisible.

"So what the hell we gonna do now?" Tiny asked.

John looked up at the well's opening and the moonlight which would soon be sunlight painting the well's stone walls and bringing their death. Then he looked at the door. "If you can help me open this, maybe we can get out of here. Shadow did something to me. I'm a lot weaker than I was. I can't get the thing to budge. And I can't climb or jump for shit."

Tiny pushed at the door, shoving his shoulder hard enough against the metal to nudge a groan from his mouth. The door didn't move, or flinch in its frame, so Tiny took a few steps back and ran into it like a bat to a ball with the bulk of his body. Still, the door didn't budge.

"Shit!" Tiny said. "I'm weaker, too. What the hell?"

"I don't know," John said, scrounging the well's bottom with his eyes, searching for something, anything among the dirt and debris in the darkness that might help them escape the well.

John focused again and tried to reach Larry.

Still nothing.

John wondered why he could reach Tiny but not Larry or Abigail. Tiny shared the Darkness with him, same as Abigail — with the same parasite bred into them both. They were, in essence, his parasite's children, and if he'd been able to connect with Tiny, he should've been able to connect with Abigail. If he could contact her, she could tell Larry to save them.

John tried reaching out to her again.

Abigail?

Nothing.

A round of automatic gunfire cracked the pre-dawn silence.

"Shadow!" a man screamed out. "Just give us the crystal."

John looked at Tiny. "You bring friends?"

"No, didn't have time to round up the crew, though I wish I had."

John closed his eyes, absorbing the outside world in his mind — he felt several people closing in on Shadow.

What the hell? What crystal?

Another round of gunshots punctuated the darkness as Shadow's fear continued to balloon, so swollen it pulsed inside of John as though it were his own. Shadow's fear was a rising tide of confusion. Shadow knew at least some, if not all of the people in his ambush.

John turned to Tiny. "I think his people turned on him."

"How you know that?"

"I can sense some of Shadow's thoughts. You can't?"

"Hell, no. It's not like you gave me an instruction manual with these powers, bro."

John laughed. "I don't know how I do it. I just do. Afraid I can't help you there."

Sudden movement skittered on the other side of the door, like an injured animal thrashing.

John turned to Tiny. "Get ready, he's coming!"

Tiny balled his fist. John stood back from the door, ready to pounce.

The door burst open and Shadow threw up his hands. "Wait, wait! I'm not going to hurt you!"

Tiny moved in to take a swing, but John waved him back. "Hold on," he said, studying Shadow as he closed and locked the door, sealing them off from his enemy despite the large opening above. John imagined the men aiming their weapons down and firing.

"My people turned on me. They brought Harbinger here."

"Why?" John asked.

Shadow looked Tiny up and down. "Who's he?"

"A friend," John said, figuring Shadow could get four from two and two, see that Tiny was a vampire, and maybe even sense he was John's. "Why did your people turn on you?"

"Because my father, until he died two weeks ago, was a vessel. Now someone wants what he had."

"What the fuck is a vessel?" Tiny asked.

"We don't have time for a long story. You just need to know that I, and four others, are all that stands in the way of the world's utter destruction. Help me escape, and I'll tell you everything you need to know."

Tiny said, "And you ain't gonna try an' kill us again?"

"I wasn't trying to kill you," Shadow said. "I was trying to get away from you. I don't know who I can trust, and when John here rolled up on my hotel with the men in black, what the hell was I supposed to do?"

"So, how do we escape?" John asked. "Can you make another portal?"

Shadow laughed, "I'm good, but I'm not *that* good. Those things take time to prepare, and ingredients I don't exactly carry with me. There's a network of underground tunnels leading into the sewers. We make our way through them, find a way topside, and get to where I stashed the list."

"What list?"

"The list with the names of the other vessels. If Harbinger's after it, that means they're looking to kill everyone on that list."

"We're in," Tiny said before John. "But first, you need to give us our powers back."

"Don't worry, you'll be fine once we get out of here. I put damper spellstones at the bottom of the well to prevent feeders from escaping."

"Damper spellstones? That some kinda kryptonite or something?" Tiny asked.

"They won't kill you, so not exactly, but yes, you can say that."

~

THE TUNNEL WALLS were slimed with moss and something black, smelling like death at its dankest. They moved across the slippery ground, squinting through the dark amber glow of Shadow's lightstone, not that John needed it, as his senses had quickly grown used to the lack of light once he'd left the well's dampening effects behind.

They wound their way through the old man-made structures, mostly going straight, but taking a right once, and a left twice, walking in mostly silence for nearly 10 minutes.

"I didn't even know these tunnels were here," Tiny said.

"They were built back when the city was made," Shadow explained. "They were used by Otherworld Smugglers who would traffic artifacts, and people, into and out of town. Some were used during prohibition, with a lot of the tunnels leading to the basements of speakeasies. Most of the exits have long since been sealed off, but a few are still active. We're not too far from where the tunnels split into three different paths. The one in the middle leads to old sewage systems."

"That's probably where they'll be waiting," John said.

"For sure," Tiny agreed. "They have these freaky magick knives like you?"

"I don't know," Shadow said. "I doubt they figured they'd need anything other than guns against me. Bullets will do the job fine. I'm half-human, and all human weakness."

"So you might wanna stay back and let the vampires take care of business," Tiny winked.

Footsteps splashed through the shallow water, just ahead. Lights bounced off the wall — Harbinger soldiers, no doubt.

"Stand back," John thrust his hand in front of Shadow, then stepped forward to block his movement. Splashing grew louder. Shadow extinguished his stone's red glow.

Eight guns with lights rushed at John, Tiny, and Shadow. "Get down, hands in the air!" one of the Harbinger soldiers shouted as if they had any authority.

"Stay back," John repeated to Shadow, then turned to the soldiers.

John sensed the first soldier's itch for his trigger before he pulled it, so he pivoted out of the way. Shadow dipped into a swath of the tunnel's darkness, drawing it like a cloak around his body.

Shots fired from a soldier's gun, bullets whizzing off concrete as Tiny went into motion, a blur of darkness descending upon the gunman. Within seconds, the gunman was reduced to a screaming, burning heap as Tiny yelled, "Yeehaw!"

Gunfire erupted around them as the other soldiers fired on Tiny.

With seven left for John, he started two at a time, leaping toward the closest two soldiers and landing hard with a hand on each one. The soldiers struggled, but never stood a chance. Their screams died inside their helmets, as everything they once were and ever would be flooded into John, teasing his hunger for more.

As the soldiers' lifeforces, and memories, swirled inside John, he swatted the guns from the three soldiers Tiny wasn't taking care of.

As John circled in on the now unarmed soldiers, two of the three drew pistols from their holsters. One of the men Tiny was tussling with, managed to break free of his grasp, as Tiny must not have found a way to breach the man's suit yet to burn him. John looked up just in time to see the man's pistol aimed at his head. While John could take numerous shots to his body, a headshot could be mean death.

Tiny shoved the soldier he was fighting with aside and leaped on the other man just as he squeezed a shot off at John. Tiny smacked the man's hand just before the shot got off, knocking the gun to the ground and sending the bullet into John's right calf.

"Sorry, John!" Tiny yelled, then grabbed both soldiers, wrapping them both in a giant bear hug, his hands finding their way under the men's helmets, sending them both into screaming spasms.

One of the three remaining soldiers got a hold of his fallen rifle and began spraying the tunnel in a desperate panic. John threw out his hands and sent a blast of energy into the man, sending him flying backward into the two men who had gotten behind him for safety.

As the men fell back, John raced forward, and was on them in seconds, feasting on their energy, feeling it surge through his body like a thousand fires, but without the pain.

John heard Tiny yelling in victory as he finished off the last of the soldiers, but John was in too much bliss to open his eyes. He basked in the power, feeling it heal him entirely, replenishing his strength, and making him feel unstoppable, like the perfect killing machine.

He opened his eyes to the sound of Tiny calling out for Shadow, "OK, it's safe to come out now."

But Shadow wasn't coming.

"Shadow?" John asked, an uneasy feeling ruining his good buzz.

But there was no Shadow — he had used the distraction to escape.

"So what the fuck do we do now?" Tiny asked.

John said, "We keep walking. Follow Shadow's scent."

"Think we'll find him?" Tiny asked.

"We don't have a choice," John said.

SIXTEEN

Abigail

IN THE DREAM, Abigail was in school, and not a vampire.

She was a normal 11-year-old girl, sitting at a desk watching the boy beside her, trying not to stare. He was cute, with brown hair and blue eyes. He looked like a baseball player. Abigail wasn't even sure what a baseball player was supposed to look like, but the boy definitely looked like one in her dream.

He turned to her, then smiled and said, "Hi, my name's Bobby."

It was weird, him introducing himself in the middle of class. The teacher, who was only vaguely there, stood three feet from the front row, wrapped in a thick fog like the rest of the room. In Abigail's dream, the only things that mattered were her and the cute boy — Bobby.

She wasn't sure what to say. Abigail had never spoken to a boy her own age, not since she was much younger, and back then they were gross, not ... *cute*.

"I'm Abigail," she said, looking down shyly.

Still smiling, the boy said, "Abigail, that's a pretty name. What are you doing here?"

"What do you mean?"

"Why are you here?" he repeated, his smile now faltering, creeping to fear, matching the concern in his eyes.

He disappeared, and Abigail woke to the sound of a man screaming, immediately followed by a woman's screech.

She opened her eyes, confused to find a man and woman lying in her bed. The man was large, with curly dark hair, in his 40s, Abigail guessed. His wife was big too, blonde, a bit younger, maybe. They looked vaguely familiar, though she couldn't remember where, or if, she'd seen them before.

What are they doing in my room?

Abigail finished the thought, then realized it wasn't they who had come into her house — she was in theirs.

Abigail screamed.

"What are you doing in here?" the man shouted, reaching into his nightstand.

The man fished out a pistol and aimed it at Abigail before she recognized the danger.

"Where am I?" she asked, shaking, looking around the unfamiliar room, trying to figure out how she'd gone from her bedroom to this one, and how far she was from home.

"We don't have any money!" the man shouted, waving his gun. Anger rolled from his body in waves, tinged with fear in bright orange waves of aura.

"I don't want any money." Abigail glanced at their nightstand clock: *5:30 a.m.* She vaguely remembered going to bed early, not feeling too well, sometime around three.

How did I get here?

"I don't know how I got here, sir," she cried out to the man, backing away from the bed.

"Look, Jack, she's just a kid," the woman said, leaning

closer and looking at Abigail. "Put the gun down for Christ's sake!"

"No! She might not be alone. You call the police." Jack reached out for the nightstand, handed the phone to his wife, then stood, cautiously holding the gun on Abigail. "You come with me, missy."

"Where are you going?" his wife asked.

"To check on Bobby."

Bobby?

As the man flicked the lamp on, her eyes found a framed photo on the dresser — the boy baseball player from her dream. *Bobby.*

He's real?

"No, please don't call the police," Abigail begged. "I swear, I'm here by myself. I don't even know how I got here. I just want to go home, I think I might've been sleep-walking or something, I swear, I don't know what's happening."

"Call the police!" the man repeated his order.

"Please," Abigail said, bursting into tears. "Please don't call. I'm so scared." Not sure what else to say, Abigail went with a lie. "I can't go back home … he'll hurt me."

The woman paused, clutching the phone to her chest.

The man said, "What?"

"My Daddy likes to hurts me. Tonight he was going to hurt me again, so I snuck out of the house. Now he's looking for me. I was trying to find somewhere to hide."

Jack looked at her, licking his dry lips, likely trying to decide if he believed her or not. Abigail's tears must have been convincing. He turned to his wife.

"Hold on, Marge. She'll wait here while I check on Bobby."

"Thank you, mister," Abigail said with her best feigned sincerity. She wasn't sure what to do next, how she'd get out of the house without telling them where she lived, who her *daddy* was, or something to keep them from calling the cops. She realized with dread that telling them she was abused probably wasn't buying much time.

Jack looked annoyed, like he thought the girl might be messing with him, but he couldn't be certain and didn't want to be a jerk to a child whose father was abusing her. He left the bedroom, leaving Abigail with Marge. She held the phone without dialing, but her eyes, filled with glassy suspicion, were all over Abigail.

"What's your name, Honey?"

"Alice," Abigail said, thinking of *Alice in Wonderland*, which was exactly how she felt, trying to piece together where she was and how she woke in a strange house. "What street are we on?"

"1215 Elm Street," the woman said.

Abigail was five doors down from her house. That's probably why they looked vaguely familiar. She must've seen them on one of the few occasions they might have passed after sundown.

Jack screamed from down the hall. "Bobby! Oh, God, Bobby!"

Though Abigail had no memory of feeding on the boy, his father's grief-stricken scream could mean only one thing.

Oh, God, what did I do?

Marge's eyes lost their concern and crackled with fear. She fell back from Abigail and started to dial.

"No!" Abigail screamed, launching herself onto the bed and swiping at the phone. Her hand locked onto Marge's wrist and the feeding started, whether Abigail wanted it to or not.

The woman screamed as her life force flowed from her burning body into Abigail's, slowly at first, then faster.

Abigail's vision was replaced with a sudden cascade of memories from the woman's life.

Seven years old, bullied and running to tell the teachers: "They called me Large Marge the Sailing Barge!" Then she was 8, going to see a sneak preview of *E.T.* with her parents. They didn't get home until two in the morning because of the flat tire after the movie, but it was an awesome night, anyway.

Nine years old and terrified of riding the bus, Marge was intimidated by the other kids who always made fun of her. Mom gave her a small stone heart, and told her that whenever the heart was inside her pocket, she was never alone. For five years the stone never left her pocket, until one day Marge lost it at the park and couldn't stop crying.

Graduation from Duke, meeting Jack, getting married. Then Bobby, followed by countless merry memories of a loving family.

UNLIKE THE OTHERS Abigail fed on, Marge was mostly happy. Her memories swirled through Abigail's head, making her feel warm and pleasant, erasing many of the darker pasts she'd gathered over the year.

A sudden gunshot — and intense pain splintering inside her gut — interrupted the flow and killed her connection to Marge.

Abigail's eyes blinked back to the bedroom, staring at Jack, gun in hand. She looked down, saw the hole in her stomach, and involuntarily whimpered at the blood pouring out from inside it.

Jack fired again.

The second bullet slammed into Abigail's chest and

threw her back to the headboard where she lay still beside Marge's burned body.

"What did you do?" Jack screamed, running toward her, gun still aimed.

Pain pounded through her body, reminding Abigail of the agony she'd felt when shot a year before, back when she died in the motel parking lot. Before John saved her with his curse.

She looked up at Jack, seeing him through the filter of Marge's memories. He was a good husband. Kind, caring, loving. He'd worked hard to provide for their family. Marge truly loved him, even if they weren't as intimate as they'd once been. Jack was her everything. To see him in so much pain cut like a knife in Abigail's heart.

"I'm sorry," Abigail said through tears and torrents of pain, wanting, in the current of Marge's memories and feelings, to reach out and console him. But she was frozen, dying from the gunshot. Though John said she was nearly invincible, nearly wasn't *completely*. And this time her angel wasn't there to save the day.

This time, death was permanent.

Abigail couldn't move her limbs. Her eyes drifted in and out of focus as Jack kneeled beside his wife, mouth agape, unable to fathom what could have possibly happened to his sweet Margie.

"What are you?" he trembled, holding his wife's ashen remains, glaring at Abigail. "What kind of monster are you?"

Abigail continued crying, "I'm sorry," she said, fresh blood spilling from her mouth.

She said, "I'm so sorry, Jack."

When Abigail said his name, Jack's eyes narrowed on hers, grief and shock igniting a fire in them.

"Fuck you!" he said, dropping his gun, jumping over his wife's body, and attacking Abigail with his bare hands.

His hands found her neck, ending his life for hers.

She fed again — this time with happy memories crushed under the agony of a man finding his son and wife dead, killed by a monstrous girl.

Jack's darkness festered inside her own, killing the flickers of joy from Marge's memories, salting her wounds with misery and death.

SEVENTEEN

Hannah
_____

ARBOR FALLS, California

THE PICNIC LOOKED LIKE A POSTCARD.

Their basket spilled out from its spot on the blanket, laying on a bed of deep green grass a dozen yards from a glassy lake, nestled at the base of two smallish mountains. Greg said it was his favorite spot in California, if not the world.

Hannah looked out at the gorgeous landscape, and then to the gluttonous spread, smiling. She was tipsy, if not drunk. They were each responsible for preparing what they thought the other wanted, and while there was some over-lap, mostly with the skewers — melon, ham, mozzarella, cherry tomatoes, and artichokes — and sandwiches, with both sliced muffalettas made by Greg and tea sandwiches from Hannah, there were also small plates of fresh sushi, piles of finger fruits, though only cherries and grapes remained, and a copious amount of Hannah's homemade sangria.

"More sangria, my lady?" Greg proffered the large carafe in the nook of his arm as if it were a wine bottle and he a steward.

Hannah was already warm, and on the verge of three glasses too many.

"No, no, I'm good," she said, holding up a hand and giggling at his impression.

"That's good," Greg said, holding the carafe close to his eyes and lightly swirled the remaining liquid. "Not much more than a sip left, anyway." He lifted the large carafe to his lips, finished it off, then dropped it into the wicker basket.

"Wow, we finished all the sangria?" Hannah said, genuinely impressed.

"No, you finished most of it, you lush!" Greg jabbed his finger between her breasts, smiling.

"No, I didn't! You did." She set her glass on the blanket, crawled toward Greg, climbed on top, straddled him, then leaned into his body, kissed his mouth, and teased his lips with her tongue.

Hannah imagined they'd have a nice romantic evening in their bedroom after a long romantic bath in the oversize whirlpool Jacuzzi, but she was horny now, and no longer willing to wait. Greg's hardness pressed against his pants, and her dress.

She looked around to see if they were still alone. They were beside a lake in the middle of nowhere, save for a few other cabins in the distance. She couldn't imagine anyone sitting in their windows, watching with binoculars. If so, screw it, let them enjoy the show.

She laughed at the thought, and her current level of daring, then reached down to unbuckle his pants.

"What are you doing?" Greg asked, also looking around as if they were in the middle of Hanley Park back home, surrounded by joggers, kids playing, and people walking their dogs.

"I think you know," Hannah said, winking.

Greg laughed. "Wow, you are a terrible winker!"

"What?"

"Yeah, you're wink was kind of like, I dunno, Quasimodo?"

Hannah slapped him playfully across the chest, "Bastard!" then climbed off his crotch and pouted.

"I'm sorry."

"Nope, I don't accept your apology," she said playfully.

"You have to."

"Why?"

"Um," Greg looked to the violet sky as if there was a clever comeback hiding inside it. He opened his mouth, but his cell rang from inside the basket.

"I thought you turned it off!" She turned from Greg, reached into the basket, and looked at the display: *PRIVATE: BLOCKED.*

"Who is Private: Blocked? Is he related to General Pain?" She smiled, trying to make a joke.

"Gimme the phone," Greg said, rushing to answer.

Something, Hannah didn't know if it was because she was drunk, or annoyed that he was letting his work invade their time, made her hold the phone just out of reach. "Nope. No business. It's Us Time, remember?"

Greg reached for the phone and she pulled it back, hopping to her feet and sprinting away, laughing. Three steps from Greg, Hannah's foot knocked over her wine glass, and she fell to the grass, dropping the phone on the blanket.

Greg grabbed the phone, glared at her, then took the call.

"Greg here."

He began to walk off, likely looking for privacy, when Hannah felt a pang of hurt, from both his glare and indifference. He could have helped her to her feet, but had grabbed the phone instead.

What a jerk!

Hannah sat at the blanket's edge, watching the spilled red wine spread through the fibers. She fumed as Greg walked farther away from their cozy spot, into the woods along the trail they'd taken from cabin to lake, until he was nearly out of sight. What was so important that it couldn't wait? And what was with the blocked number?

"He's having an affair."

Her inner whisper was so sudden, insistent, and out of the blue, Hannah almost had to laugh. The whisper, as if it was from someone else, even though it was her voice and tone, demanded her attention.

"Think about it. He's always working late. Sometimes he takes calls in front of you for work, then other times, he goes off to another room. When he does take calls in front of you, it sounds like he's talking in coded language, like a parent who doesn't want their kid to catch on to Christmas planning."

No, he's not cheating! Greg is like the nicest guy I've ever known. Sure, he works a lot, and that's annoying, but so do I, and I'm not sleeping around. I truly doubt he is.

"Yeah? How would you know?"

Because I know!

"You don't even know what you don't know."

Hannah sat wondering what the hell that even meant. It was like she was arguing not with herself, but some other part of herself.

Maybe it fear was having her say.

She and Greg kept getting more serious, and her fear was searching for reasons to ruin things. Some part of her was so afraid of living the unknown with a man she loved,

Hannah was willing to trash it and stick with the known of isolation.

Hannah wished she had a girlfriend close enough to help her sort things out. Jenny was her only friend besides Greg, and an employee. Hannah had to distance the personal stuff. Even though Jenny's sordid life was an open book to Hannah, from her favorite sexual positions to her scariest dreams, Hannah never felt comfortable reciprocating.

Jenny often joked that Hannah needed to step out of her shell, trust more. And while Hannah *was* trying, it wasn't easy. As she watched Greg surface from the woods, some part, if not most of her, wondered who the hell he was talking to and why one phone call could make her feel like everything was wrong.

HANNAH SPENT the rest of the night trying to pretend she wasn't annoyed, until she finally lost it.

"I can't believe you didn't help me up." She turned to stare at the mountains, to keep from crying and hopefully hide the truth if she did.

Greg didn't apologize like Hannah expected. Instead he said, "I spend most of my day putting out fires, Hannah. You tripping in the grass isn't an emergency. That phone call was."

He should have punched her in the stomach. Less painful, and over quicker. His tone was so cold, and workmanlike, that it caught her by surprise. While he worked a lot, Greg was usually tender when spending time with her. Now, it seemed like he was being Work Greg, all business, no emotion.

They fought for a half hour. The closest Hannah and

Greg had ever come to fighting before, was when he didn't want to see a Jon Conway movie because "Conway was a douche bag." He was her favorite actor so she dug her heels in, but only for a few minutes until Greg offered to take her to dinner instead.

That was a silly fight, but this one was real.

It was horrible, but over quickly, with verbal anger erupting from either side. Greg eventually apologized: for the stresses of his work, for letting them bleed into their personal time like the wound they were, and for his job being so complicated and boring that it could barely be explained without a fresh cup of coffee for each of them, let alone added to their general conversation.

During the most heated flare of their battle, both were near snarling, just as they were when making up between the sheets.

HANNAH WAS DRIFTING between sleep and waking when her inner whisper came back.

"He's watching you."

What do you mean he's watching me?

"He's watching you sleep. Can't you feel him?"

No.

"Go ahead, open your eyes. You'll see that I'm right."

Hannah lay still for a moment, then decided to take a peek rather than open her eyes all the way. She peered from a barely fluttered lid, and saw Greg lying beside her, staring.

Startled, Hannah's eyes shot open.

She bolted up from the mattress.

"What the hell? You scared the crap out of me."

"Sorry, Baby," he said from behind a calm smile. "I was just watching you sleep."

She glanced at the clock beside his nightstand: 3:14 a.m.

"Why are you even up?" she asked as Greg pulled her close to his warm, naked skin.

"Couldn't sleep, I was horny."

"So, you what? Just stare at me, hoping I'd wake up?"

Greg smiled. "Worked, didn't it?"

"Yeah, you creeped me the hell out, if that's what you meant by 'worked.'" Hannah rolled over, as far from him on the bed as possible, yanked the covers around her, and turned toward the wall.

His cock found her backside as his left hand slithered up her torso to cup her breasts. His right hand trailed down between her legs. He slid three fingers inside her. Hannah swallowed, turned, and kissed him.

As she drifted from climax to slumber for the second time that night, her inner whisper hissed.

"He's lying to you, Hope."

Hope?

Hannah turned the thought in her mind for a moment, until its weight was too heavy to hold. Then she lost the thought and drifted to sleep trying to find it again.

HANNAH WAS SURPRISED to find Greg still sleeping when she woke the next morning. She lay in bed, thinking about their argument and trying to remember her dreams as a craving for melon claimed her. It took 10 minutes or so before the craving was sharp enough to pull her from the cozy bundle of down and blankets. Hannah peeled the covers from her

SEAN PLATT & DAVID W. WRIGHT

body, about to climb from the bed, when she noticed Greg's phone — which had been in his pants when they slipped into bed — sitting on top of the nightstand.

Did he check messages, or make a call? And who the hell is he calling? PRIVATE: BLOCKED?

An idea nudged itself to the front of her mind, either brilliant or horrible, depending on the outcome.

Hannah eased herself from bed, her eyes on Greg in the early morning light, watching as he slept, face down, on his stomach, snoring hard. She crept toward the spacious bathroom where she left her purse, slipped inside, softly closed the door, grabbed her purse, and sat on the toilet.

She rifled through her purse and retrieved her phone as she peed, thumbing through her apps until she found The Dictator, a funny but effective dictation app she used to record her ideas, everything from ways to mine more business from her standing orders, to ways she could reduce her spoilage. The app was voice-activated, meaning she could leave it running, and it would start recording only when she spoke.

But in this case, the app wouldn't be recording her voice.

She clicked *RECORD*, left the bathroom, and crept back into the bedroom with a hush. She scanned the room for somewhere discreet to bury her phone, then decided on the dresser, tucked behind a vase of fresh cut flowers. The dresser was close to the bed, as well as the doorway leading out to the balcony, and Hannah figured it would likely capture voice from either location.

I shouldn't do this. It's spying!

"No, it's called discovering truth, and you need to do it. If Greg is innocent, there's nothing to worry about, right?"

Right, she thought, hating herself anyway.

Hannah finished hiding the phone, then hopped onto the bed like an exuberant child.

"Rise and shine, sleepyhead!" she yelled, feeling almost as if she were faking an orgasm. "Still wanna go to El Montaño today? I was hoping we could get drunk on great wine, then pig out on amazing food."

"Yeah, yeah," Greg said groggily, maybe hung over. "Of course."

"Okay, I'm going to enjoy the Jacuzzi, then I'll need to dry my hair, put on makeup, and all that jazz, so you probably have another hour of snooze time."

"Well, gee, thanks for waking me up *now*," Greg said, turning over and burying his head under the pillow.

Hannah laughed, smacked him playfully on the ass, then went into the bathroom and turned on the faucet.

As she sank into the warm, bubbling water, Hannah closed her eyes, trying her best to relax, and stop wondering what she'd find later.

She thought about it every second anyway.

EIGHTEEN

Duncan

DUNCAN WOKE IN HIS BASEMENT, hungry and cold. Shaking, and feeling every bit of his thousands of years. Yet, he was glad to be alone in the dark, spared the indignity of what had happened in his home.

Upstairs, Jacob and his freaks — Harbinger soldiers and monsters — had commandeered his house. God knew what they'd done to the place and his life's work: collections of rare art, books, and artifacts from Otherworld, all now in the hands of the monstrosity, Jacob, and the creatures he'd brought with him. Duncan's estate had become, it seemed, Harbinger Central, at least while the monster plotted his evil plans for whatever the hell it aimed to do.

He sat up on the mattress that Jacob's beasts had brought down for him and looked up at the windows. Someone had nailed boards across them while he'd slept. There were no lights on, and the basement should've been pitch black, but Duncan could see well enough. Most of the large basement was filled with old furniture he'd not yet parted with, or stuff he'd told himself that he'd restore if he ever got back into restoration. Then there were boxes of stuff whose contents he couldn't remember, and the remnants of a food supply he'd kept in the basement, which Jacob's minions must've raided. Nothing screamed, *Use this to escape!*

Even if I could escape, where would I go like this?

He thought of the parasite inside him, evolving his body to turn him into the very things he'd been hunting for so much of his life — feeders, vampires, whatever the hell you wanted to call them.

Now he was one of them.

Duncan wished he could reach inside himself and pluck the disgusting monstrosity from his body, but it was now one with him, controlling his urges — more by the minute — and now some of his thoughts. Jacob used their psychic connection as a leash, making Duncan his dog.

Duncan had never been anyone's bitch.

The swirling regret, circling his mind ever since he was thrown down into the basement, was that he'd wasted his one shot on Jacob, when clearly he should have used it on himself.

Jacob tried prying information from inside him — chiefly where Jacob's brother, John, could be found. Duncan was trained in psychic warfare well enough to keep Jacob from the most sensitive information inside his mind, but it was difficult to maintain his vigilance with the parasite's constant sniffing for weaknesses in his mental firewall. It was only a matter of time before Jacob would break through his defenses.

Duncan had to find a way out of the basement. He didn't know where he'd go, but couldn't just wait to be used as a pawn in Jacob's game.

Duncan was considering his limited possibilities when

the door at the top of the stairway creaked opened and bright light from above pierced the gloaming.

"Hello, Mr. Alderman," Jacob said in the same cheerful voice that made Duncan want to rip the flesh from his face.

Duncan said nothing.

"How are you feeling?" Jacob asked, descending the steps. "Oh, wait, how silly of me. Why ask when I can simply tap into your head? Ah, let's see. Seems you're hungry. Is that right?"

Duncan said nothing.

"I can *make you* answer me, you know."

Sharp pain twisted through Duncan's brain, as if someone were sliding a knife through his skull. He screamed out, clutching his head with both hands, as if he could pry the dagger from inside him, and somehow kick Jacob out of his head.

"You can't evict me," Jacob said, reading his thoughts. "I'm a part of you now, Mr. Alderman. The pain ends only when I allow it to. Understand?"

He nodded, eager to end his torment. Duncan wanted to vomit, though he surely had little to lose.

"Say it," Jacob said, his voice dripping with sick glee.

"Yes!"

"Good," Jacob nodded. "Glad to see we're speaking."

The pain ended and took his urge to vomit.

"Now, I understand you don't want to tell me where John is, and that you're going to resist me. That's OK, Mr. Alderman. I admire your loyalty. And fortunately, for you, I don't really need to find him right now. I'm more concerned with the vessels, of course. But mark my words, a time will come when I ask you again. And you *will* answer when I do."

Duncan said nothing, glaring out from the shadows at the monster, standing at the foot of the stairs like a conqueror awaiting coronation.

The monster sighed and stepped toward Duncan. "You look at me with such hate, as if you're better than me."

Duncan said nothing, nor did he flinch when Jacob drew closer, stopping just inches from his mattress.

"Get up," Jacob ordered.

Duncan held his stare, already disgusted with himself for his surrender. Jacob was chipping at his will, and while Duncan had little doubt he'd eventually be broken, he refused to make it easy.

"I said get up." Jacob narrowed his eyes at Duncan.

He felt the thing inside him, worming its way through his brain until it found what it was looking for. One moment, Duncan was actively defying Jacob. The next, his body was rising from the mattress against his will, obeying its master.

Jacob smiled, smug and disgusting. Duncan longed to reach out and slit his throat. Somewhere upstairs, assuming Jacob had not found and destroyed them, he had two Otherworld onyx blades which would do the job perfectly.

"Wow, such violent thoughts, Mr. Alderman," Jacob laughed. "You and I, we're not so different."

"You're a monster," Duncan said, surprised he could speak since his limbs were ignoring commands to sit, strike, or do anything other than obey.

"Correction, *we're* monsters," Jacob said, jabbing his index finger sharply into Duncan's chest. "You and I are now the same. We are one. And soon, there will be many, many more. It's pointless to resist. Why put yourself through the pain of denying what must be?"

"You may have infected me, but I'm not a monster."

"We'll see about that,. Jacob smiled, then turned and headed back to the stairs, releasing control of Duncan's body.

He was a rag doll falling to the mattress. Duncan ran his hands over his limbs, feeling his true self slowly return to, staring at Jacob ascending the stairs. He stepped through the door, then leaned back through the doorway and said, "Oh, that was rude of me to leave without offering you a meal. I'm so sorry. Where *are* my manners?"

Someone else stepped through the doorway and was shoved by one of the Harbinger soldiers for hire: an attractive brown-haired woman — Duncan wasn't sure of her name — in her mid-20s. Until a couple of days ago had been one of his housekeepers.

She looked down, saw Duncan, then turned back at the top of the stairs where Jacob was closing the door.

"Bon appétit." Jacob laughed and closed the door, leaving Duncan to his *meal.*

∾

"ARE YOU OKAY, MR. ALDERMAN?" the housekeeper asked, slowly approaching him, hands bound behind her. He looked down, past the length of her black dress, noticed her missing shoes, and wondered if Jacob's men had taken them to keep her from trying to leave.

"I'm fine. Are you?" Duncan asked. "Did they hurt you?"

"No, but they killed Helga and Trina," she said, her voice cracking with grief. She seemed on the verge of tears, perhaps finally glad to see someone she knew still alive. Little did she realize she'd only been spared to feed Jacob's newest vampire. Duncan didn't have the heart to tell the woman that he had no idea who Trina was, let alone know her name.

"May I sit?" She stepped toward his mattress, the only place in the dark basement to sit, unless she wanted to use one of the dusty crates or boxes filled with stuff he hadn't seen in years.

"Yes, but don't touch me," he said sharply.

"Okay." She sat on the corner of Duncan's bed and he fell back, as far as he could into the corner where the mattress met the wall. She looked at him confused, as if unable to understand his repulsion. Or maybe, he figured, she thought he was afraid.

Her sudden nerves stirred a hunger inside him. Duncan could see a shimmering orange aura swimming around her. He wasn't sure what that meant, but the parasite inside him was salivating, chewing at his insides. Duncan wanted to touch her, to draw her life from inside her, and feed. He wanted it more than a beggar starving for food, or a teenager with a hard-on desperate for somewhere to put it.

Duncan wanted the life from inside her more than the air in his lungs.

He closed his eyes and tried to drown his bloodlust.

"Who are these people? What are they going to do to us?"

He wondered why she'd said *people*. Had she not seen the monsters?

"They're going to kill us," Duncan said, unsure why, except that he enjoyed the scent of her terror. Her colors went from orange to red. He closed his eyes to deny the parasite the joy of stoking the woman's fear.

"Kill us?" she asked, suddenly on the verge of tears. "Why?"

Duncan struggled to keep his eyes closed, knowing he

would reach out and grab her the second he saw her. He tried to think of anything other than feeding, disgusted by his irrepressible animal urges. He was a man of tremendous self-discipline. He'd worked for decades to master his every impulse from food to sex. Now it was as if some impetuous, psychopathic child had jumped into his driver's seat and was taking control, eager to run him off the road just to see what would happen.

No, you don't have to do this. You aren't a feeder. Or a monster.

He thought again of his words to Jacob:

You may have infected me, but I'm not a monster.

"We'll see about that," he'd said with a shit-eating grin.

Duncan now knew what he meant. Jacob was proving they were one and the same, forcing Duncan to acquiesce to his new parasitic instincts. He could almost feel the pompous fuck laughing upstairs, imagining Duncan's struggle to control his hunger. It was like locking a starving vegan in a room with a juicy steak, knowing full well that no matter how much he claimed to love animals only his animal nature would help him survive.

No, I am stronger than this.

Duncan tried thinking of better things, like Caleb.

Not Caleb now, wherever he was, assuming he was still alive since he'd vanished into Jacob's portal. He thought of Caleb as a child, and how much he'd loved the kid. Caleb looked up to his *Uncle* Duncan, and gave the old man the closest thing to a paternal role he would ever have. He wished Caleb's adopted father hadn't felt so threatened, and hadn't made Caleb feel guilty as a result. Hell, his dad had made Duncan feel guilty, and that was almost impossible.

Duncan remembered going fishing with Caleb when the boy was 11 and first starting to notice girls. Caleb asked

Duncan what to do when a girl didn't like you like you liked her. He pointed at the lake. "See that lake?"

Caleb nodded.

How many fish do you think are in there?"

"I dunno, maybe a few hundred."

"And how many fish do you think are in all the other lakes in the world? How many in all the seas?"

"Millions?" Caleb looked confused. "Why?"

"Let me ask you, Caleb. Remember that brim you nearly caught last time we were here? Just as you were reeling it in, it popped off the hook?"

"Yeah!" Caleb laughed.

"You didn't get all bent out of shape about that, right?"

"No, not really."

"Why is that?"

"I don't know. I figured I'd catch another one."

"Exactly," Duncan said, holding up a finger. "It's the same with girls and women. There's no shortage, and never will be. Getting hung up on only one will end in nothing but heartache."

"But she's not a fish, she's a girl. A beautiful girl. She's smart, pretty, and even likes soccer!"

"Yeah, but there are plenty more out there too, son. There's always someone else. Trust me."

Caleb's line went taut as another fish bit on his line, almost on cue, as if to prove the old man's point.

Duncan couldn't remember what happened with that particular girl, or anything about her outside their shared conversation on the lake. There had been many girls in Caleb's young life until he finally met his wife. Duncan never once considered that he might've been wrong. There *was* always someone else to occupy a space in your heart. Maybe that sort of realization could only come after living through centuries and watching everyone you love die, until you finally stopped allowing people to get close enough to miss them.

Now, sitting with no one to care one way or the other if he lived, Duncan wondered if he'd been wrong from the start. Some people, whether lovers, or someone welcomed into your family — there were *some people* whose absence could never be replaced.

The housekeeper's voice cut through Duncan's thoughts, and his attempts to forget she was easy prey beside him. "Can you untie my hands, sir?"

"I'm afraid not," he said, meeting her eyes.

She paused, then asked, "Why not?"

"Because if I touch you, you'll die."

The woman's eyes widened. "What do you mean?"

She scrambled to her feet. Her aura darkened to deep crimson. Something in her scent changed and stirred his hunger further. He also found himself sexually aroused, which only disgusted him more.

"The man who brought you in here, did you see him burn anyone by touching them?"

She nodded, shaking, her eyes brimming with tears.

"That man is a monster. And now I am, too."

She stared at him, unmoving.

"What are you, fucking stupid?" Duncan barked. "Go away!"

She turned from him and ran up the stairs, as fast as she could with her hands tied behind her back. She banged her head on the door and wailed, "Please, please let me out!"

Her fear escalated and stirred Duncan's inner monster, like a stomach growling over the scent of baking bread. His cock was rock-hard.

Duncan was at the top of the stairs a second later,

surprised by his speed, once he surrendered to the creature's will and let it guide his actions.

The housekeeper screamed.

Duncan reached out and silenced her forever, drinking her soul, feasting without thinking of the monster he'd become. He ingested her life force and memories, finally learning her name: *Melora*.

NINETEEN

Abigail

ABIGAIL STOOD, unable to move, staring at the charred bodies in bed.

"Oh, God; God; oh, God. What do I do?"

She spun in a circle, looking around the room as if the answer might pop out, maybe from the closet. She thought about calling Larry. Surely, he could help her cover this up.

No way. He'll freak out, and want to leave. No questions asked. Take no chances. Adios, Katya.

Abigail looked down at the burned corpses again, wondering if the police would tie the murders to her. Or worse, what if John's agency was investigating.

They would definitely tie it to her.

Unless they think there was a fire.

Abigail ran from the bedroom and bounded down the stairs, through the dark living room and to the garage. On the ground, beside the lawnmower, she saw it: a big red gas can.

Please be full, please be full, please be …

It was.

She picked it up and carted it into the living room, running back up the stairs as fast as she could, gas sloshing all along the way.

Okay, where do I start?

She thought of Bobby. She'd killed him first, even though she held no memory of doing so. She went into the boy's room. Seeing his charred body triggered a store of memories, and a fresh wave rolled through her mind.

BOBBY FOUND A TINY, filthy dog with a broken back sprawled in the middle of the street outside his house, and cried until his mom agreed to make Dad find a vet.

He was trick-or-treating too many streets over. He got lost, bag snatched, then beaten up by three boys, ironically all dressed as members of the Justice League: Superman, Batman, and the Flash.

Bobby petted his mom's head for who-knew-how-many hours after losing his baby sister, two months before Rebecca was supposed to be born.

BOBBY'S MEMORIES softened from boil to simmer, and Abigail stared down at his charred remains feeling as if she'd lost a close friend, despite not knowing the boy for more than a few fleeting seconds inside her dream. She imagined a different life where she met him not as a vampire, but as a girl instead — a life which would never be, and was agony to think about.

She uncapped the gas can and shook it over his body, like she was watering the lawn.

The gas was pungent, burning her throat, as Abigail went from his room to his parents', spilling a trail of fuel along the way. Once she reached their room, Abigail poured the gas all over his parents, making sure to save at least a little for downstairs. She emptied more gas in a line down the stairs then in front of the couch and in a long wavy line running along the front door and window until the can was empty.

Abigail went into the kitchen, searching for a lighter or matches.

She pulled out one drawer after another, heart pounding, utensils rattling and drawers banging back into place.

Hurry, hurry, hurry …

I've gotta get home before Larry notices I'm gone.

Finally, Abigail found a junk drawer and seized a green plastic lighter from inside.

Yes!

She ran upstairs clutching the lighter, afraid she'd drop it. She froze in front of Bobby's room, unable to move.

What have I done?

She stared at Bobby's body again, trying to figure out how she'd managed to get inside the house to begin with.

Was I sleepwalking? And if so, what's to stop me from doing it again?

She thought of the incident in the restaurant, overcome by memories, and the overwhelming sadness she'd not only experienced through her victims' memories, but that which she inflicted herself.

She thought of Bobby's father screaming:

What are you?

She swallowed, tears streaming her cheeks.

I'm a monster.

Abigail moved closer to Bobby's burned body, then sat on the bed beside him, allowing the gas on his sheets to seep into her pajama bottoms. She lay on the bed and let the gasoline soak into the back of her shirt. It was ice cold — ironic given its flammable properties.

More memories raced through her mind, more misery, more sadness.

She raised the lighter above her, staring at the little gray wheel, then realized she'd never lit a lighter, though she'd seen people do it plenty and it surely seemed easy enough. She ran her thumb along the wheel, waiting for fire.

Nothing.

Abigail looked closer, and saw a plastic red tab, probably there so kids didn't accidentally start fires. She pressed down on the red tab and started to run her thumb over the metal wheel again, bracing for death.

Abigail wondered if she'd die quickly. She hoped so. Life was too damned hard, and all she wanted was for the pain to finally end.

Suddenly, Abigail heard a voice in her head that wasn't hers, or any one of the many memories rattling inside her.

"Abigail?"

An unfamiliar girl's voice she couldn't remember ever hearing before.

She opened her eyes and moved her head to search the room, but saw nobody.

"Hello?" Abigail called out.

"Don't do it," the girl's voice said.

Abigail realized the voice was in her head, like John's used to sometimes come.

Who is this? Abigail thought-asked.

"My name is Talani. I'm a vampire, like you."

How do you know I'm a vampire? Abigail thought, suddenly afraid. Someone out there knew her secret. Someone she didn't know. How could Talani speak to her? Was she nearby, Abigail wondered, knowing as she did that Talani could read her thoughts and fears.

Leave me alone!

"*Relax, Abigail. I'm just like you. I'm only 15. You and I are a lot alike.*"

You don't know me, Abigail thought, feeling violated, wanting to run off and be left alone. She tried to shut the girl from her mind, but didn't know how. She never had to defend herself against an intruder to her thoughts. Before now, only John had communicated with her like this.

"*I just wanted to tell you, you're not alone. There are others out here like us. Good people, forced to hide from the world because of what we are. I don't want to intrude on your life. I don't want anything, really. I wasn't even going to bother you, but I felt your pain. I couldn't sit and do nothing, especially if I could make a difference. I just want you to know, you're not alone. Don't kill yourself, Abigail. I have to go. I can only do this for a little bit at a time. But please ... *"

And then she was gone. Though Abigail hadn't felt the presence enter her mind, she felt its departure, draft from an open window in her brain.

Talani? Abigail asked, testing to see if the girl was really gone.

No response. As she lay in the gas-drenched bed, fumes stirring her nausea, she thought of Talani's words, "You're not alone." Abigail wondered how many of her kind there were. She'd known there were some, and that many were bad, monsters feeding off the good. But what if there were others like her, like John, good people cursed through no fault of their own?

She thought of John and wondered if he would miss her, or be happy to be free of the burden of looking out for a perpetual child? Then she thought of her new friend Katya.

Will Katya miss me?

She'd been so concerned when Abigail was sick at the restaurant. She actually cared. And though he wasn't good at showing it, Larry cared, too. And of course, there was John. She thought back to the last time she'd seen him, and how he'd hugged her as though he never wanted to let her go.

If I kill myself, I'll hurt them all.

They don't deserve that.

Abigail's tears were in full flow. She closed her eyes, trying not to think of the hurt she'd visit on those she loved most if she were to murder herself. She didn't want to hurt anyone else. Taking her life was selfish. Yes, she'd be silencing her torment, but didn't everyone have to deal with some amount of personal pain? Killing herself would add to her friends' agony, especially John's.

Abigail couldn't bear to cause any more pain.

There had to be some other way to quiet her anguish, some other way to deal with her victims' memories. She hadn't even given John a chance to help her.

Abigail sat up, looked down at Bobby, and said, "I'm so sorry."

She grazed his ashen cheek with her trembling finger-tips. His skin was hard, like scorched leather. She wanted to say something more that the boy might hear, but Bobby was gone, and Abigail was whispering to ghosts.

She rose from the bed and headed downstairs. At the bottom, she managed to get the lighter's wheel to turn and the flame to spark, then pulled a gasoline-soaked pillow from the couch and held the flame to its body until flames licked the cotton.

She threw the pillow to the floor and watched flames race in a line upstairs, mesmerized by the sight of fire licking the walls. Abigail wondered if she had stayed and died in the fire if she would see her life's memories race before her as death came to claim her. Or would she be forced to witness the lives of others pass before her eyes?

The fire alarm screamed through the house and sent her running outside, flying toward home as though one with the wind.

TWENTY

John

JOHN AND TINY followed Shadow's scent through the tunnels.

John was damned good at hunting Otherworlders and Halfworlders alike. Shadow had left his stink all over. They followed him on foot into the old sewer system, and eventually to where his path ended, in an ancient looking dusty basement. From what John could sense, they were in an apartment building basement, filled with residents, many still sleeping.

"He here?" Tiny asked.

"Yes, though I'm guessing if we can sense him, he can sense us, and is waiting."

"Waiting with more of that magick voodoo shit, I bet."

"Maybe. So, you wait here. I'll stay connected."

"I ain't letting you go up there alone."

"Just pay attention to me, okay. I'll be fine. I don't think he's looking to hurt us, anymore. He's looking for something. I'll see if I can help him find it, and send you a flash if something goes wrong."

"A *flash*? Is that what you call that shit where you're talkin' in my head?"

"Got a better word for it?"

"An instant message? Maybe a poke?"

"A poke?"

"Yeah, a poke, like on Facebook."

John shook his head. "You crack me up, Tiny."

"What? You're not on Facebook?"

"No. What the hell am I going to do on Facebook? Make friends?"

"Ah, I see, you're probably all on MySpace and shit like Larry."

John laughed again, heading out the basement door to the stairs. He made it six flights before the stairway ended on the top floor. There were more than 20 apartments at the top, all filled with either sleeping, or at least relaxed, people. Except for one.

John could sense Shadow's frantic energy. He tried to focus on the man's thoughts, but couldn't read them, which likely meant that Tiny was right. Shadow was waiting, like before. He couldn't afford to be taken by surprise, again. John considered finding a phone and calling Mike Mathews, telling him to light the place with agents.

But then John might not learn who the vessels were, or how to find them.

He could sense Shadow's desperation and fear. John hoped Shadow's betrayal would favor his fortune. He could protection from his enemies, assuming Shadow believed he could trust John to keep him from Omega.

John approached Shadow's apartment, stopped outside the door, and lightly knocked.

"Shadow? It's John. I want to help you."

"Go away, John!" Shadow's voice came high-pitched and stressed. "I don't need any help."

"You know I'm not leaving. And you know you can't make it alone any longer. They'll find you. If I did, they will too. Let me help. We can protect you."

"Like you protected my family? No thanks, John. I'll take my chances going solo."

"*I* will protect you. You have my word."

Shadow was silent. John waited anxiously for something — an opening door or deafening explosion, but was answered only by silence.

He's making another portal to escape!

John wondered if he should bust the door down. If Shadow was armed, or waiting with more magickal weapons, bursting in was a death sentence. But too much was at stake to play cautious now.

Before he could act, the door opened to Shadow. He looked cautiously into the hallway and said, "Where's the Hulk?"

"Standing guard nearby, to make sure we're safe."

Shadow nodded and opened the door wider. John stepped inside and saw several duffel bags sitting in the middle of the otherwise empty apartment. There wasn't even furniture, at least in the living room. John wondered how many such places Shadow had at his disposal. As many as Larry? More?

"What is this place?"

"My last resort," Shadow said. "I can't trust that no one knows about it, but at least I have a head start."

"Where are you going to go?"

"Like I'd tell you."

"Fair enough," John said. "But I need to know about the vessels, please. Shadow, tell me while you get ready."

"Okay, but pay attention, because I'm only saying this once. I need to get the hell outta here."

"Okay." John watched Shadow move supplies and

wads of cash from smaller bags to a larger one, stuffed with weapons, of this world and John's.

"Your mom was helped by a powerful wizard when she crossed over. The last of his kind, after the Great Purge." Shadow turned to John. "You know about the Great Purge?"

"Yes," John nodded. "I've read in *The Unwritten Tomes*."

"So, this wizard was taken in by your father when the North initiated the genocide of all magick users within the Northern Realm. Your father appointed him as his realm's Head Wizard. After he betrayed your father by helping your mother, you, and Caleb escape, Jacob forced him to create a new portal to follow you."

Shadow stopped moving boxes and turned his full attention to John.

"The wizard knew he had to do something before your father came over, so he had an apprentice make one last portal, then had her kill him, split his soul, and spread it to six separate crystals, so he couldn't be forced to do whatever it was your father would have him to do. The apprentice then came, placed the gems inside five people, or vessels, then sent each of them here. The vessels had no idea what was inside them. Once here, their minds were wiped, and they were blended into society never knowing what they were or what they were carrying."

"How the hell is that even possible without anyone knowing?"

"Because my father organized it on this end. He was the only one on this side the wizard could trust, and in turn, the wizard put the sixth crystal inside him. My father was so committed to keeping the secret, he killed everyone who helped, and was the only person who knew anything on this side. He hid his secret until he was dying. He said I had to take the gem from his body before anyone found it, then told me there was a list of the other vessels, which he'd written in the Old Language, just in case."

"In case of what?"

"I don't know, in case all hell broke loose on Earth."

John held up a finger. "Wait a second. If this wizard was so 'all-powerful,' why didn't he just go after my father and kill him?"

"Because your father had infected him years before. He controlled enough of the wizard to prevent him from ever harming your father. It was surprising that he'd been able to help your mother escape without your father finding out beforehand."

"Shit," John said. "So, where is the list?"

"Do you think I'm just gonna give it to you?"

"What choice do you have? You think you can keep it safe after your people betrayed you?"

"How do I know you won't turn it over to Omega? If my father didn't trust them, why the hell should I?"

"Because I'm not them, and would never let them have the list."

"Yeah, what if they use your woman as leverage? They obviously earned enough devotion to buy your betrayal for a year. What's a little thing like a list?"

"I don't know how to change your mind," John sighed. "But I do know that if Jacob's after you, he *will* find you. What happens when he gets the list?"

"I imagine he'll go after the crystals and get them, one way or another. If he gets them all, my father said the wizard's soul, and his power, can be brought back and either absorbed by someone, like Jacob, or another host. Whoever brings him back, will have all of his power and knowledge."

"Then you need to give that list to me."

"What will you do with it, John?"

"We destroy it. With the list gone, *no one* has the power, right? Everyone on the list is protected. Nobody, on either side of the war, will ever find the crystals."

"I don't know," Shadow said, then fell into silence.

"What?" John said.

Shadow stared, his expression slightly off, standing frozen, mid-thought. Then eyes widened, staring behind John.

John turned, too late. A sharp pain sliced into his back and sent him to his knees. His world erupted in pain and he fell to his side as something burned through his body.

He looked up and saw Jacob in black robes, staring down with a smile.

"Hello, brother," he said, stepping over John and walking to where Shadow was still frozen stiff, likely captive in some spell or enchantment.

John flashed out to Tiny:

Tiny! Help!

No response.

Jacob is here! Jacob is here! He stabbed me!

"Where is the list, boy?" Jacob asked.

Shadow's mouth opened, gasping as if Jacob had just given him the ability to use it. "I don't know," he said.

"I let you use your tongue, and you *lie?*" Jacob shook his head, looming closer to Shadow until he was inches from his face. "Open your mouth, boy."

Shadow shook his head. His shaking turned violent as Jacob took control, parting the man's mouth against his will. Jacob's gloved right hand reached into his robe and drew a dagger. His left, also gloved, moved to Shadow's mouth and pulled at his tongue.

Shadow screamed. Jacob raised the dagger, tracing the black blade against Shadow's cheek, drawing blood as it moved.

John reached behind his back, trying to feel the pain's source — another dagger, stuck in his back. He tried to grip it, but his fingers locked when they touched it.

Shadow screamed as Jacob cut his tongue off and threw it to the ground in front of John, where it landed with a sickening splat. Blood gushed in rivers from Shadow's mouth, but he couldn't bring his hands high enough to stop the flow with Jacob controlling his body.

"Now," Jacob said, "I want you to use your hands and get me that list. Remember what I did when your tongue disobeyed.

Shadow's hands went to his mouth, feeling his severed tongue and crying in anguish.

"Now!" Jacob shouted.

Shadow kneeled unzipped a green camouflage knapsack. Jacob watched carefully as John tried to hold his focus through the burning sensation.

Tiny! Come on!

Shadow handed the list to Jacob. "And where's your father's crystal?"

Shadow reached down the front of his shirt, hands trembling as he retrieved a crystal pendant, glowing a dusty red and fastened to a black leather cord.

He handed it over to Jacob.

"Thank you," Jacob said, then thrust his blade into Shadow's chest and shoved him to the ground.

John screamed, "You fucker!"

Jacob turned to him, smiling. "Now, little brother, what to do about you?"

Tiny barreled into the room and charged Jacob.

He spun out of the way seconds before Tiny could get a hold of him. Tiny fell forward, nearly colliding with Shadow's fallen body, missing the wounded man by inches.

Jacob's eyes fell on John, then went to Tiny and back. He smiled and ran from the door.

"I'll get him!" Tiny jumped to his feet.

"No!" John said, "Get this knife out of my back."

Tiny's eyes went wide, almost scared. "Oh, shit."

"Put your gloves back on or else it might burn you."

Tiny retrieved then gloves from his jacket, slid them on, then yanked the blade from John and dropped it to the carpet beside him. The fire was gone, but the pain remained.

John looked up as Shadow crawled toward the duffel, blood spilling in pools from his wound. He pulled out a notebook and pen, then opened it on the floor and scribbled across the pages.

"What is it?" Tiny asked Shadow.

"Jacob cut out his tongue," John said as he stood and went to see what Shadow was writing.

The top of the paper read, *5.*

"You remember the names?" John asked.

Shadow nodded, keeping his eyes on the paper as he struggled through dying breaths to move his pen and get names on the page.

But they were social security numbers, not names. John stared as Shadow scrawled numbers, fast as he could.

He'd written three sets when he had to stop, surrendering to a violent fit of coughing that lasted for nearly a minute as bloody nuggets spewed from his mouth.

Shadow returned to the paper and scrawled. He reached the fifth set of numbers when John's eyes locked on the last set in disbelief. His heartbeat nearly tripled in speed. He knew that Social Security number. Could never forget it.

No. It can't be.

John kneeled next to Shadow. "That last number, are you sure?"

Shadow looked at the paper, then back up, coughing more blood into his hand. He smeared it on his shirt and nodded.

"You know it?" Tiny asked.

"Yes. It belongs to Hope."

TWENTY-ONE

Hannah

THE MORNING CRAWLED, as did the afternoon to follow.

After Hannah took the thousand years she promised to prepare for the day, she took her phone from the dresser and packed it in her purse, anxious for the minute she could be alone with her phone.

It didn't happen on the drive to El Montaña, anywhere on the vineyard tour, or at any time during her one chance to slip into the bathroom alone. The bathroom was small, quaint like the rest of the winery. She was only inside for a moment, barely having closed the door and not yet locking it, when Greg slipped in behind her. He said it would be "romantic" to use the bathroom at the same time.

Hannah smiled like she meant it, glad she didn't have to go number two, and emptied her bladder while cursing the interruption and ignoring the phone like a brick in her purse.

Only later, after the tour once sitting in the restaurant, after wine was poured and appetizers ordered, but before bruschetta was brought to the table, Greg got a call and excused himself, looking at Hannah with apologetic eyes.

She nodded, feeling grateful but looking patient, then Greg left, and she yanked the phone from her purse. She inserted the earbuds, then pressed play on her recording as her heart raced even faster.

At first there was nothing, but as Hannah scrubbed her finger across the recording, she found a spike in the volume. She rewound the recording a few seconds, stopped, then started it back from a spot where Greg had stress in his voice.

"She dreamed about John again last night."

Pause ...

"Yes, I'm sure. What do you want me to do?"

Another pause ...

"Are you certain, Mr. Cromwell?"

The longest pause so far ...

Then, "Yes, I'll do it before we return to the house. Don't worry. Hannah won't suspect a thing.

She looked up as Greg pulled his chair from the table and sat, smiling.

An earbud fell from her ear.

"Whatchya' listening to?" he asked.

TWENTY-TWO

Duncan

IN HIS DREAM, Duncan relived the funeral of his closest and last true friend, Ed Baldwin.

Caleb's adopted father died of a heart attack just shy of Caleb's sixteenth birthday, and the boy was devastated. He spoke to no one: not his friends, girlfriend, or even his mother, Myriam. He stood outside the funeral home, pacing the parking lot, eyes wild and hair disheveled.

Duncan went outside, and unsure what to say, said nothing. He stood beside Caleb, waiting for the boy to speak.

The young man looked up at Duncan, angry, and confused, his eyes brimming with tears.

"Why?" was all he could manage.

"I wish I knew," Duncan said, pulling the boy into a strong but gentle hug.

Duncan had buried more friends and loved ones than he could count. While he missed Ed, sympathy and sadness were only practiced. Truth was, he no longer felt the pain of loss. At funerals, Duncan often found himself mourning his missing feelings more than anything else.

Available Darkness: Book Two

Time marched on. People came and went. Same as ever.

Little did Caleb know he was an Otherworlder who would stop aging in his 40s and bury many people himself. Perhaps, he, too, would one day be jaded like Duncan.

The first funeral was always roughest.

Caleb collapsed into tears, and turned away, red-faced. "This is all my fault."

"What do you mean?" Duncan had asked.

"I killed him."

Duncan woke from the dream.

TWENTY-THREE

Duncan
_____

DUNCAN PACED his basement wondering what Jacob planned next.

He was growing restless, and, oddly enough, hungry again. Duncan felt near starving, though not for food. He was craving another life. The housekeeper, Melora, left him feeling more alive than he'd ever felt. The energy surge, along with her vicious flood of memories and experiences, was more powerful than any drug he'd ever taken — and Duncan had taken a great many over the years: for recreation, experiments in self-improvement, and general need.

Feeding was like acid and opiates, rolled into a tantric orgasm, multiplied by a million. A bit like a bad trip, but only for a fat handful of flickers, as he was forced to sort through Melora's worst memories, fears, and pain, like when she lost her child three hours after birth.

Duncan quickly found himself riding through her currents of thought until he found himself swimming in calmer seas, basking in the pleasures of her life as if by instinct. He'd even relived her more erotic moments, which left him surprised in both the depths of her kink, and that such a plain-looking woman had so many sexual escapades with men and women of every shape and size. Melora was one book Duncan could never have judged by its cover.

He wanted out of the basement, and to experience the rush again. Yet, Duncan was also shrouded by guilt. He hadn't wanted to kill Melora. The parasite's instinct and his own sense of self-preservation compelled him to feed from her screaming body. As he sat, imagining feasting on others, Duncan felt disgusted.

I can't just go kill people.

I am not them.

I am above them.

He could almost feel Jacob's laughter as the monster descended the stairs, looking down at Melora's charred remains, which Duncan couldn't bring himself to move from the bottom.

"So, how is superiority treating you? Is that whole 'I'm not a monster' thing going well?" Jacob smiled and tutted. "For so long your people have treated ours like monsters, as if we'd chosen our paths. Chosen to be infected with the parasites. As if we decided on a life of murder. People love to feel smug, but when it comes down to it, they're all pigs wallowing in the filth, eating whatever they must to survive."

Duncan said nothing since Jacob was right. He was now no better than the monsters he'd hunted for so long, but that didn't mean he had to admit it.

Jacob circled the body. "So, are you ready for your next meal?"

"No," Duncan lied.

"You say no, but you forget, I can feel what you feel. I feel that hunger within you, Mr. Alderman." Jacob smiled. "Why deny what you can embrace? I've elevated you past the rest of your species, and above the humans! You should be thanking me. I'm setting you front and center for the next evolution of our kind. We will be Gods among beasts, and the world our buffet."

Duncan still said nothing, staring down at the concrete floor.

Jacob said, "It's okay, you'll come around. In the meantime, I've a small favor to ask. It seems I've come into possession of some numbers, Social Security numbers to be precise. I need to find the people attached to the numbers."

"Are these your so-called 'vessels?'"

"Why, yes they are. See? You and I make a good team, Mr. Alderman."

"Why should I help you?"

"Well, let's pretend for a moment that you have a choice, and that I can't bring you to your knees in crippling pain by merely thinking it. In that case, you would help me because you're helping yourself. Now that you're with us, our goals are as one."

"I want out of the basement. I'm tired of being cooped up down here. Plus, I'll need access to my computers if you expect any answers."

"Fair enough, consider it done." Jacob stepped closer to Duncan, locking eyes with the old man as sharp force suddenly pressed into his skull from all sides. "But just so you know, I can see your every action and hear your every thought. If you even think about doing anything to interfere with me, I'll know, and make you wish I had killed you." Jacob snarled, yet still sounded almost pleasant. "You think killing the hired fucking help was difficult? I'll lock you in a room with a newborn infant if you cross me. See how that weighs on your conscience."

Duncan nodded. "You don't have to threaten me."

"That's excellent news," Jacob said, losing his snarl. "I've taken the liberty of blacking out the second floor windows, so I'll have a room prepared for you."

"Can't I have my bedroom?"

"No," he said, "I've grown quite accustomed to your bed. It really is quite the luxury."

~

An hour later, Jacob released Duncan from the basement. The old man ascended the stairs to find his entire house commandeered by Harbinger, as he had suspected. Armed men in black crowded the bottom floor, and a few others wearing civilian clothes. Duncan figured they were Otherworlders or Halfworlders sympathetic to Harbinger's cause.

He was led to the second floor guest rooms where he hadn't set foot for several years, except for during a minor remodeling job three years earlier. He was placed in the room at the end of the hall, farthest from his bedroom. The room's window was painted black, a clearly hurried mess, with black paint dripping stains along the wooden sill and hardwood floors. While Duncan noticed the mess, he didn't allow it to worm its way under his skin since his house was filled with far worse atrocities than spilled paint.

His laptop was set up on a small desk, waiting for him.

Duncan sat and lifted the lid.

"Remember," Jacob said, "do as instructed and nothing more. Do not attempt to send a message to anyone or I will turn threat into reality."

Duncan signed into the Agency's database, while Jacob probed his brain, searching for any sign of betrayal. He could feel the monster skittering through his mind, reading his thoughts. He tried to bury his revulsion, but Jacob kept digging, deep as he wanted.

Fuck you.

"And fuck you, too," Jacob said aloud, delighting in his demonstration of power. "Here," he said, handing Duncan a piece of paper filled with neatly printed numbers in the Old Language. "You can read this, correct? Get to work."

Duncan began typing in the numbers, retrieving names of people he didn't even know existed, and who had never raised so much as a blip on the Agency radar, lest their names would've been flagged. As he pulled up each name and address, he asked Jacob if he wanted to record any of the details.

"Not necessary," Jacob said. "I never forget … anything."

Duncan typed, feeling Jacob's presence in his head, as if the man were pressing on his brain like a full bladder. Duncan decided to experiment, compartmentalizing a thought as if imagining it in a hidden box, then waited to see if it would register. The tricky part in compartmentalizing was that the mere act would often tip the infiltrator off to what you were doing, even if not to the precision of your thought. Tell someone not to think of an elephant, and all they can see are large floppy ears, the color gray, and two long tusks. Trying to disguise the act of concealing a thought was similar. You had to think the thought and then quickly place another on top of it, almost forcing yourself to forget it. And then there was the act of thinking through a series of thoughts while covering those with others — a task which had taken Duncan decades to master.

I know your weakness, Jacob, and will use it against you.

Duncan kept typing, thinking of the names and numbers he pulled from the database, waiting to see if his secret thoughts were properly concealed from Jacob. He'd never been up against anyone with powers like Jacob. Nor had he masked a thought for longer than 10 minutes before the mental exhaustion tripped him up.

Jacob continued staring at the computer screen while probing Duncan's mind.

He typed in the final number, and noticed the name attached. "Hope Barnett."

Her? How can it be?

The errant thought flew into the wild before Duncan could capture it back and toss it in the box.

"Is that *John's* Hope?" Jacob slithered down past Duncan's shoulder like a snake. "Where is she?"

"I don't know," Duncan lied, trying to bury what he knew of her protected identity before it slipped into Jacob's head.

Do not think it, do not think it.

Hannah Quinn.

Too late.

It was almost as if Jacob reached into him mind and plucked the name before Duncan could hide it.

"Ah, she's changed her name, eh? And the Agency's hiding her? Is that why it says 'location unknown?' Tell me where she is." Jacob narrowed his eyes and burrowed deeper into Duncan's head. If Jacob dug too deep, he might discover Duncan's plan. And if he did that, Hope was lost, both John's and humanity's.

"I don't know, it says 'location unknown' because we don't know," Duncan said in a commanding tone crafted to push Jacob's buttons. "Now get out of my head."

"You are my pet, and I shall do as I wish," Jacob smiled, edging himself deeper into Duncan's brain.

Duncan's eyes seized on the pen and pencil holder. He reached out, grabbed a pencil, gripped it hard in his right hand, then drove it deep into the middle of his left. He screamed, but not alone. Jacob's scream was equally loud, an echo of his pain.

Behind the scream Duncan felt the monster withdraw from his mind.

"What the hell?" Jacob reached out and grabbed Duncan around the neck. "You think you can hurt me? You think you can hurt *ME?*" The monster picked Duncan up by the throat and stared at him with burning eyes.

"Where is she?"

"I don't know," Duncan said, burying the secret in hurried layers of thought, bracing his mind before Jacob entered again.

Jacob scowled and threw Duncan across the room, slamming him into the wall beside the bed. "Do you think you're the only one with information? Do you think there is anyone in your organization I can't reach?"

Jacob grabbed the laptop and left the room, locking the door from outside. His anger seemed to soften on the other side, and when he spoke his voice was again sickeningly sweet. "You know, I'm starting to think I should find a new second-in-charge if you're going to pull stunts like that, Mr. Alderman. I'd think long and hard about your attitude."

Duncan glared at the door, yanked the pencil from his hand, dropped it to the ground, and watched as the wound began to heal itself. Pain receded and brought his resolve into bloom.

Duncan now knew what he had to do, though he didn't dare to think it while Jacob was still in the house.

TWENTY-FOUR

Larry

LARRY WAS RUDELY TORN from his pizza coma as sirens screamed outside.

He reached up, fixed the glasses askew on his face, hopped from couch to floor, threw his Xbox controller aside, then ran to the window and parted the thick curtains. Flashing lights split the darkness to a garish rainbow blur as a mile-long fire truck drifted in front of the house. Larry grabbed his gun, slid it into the waistband of his jeans, then stepped out into the cool night air.

He stood on his porch, staring at the house down the street as it was licked by walls of curling fire. The scent of gasoline permeated the air, but seemed too close to be coming from the burning house. Another fire truck, this one shorter, was followed by a pair of police cars and a lone ambulance.

"What the hell?"

Larry was about to step back inside and let Abi know what was happening when he heard the soft sound of nearby crying. He looked down and saw Abi crouched in a ball behind the thick row of shrubs beneath their living room window, staring up at him as if something unimaginably horrible had just happened.

Larry swallowed. The flickering in her eyes made him weak in the knees, but he managed to hold himself steady. "What's wrong, Honey?"

"I did it," she said.

"Did what?" Larry said, dreading the answer.

Abi slowly lifted her arm and extended a shaking finger at the house with the fire trucks in front.

"Come inside, Abi." He waved his arm and wished he could hug her. She looked like she needed one. Yet, so far as he knew, he was only safe from John's touch. She slowly stood, and as her body rose above the bushes, Larry could see her pajamas were soaking. The pungent scent of gasoline wafted from her body and into his nostrils.

What the hell happened to her?

Abi stepped inside the house, her eyes holding the floor like a scared, or ashamed, animal.

Larry closed the door, locked it, and looked at Abi, shuddering in front of him as if awaiting trial. "What happened?"

"I don't know," she cried. "I woke up in their house after I killed their son. I think I was about to kill them, too."

"Killed? You mean fed?"

"Yeah," she nodded, her voice cracked and fragile. "The parents saw what I did, and the mom was going to call the police. I tried getting the phone, but we touched … " Abi sniffed back her tears and swiped at her eyes. "Then the dad shot me, and tried to choke me or something. Then *he* touched me. Pretty soon, everyone was … dead."

"So, how the hell did the house burn down?"

"I didn't know what to do!" Abigail cried. "I didn't want the bad men to come and take me again. So, I started a fire. I thought maybe the police would think someone burned them with gas."

"Jesus," Larry said, sighing as he removed his glasses, pinching his nose at the bridge. He set his glasses on the dining room table.

"What are we going to do?" Abigail asked, with enough fear in her voice to keep Larry from daring to yell.

He breathed himself into a calm, then said, "How did you get inside their house?"

"I don't know. One minute I wasn't feeling well so I went to sleep, and the next minute I was in their house. I even slept through killing Bobby. I didn't wake up until I was standing over his parents' bed. I think something is wrong with me." Her voice cracked, forcing Abi to breathe before she could finish her thought. "I think I'm broken."

Larry remembered how, a decade ago in Florida, John had thought he'd been going out on midnight kills and not remembering them. Of course, it turned out to be his brother Jacob. But what if Abi *was* killing in her sleep? This added a new wrinkle to caring for the girl, a wrinkle that Larry didn't know how to iron.

"We'll figure this out," he said, even though Larry wasn't convinced in the slightest they would. "I'm gonna grab some stuff from the kitchen to help get rid of that gas smell, so go get undressed and ready to shower. I'll bring it to you with some fresh clothes."

"What are we going to do? Are we going to move again?"

"I don't know."

"I don't wanna move," Abi cried.

"I *don't know*," Larry said, trying to keep the annoyance from bleeding through his fraying calm. The only thing Larry knew for certain was that he couldn't handle this on his own. He *had* to reach John.

"Okay," Abigail said, then turned from Larry and trudged up the stairs.

Larry didn't even have to try and reach John. The soundtrack of rushing water only played for a minute upstairs before the doorbell dinged. Larry crept to the peephole with one hand wrapped around the hilt of his pistol, then opened the door to John and Tiny standing on his porch, covered in blood, looking like they had a problem far larger than Abi's.

TWENTY-FIVE

John

"I THINK I'm going to need another Mountain Dew," Larry said as John finished updating him all the way to Shadow's death and betrayal by his people.

John and Tiny followed Larry into the kitchen. He handed them each a cold can of soda.

"The Agency probably thinks I'm dead, or Shadow's captive, so that's our advantage," John said. "I need to find Hope. The two people most likely to know are Duncan Alderman and Bob Cromwell, one of the Agency bosses."

Larry said, "Can't you just ask Alderman?"

John shook his head. "I'd rather not have to kill him."

"What? That dude used Abigail as a pawn to get you to join his little Omega death squad. He also used Hope to keep you on a leash. Fuck that dude."

"Fair points," John said, taking a swig of soda. "But he also took care of my brother, Caleb. He did what he did to protect him. I can't fault him for that."

"So, Cromwell's the target?" Larry asked.

"Yeah, do you have info on him? Where I can find him?"

"Let me make a few calls. I'm pretty sure we can get to him. You wanna do it now, with the sun coming up? Or wait until tonight?"

"Well, it depends where he is. If he's at the office or anywhere near Omega, we'll have to wait until tonight," John said, sighing. "I need Mathews and everyone else to still think I'm missing. Besides, I don't have my lightproof uniform, which is just as well. And Tiny doesn't have one, so we'd be screwed if we're fighting anywhere near daylight."

Larry looked at John, "So, what are you gonna do if you find her?"

"*When* I find her."

"Okay, *when* — what are you going to do? We've got Jacob to deal with, again. And you're probably gonna piss off Omega if you strike at Cromwell."

"I don't know what I'm going to do. I only know that once I have her, I'm never letting her go again. Not ever."

"I still don't get how *she's* from your world! This is way too trippy."

"Tell me about it," John said. "I don't know how I couldn't tell. Humans give off a different aura from Otherworlders. It must be a mistake. The list *has* to be wrong."

"A bit too convenient to be wrong, don't you think?"

"What do you mean?"

"Think about it — you were willing to end your life for her," Larry explained. "You love her with the kind of love I've not seen outside of chick flicks. Maybe you two are so deeply connected because you're from the same place."

"Hey, guys, I love all this Hallmark stuff, but we need to catch some sleep a bit even if we wind up heading out today." Tiny turned to Larry. "You got a dark spot where we can crash?"

"Yeah, I have a spare room upstairs I blacked out just

for Johnny, so you guys can share. Sorry, but there's only one bed. You're gonna have to bunk together."

Tiny smiled, "I dunno, can you keep your hands off me, pretty boy?"

John smiled. "I'll try my best to resist."

Tiny said, "Okay, I'm gonna shower. You wouldn't happen to also have some fresh clothes?"

"Got some for John, but we don't carry size giant."

Tiny laughed. "It's good to see you again, Larry. Forgot how damned funny you are. So, you got a washer and dryer, then?"

"Yeah, right through there." Larry pointed at the hallway leading out to the garage. "But I don't want you walkin' round my place all naked 'n' shit. We got a kid, ya' know."

"Yeah, yeah, I'll wear a towel," Tiny said. "How is Abigail doin' these days?"

"She's okay. I think she's actually taking a shower in the guest bathroom, so let me show you to the master bath," Larry said, leading Tiny upstairs.

John could feel Abigail — still upstairs in the shower, upset. He couldn't tell why without probing her mind, and didn't want to invade her private thoughts. He paced the kitchen, waiting for Larry when his eyes were drawn to the front of the fridge where three of Abigail's drawings hung, all in crayon.

He moved to look closer.

One was of a dog playing with a ball on a field. John wondered if it was someone's dog that she knew, or perhaps a dog she had as a child. He couldn't remember seeing a dog in any of her previously shared memories. Maybe Abigail wanted a dog, but was afraid she might kill it with her touch. John made a note to tell her she wouldn't. Their touch was only deadly to humans, non-vampire Otherworlders, and some — but not all — of the monsters from his world. Pets were fine. The second drawing looked like a mermaid, with long blonde hair. The third drawing showed Abigail, Larry, and a woman standing side-by-side, almost like a family portrait.

This must be Katya.

John was happy to see Abigail accepting the woman Larry hired, but felt a twitch of jealousy, or maybe regret, at his omission from the drawing.

Larry came back downstairs with a serious expression and a hushed, non-hyper Larry voice. "We need to talk."

"About what?" John asked.

"Abigail. She's not doing well."

"What's wrong?"

"I don't even know where to start, man. But I suppose the squad of fire trucks down the street is as good a place as any."

TWENTY-SIX

Hannah

HANNAH FROZE as Greg pulled his chair from the table and asked her what she was listening to. Her mind flashed back over what she'd heard him say in the recording — what seemed like certain betrayal. Questions screamed in her mind.

What is he doing?

What's going on?

Who was he talking to?

What is he planning to do to me, or with me?

Who is John?

A second voice split through the madness, the same inner whisper that led her to record Greg in the first place — some wiser part of herself that saw through her "boyfriend's" charade.

"Don't let on that you know anything. Play dumb or you'll never escape."

Escape?

The thought of suddenly having to escape a man she loved, a man she trusted, seemed ludicrous to Hannah, bordering on insane. Yet, she definitely didn't imagine

Greg on the recording. Those were his words, and his voice. The trusting part of Hannah wanted to believe there was some sort of logical explanation. It wasn't as though she heard the entire conversation. Maybe there was more. Greg could have said something to clarify his comments a few seconds after the part where she had to pause when Greg appeared in front of her asking what she was listening to.

I must've misheard him.

"You heard him correctly, girl. Stop second guessing yourself."

Hannah promised herself she'd listen to the rest of the recording later. For now, she would do as her inner advisor suggested: stay calm and play stupid.

She slipped the phone back inside her purse, hoping Greg didn't notice she was in The Dictator app, and not a music player. Fortunately, he never seemed to give much attention to details, especially when it came to things like her apps or music. Hannah figured her secret was safe, unless she gave it away with a look of sheer terror when he surprised her.

"Just listening to some music," she said, painting her mouth with a phony smile she hoped didn't look like what it was. Joking, she said, "So, who was that on the phone? Your other lover?"

"Yes," Greg took a sip of wine, then swallowed and said, "She's meeting us later for a threesome. Hope you don't mind."

"In your dreams." Hannah faked a laugh and hoped she wasn't overselling it. She lifted her glass and sipped, but her wine had turned from a light plum to vinegar. She winced, set the glass back on the table, then steered the subject toward tomorrow's plans, wondering if that would be when Greg did whatever it was he'd been scheming to do. Not that she expected him to announce his secret, sinister plans.

"So, what's on our agenda for tomorrow? I'd love to go shopping in town."

"Yeah, we can do that," he nodded, seemingly preoccupied.

She wondered what he was thinking. Or what sort of conversation he'd just had. Had his boss, or whomever he was talking to, told Greg to act sooner rather than later? Maybe Hannah didn't even have until tomorrow. Maybe he was planning to do something tonight.

Another sip of vinegar.

"Don't get drunk. You'll need your senses sharp."

They finished dinner, stretching it another hour with reels of small talk, as if neither were in a rush to end the evening. They even ordered dessert, which they rarely ever did, a dulce de leche cake that would've tasted amazing under any circumstances where Hannah wasn't mulling her safety or sanity.

Small talk turned slightly bigger as it fell to trips down memory lane. Greg asked, "Remember that time we had that really snooty waiter who kept enunciating everything in a horrible attempt at French?"

"Oh, God," Hannah laughed. "He was awful."

"And how he kept getting the order wrong and acting like he didn't?"

"Worst waiter ever." Hannah smiled, trying to mine Greg's true intentions from his guarded eyes. He stared at her intently, never breaking his gaze as they spoke. She wasn't sure what he was thinking — if he was jealous of the man in her dreams, or if it were something else, perhaps a part of Greg that was there from the beginning, with her blind to his existence until now. The trip down memory lane felt like a farewell dinner, which only scraped her frayed nerves.

An uncomfortable silence stretched across the table and forced Hannah's wine back to her lips. She took another sip, ignoring her admonition to stay sober. She swallowed and a glimpse of memory swirled into her head — a man with long dark hair and piercing blue eyes, staring back at her. The man she'd seen in a glimpse while making love with Greg. The imaginary man whom she fantasized about while Greg was inside her.

"John. His name is John."

The name felt familiar, not just from hearing Greg's mention, but also like something from a dream. But there was more there, just past the edge of her memory. He seemed real, like a long-forgotten love. But how could that possibly be? How could Hannah not remember someone she loved? She'd never had a much success in relationships. Hell, her luck was so bad with men, it was a running joke with her few friends in college. Though, oddly enough, she couldn't recall a single college friend's name through the haze of merlot.

Troubled, Hannah tried hard to remember her friends more clearly, but picking her brain for a minute could barely recall a reasonably hot redhead with a big mouth, her most outspoken friend.

Carla? No, not Carla. That doesn't sound right. What kind of friend am I that I don't even remember people I was so close to during the best years of my life?

"You ask this when you can't even remember John?"

He can't be real.

"If he's not real, why is Greg worried about him? And discussing him on the phone in secret?"

She thought of the accident and temporary amnesia. She didn't remember much of the hours she'd first come to, but now started to assemble bits and pieces. She'd thought of John then, too, she realized. She'd even asked Greg where he was.

But who is John?

Maybe Greg is talking with my doctor. Or consulting with a friend, unsure of what to do. Maybe he was planning to ask me to marry him this week, and now he's not sure since he overheard me talking about some guy named John in my sleep. Maybe I'm just blowing this all out of proportion.

"No, you are not. Greg isn't who he says he is. You know it, so stop denying it."

Hannah looked up from her glass and found Greg's eyes on her again, still staring. If he wasn't who he claimed to be, who was he? The whole thing seemed almost on the verge of paranoia.

"What are you thinking?"

"That you're going to kill me and dump me in the woods, you psycho."

"Nothing," Hannah said. "Just tired. Getting a migraine, I think."

"Too much wine?"

"Maybe," she tried to laugh but shrugged instead, this time reaching for her water, its ice long ago melted. She swallowed two large gulps as the waiter returned with their bill.

"Need to use the restroom before we go." Hannah stood and grabbed her purse from the table.

"Okay," Greg said, downing his wine

She went to the restroom, relieved to find it empty. It was a tiny bathroom with dark walls, a stone floor, and two stalls. White Phalaenopsis Orchids with blush-colored centers sat in potted planters on the sink, draping low between the bowls. Hannah hoped to find a window, something she could crawl out of and run, though she had no idea where she could go once she did. Her heart pounded, her breath shallow with a sudden, urgent need to escape. She wasn't sure if it was irrational fear, or some instinct for self-preservation kicking in, but Hannah wanted to run: fast, far, and without looking back.

But what do I do after I run? Where do I go?

"Don't worry about what; just go."

First, she had to pee, especially with her nerves so swollen. Hannah sat, then fished her phone from her pocket. Before she knew what she was doing, she dialed a number from an unfamiliar area code as if her fingers were on autopilot. She didn't dare stop to think about what she was doing, watching her fingers dialing, and then the numbers as they appeared on her screen.

The number seemed familiar, though she didn't know why, and was dialed so automatically, she had to have dialed it many times before.

What the hell am I doing?

Hannah brought the phone to her ear. After a long moment, a man answered with a slight accent she couldn't place.

"Hello?" she said.

"Hello," the man answered, then a moment of silence as he waited for Hannah to say something else. "Who is this?" he asked when she didn't.

"I was hoping you could tell me."

After a long pause, the man said, "Hope ... *is that you?*"

TWENTY-SEVEN

John

JOHN SHOWERED, changed into jeans and a T-shirt, then stepped out of the bathroom to find Abigail waiting in the hall, pushing her striped toe sock into the carpet, making circles. Then she saw him, and the girl who could never be a woman ran up to her angel and threw her arms around him.

"John!" she yelled, her voice muffled in his chest.

He hugged Abigail tight. Tears welled inside him and a sudden warmth spread through his heart. While John hadn't forgotten how much he missed her, he tried to bury the thoughts when they came, lest they weigh too heavily on his soul.

"Oh, God," she cried, "I missed you soooo much!"

"I missed you, too," John said, inhaling the scent of strawberry shampoo. While the shampoo was different, the girl's scent was still there beneath it, permanently imprinted on him.

"Come on," she said, "I wanna show you my room!"

Abigail took John's hand, led him to her bedroom, then opened the door to a flamboyant clash of purple, black, and pink that somehow matched her. The first thing Abigail showed him was the teddy bear he'd given her more than a year before. "Look, it's Mr. Bear!" she said, excited. "One of the cops Larry knows found it in the car I got taken away in. Can you believe it?"

She hugged the bear to her chest, squeezing almost as hard as she'd hugged him.

"Wow, that's cool." John wondered if it was in fact the bear he bought her, or if Larry had gone to the gas station to buy her another. Either way, Abigail was happy, and that's what mattered.

"And look at these!" She pointed to the purple book-case beside her bed. "I have all my favorite books, and even found some new ones!" She held up kids' books, one by one — some he remembered her mentioning, some he'd had memories of from when he saved her life, and still others he'd never heard of. She went on, her face growing ever more animated, her voice slightly squeaky, cheeks pink, an undeniable glimmer in her eyes.

In that moment, knowing how sad Larry said she was, and how happy Abigail now seemed, John felt guilt crashing down like a two-ton slab.

This is how she'd be all the time if I was here.

John tried not to think of what might have been. That was a pointless, painful exercise in futility. All he could do was try to make things right. Find Hope, then take Abigail, and Larry if he wanted to join them. Together they could run far from the madness.

Abigail prattled on at a million words per minute. John wanted to hug her again and promise that things would get better. He was going to make thing everything right.

I can't make promises to her again — it's unfair. I just have to do what I need to do, then come back and deliver. Another broken promise will only break her heart.

It was hard not to promise, and harder still to shift their conversation to what Larry had told him downstairs, but eventually John steered their exchange to the fire, and to Abigail's breakdown in the restaurant.

They sat beside one another on her bed as she told him everything that had happened. After Abigail finished, she looked at him, her eyes going from happy and excited to sad and scared.

"Larry said we might have to move. Do you think we'll have to?"

"Yes," John said.

Abigail burst into tears. "But I was just starting to like it here. I've even made friends with this girl Katya."

"I heard."

"Then why do we have to leave? Are the police going to find out it was me?"

"I don't know if the police will trace it back to you, but bad people will be looking for you once they hear about this."

"I didn't mean to do it," Abigail said, tears streaming down her cheeks. "I'm so sorry, John."

"I know," he said, feeling naked next to her sorrow.

Abigail grabbed three tissues from the box on the top of her nightstand and blew her nose a few times before her eyes met his. "Am I broken?"

John tried not to laugh, but couldn't help it. Abigail's question, and the way she asked it, seemed so innocent, almost cute. It reminded him of just how much of a child she still was, despite all she'd been through, all *they'd* been through.

John pulled Abigail into another oversized hug. "No, Sweetie, you're not broken. Not at all. Sometimes it's hard to control the Darkness. I'll help you work through it, though. I promise."

Shit, I had to go and use the p-word!

"You will?" Abigail asked, her face still in his chest.

"Yes," he said, stroking her hair until she finally fell asleep, a few minutes before he drifted off and joined her in slumber.

~

JOHN WOKE FEELING WATCHED.

He opened his eyes and saw Abigail's big brown eyes staring back at him. She smiled. "Did you know you snore?"

"I do not."

"Yes, you do. Like a big, giant bear." She imitated a bear loudly snoring and said, "That's you!"

"No, it's not." John reached over and tickled her sides.

Abigail erupted into giggles, her raspy laugh even more infectious than Tiny's deep booming guffaw. John hadn't been around many children, but there was something about Abigail's giggle that sounded like liquid joy.

"Stop it!" she said laughing and kicking his shins.

Then she stared at her blanket like she was trying to work up the nerve to make a request, or maybe tell him something. She was distracted, probably something that had happened at the house when she set the fire. John was about to ask her what it was when a knock at her door surprised them both.

"You two awake?" Larry called from behind the door.

"Yeah," John said. "Come in."

Larry opened the door, looking ripe with exciting news. "Cromwell's in town. Tiny's got some men with eyes on the place. They say he's there, and alone."

"Great! How far is it?"

"About 40 minutes. I say we get going now."

"*We?*" John said.

"Hell yeah, I'm coming and don't even try and talk me out of it because the place has security, and you need my help getting past it."

"Where are you going?" Abigail asked.

John said, "I'm trying to find someone, and we found a man who might be able to help us."

"Is it dangerous?" Abigail asked.

John didn't want to lie. "It might be, but not too dangerous."

"You just got back, I don't want you to leave again!" Abigail whined, wrapping her arms around his torso. "Please, don't leave. Let Larry and Tiny go. They can find the man, and you can stay here with me!"

John looked into Larry's eyes, feeling bad that Abigail didn't seem to mind if his best friend risked his life while being scared that John might. Larry shrugged, nodding to say he understood.

"I need to go, Abigail. But I'll be fine. I pr … I swear."

"What am I supposed to do while you guys are all away? What if something happens?" Abigail swallowed, suddenly looking twice as scared. "What if I do something in my sleep again?"

Larry took a step toward Abigail. "Katya said she'll watch you. I'll bring you to her place, and you two can have a sleepover until we get back. Does that sound fun?"

"What if I fall asleep and wake up killing her?" Abigail asked, eyes wide, terrified.

"You're not going to hurt Katya," Larry said. "Besides, we're not going to be gone long enough for you to get tired and go to sleep."

"Are you sure?"

"Yes," he nodded. "We'll come and get you in a few hours."

"Maybe you should both stay here," John suggested.

"No," Larry insisted. "You want to get past Cromwell's security, right? You need my help, unless you plan on storming inside. A guy like that, I'm sure he has a safe room."

"You sure you can get past his security?" John asked.

"I'm like freaking Rain Man when it comes to that shit, dude. Also, I've got just the thing to keep Abi awake if she's worried about sleepwalking."

"What is it?" Abigail asked.

"These special brownies. Not *those* kind of special brownies," he added, winking at John. "These are energy brownies, a recipe I picked up from this Otherworlder chick a few years back. Could keep you up for three days without a yawn. But it's perfectly safe for Abi."

"Okay," John said, then turned to Abigail. "Everything's going to be fine."

She smiled. "Well, I *do* want to see Katya."

"We gonna go or what?" Tiny was standing in the doorway. "And did someone say something about special brownies?"

John followed Larry and Tiny into the living room to go over details, feeling like he was forgetting something he'd meant to ask Abigail.

TWENTY-EIGHT

Jacob
_____

THREE OF THE five addresses on the Vessel List were within
Washington State. The fourth was smack dab in the middle
of Nevada. The fifth belonged to Hope, whose location
was unknown. Two of Jacob's Harbinger soldiers drove out
to Nevada, aiming to retrieve the vessel and bring the
crystal back. Another two agents were handling the other
Washington vessels.

He saved the closest of the three in-state addresses for
himself. His targeted vessel was a man named Albert
Koenig, a 45-year-old operations consultant who lived in
an apartment 20 minutes from Duncan Alderman's
mansion. It was still early when Jacob arrived with Mr.
Dark, a devoted Otherworlder who provided clouds and
sufficient shade on demand in addition to his job as Jacob's
right-hand man and driver.

Jacob was surprised, if not slightly startled, to find Mr.
Dark still waiting to serve him upon his return. Most of
Jacob's crew, at least among those who had survived the
firefight at the compound, had fled to parts unknown. Mr.

Dark held things in place, waiting for the day when his boss would come back.

Mr. Dark had done well the past year, continuing to recruit and pay new Harbinger members and soldiers, sewing seeds of dissent among Otherworlders as Omega initiated their campaign against aliens, half-breeds, and all known associates.

It didn't take long to rally enough soldiers to take over Alderman's place once Jacob returned. Soon, Harbinger would be legions strong, and Jacob's people, the vampiric Valkoer, on Otherworld would finally find the freedom they had waited centuries for.

"Do you need me?" Mr. Dark rasped from the driver's side, beneath a billowing umbrella of whirling shadows.

"No," Jacob said, opening the door and setting his heel on the concrete. "That won't be necessary. Wait here. I'll be finished shortly."

Jacob closed the car door, stepped out from the billowing shroud and into the night. He crossed the sweeping lawn circling the perimeter of Cooper Arms, the opulent apartment building where Koenig made his home. The doorman nodded at Jacob, looking slightly baffled but mostly dazed. Jacob nodded and walked past him.

Inside, a man wearing a well-fitted, hunter-green blazer with thin, gold stripes circling the cuff, nervously fondled the knot on his tie, swallowing as Jacob approached him. "May I help you?"

Jacob was inches away in a heartbeat, leaning over the counter and into the man's face.

"Yes," Jacob said. "I'll be going up to the seventh floor to see Mr. Koenig. Would you be so kind as to make me a key?"

The man stared at Jacob, not knowing that his next few seconds would determine the rest of his life. If he was only a stupid animal, like most humans and exactly as Jacob expected, he would make the keycard for Jacob. By the time the elevator dinged and Jacob stepped inside, the man would be well on his way to forgetting what had happened and what he'd done, just as the doorman outside had forgotten Jacob already.

If the man was the rare fighter with courage, he would sense the danger and make it his death. A fight with Jacob would last only a second, and the aftermath would see Jacob that much stronger as he rode to the seventh floor to meet Koenig.

"Of course," the man said like an automaton, averting Jacob's eyes. He went to a drawer, pulled it open, grabbed a blank card, slipped it into the machine's mouth, then tucked it into a keycard-sized envelope and handed it across the counter to Jacob.

Jacob smiled as he took the card. "Thank you, Mr. Wyatt," he said, glancing at the man's nameplate, finding his eyes despite Wyatt's resistance, then holding them to stir confusion and lose the memory.

"Of course, sir," Mr. Wyatt said without emotion.

Jacob turned from the counter, crossed the lobby, pushed a button, waited 30 seconds, then stepped into the elevator. Jacob held Mr. Wyatt's thoughts until the doors shut, then felt them fray to nothing. As the elevator ascended Jacob could feel Mr. Wyatt swatting at the surface for truth, but by the time the doors opened to the seventh floor, Mr. Wyatt had drowned beneath it.

Jacob stepped out from the elevator, walked to the end of the hallway, and slipped the keycard inside the door.

Because it was late, Jacob expected to find Koenig sleeping in a back bedroom, but he wasn't. The man was making filthy love to his woman instead. Their bloated bodies were naked, pressed into one another and turning the sofa into a sticky mess. Koenig's eyes widened in horror as he turned in mid-thrust to see Jacob racing toward them.

Koenig screamed — even louder than his woman — as Jacob picked him up by the throat, dug his fingers deep into his flesh, then lifted him high and hurled him across the room.

Koenig landed with a loud snap across the living room, his back spattered against a thick square column at the apartment's center. He smacked into the sharp corner, then fell to the hardwood floor gasping for air in a fetal ball.

The filthy woman tried to run. Jacob left Koenig gasping as if he were a wad of trash to be tossed later, then raised his hand and hurled a blast of energy at her feet knocking the woman down. She fell, face first into the coffee table, blood gushing from her mouth as she reached up to feel for broken teeth. He looked down, and yelled, "Do you want to live?"

"Y ... yyy ... yyyessss," she whimpered through a mouth of blood.

"Then have a seat on the couch," Jacob hissed. "Otherwise you die while he watches."

The woman climbed up to the couch, crying as Jacob turned toward Koenig and approached the column.

He looked down at Koenig with utter curiosity, wondering if such a simple ugly beast could possibly know anything about the power inside him. Did the man even know he wasn't human?

"Do you have any idea what makes you special?" Jacob asked Koenig, who was still writhing on the floor and gasping for breath.

Though Jacob waited, Koenig couldn't make words.

Finally, Jacob made him an offer. "I understand that it's difficult to breathe, Mr. Koenig, but I don't have all night.

Do you have any idea why someone like you would be worth the time of someone like me? If you can't answer in the next few minutes, you'll have to watch your woman become my snack."

The man gasped faster, seconds from spitting blood.

Jacob turned on his heel, then went to the couch and sat beside the woman, running his long gloved finger up and down the length of her pudgy naked leg, smiling, inhaling the room's discomfort like the scent of a rose. He waited for wall clock to lose three minutes, then calmly said, "I'm so sorry, Mr. Koenig, but you're all out of time."

With no more preamble, Jacob feasted on the woman, driving pleasure into his body from two sources: the woman's waning life force, and the petrified waves coming from the miserable man lying in agony on the floor, knowing he was next and still wondering why.

Jacob was normally a speedy feeder, but with Koenig going nowhere, and forced to watch the show, he took his sweet time, savoring seconds until the woman was cindered memory. Once done, he stood from the sofa and returned to the column.

"Hello there," he smiled, kneeling beside Koenig.

Koenig said nothing.

"Are you certain you have no clue about the magick inside you?"

The man's hollow and terrified eyes said he knew nothing.

"Oh, well then," Jacob said before making Koenig his next feast.

The man was surprisingly tasty, with many dark secrets and evils, but disappointing, without any memories to point Jacob toward a freshly discovered truth.

Who was this man, and who determined that he was worthy of being a vessel?

Jacob shoved his fist into Koenig's withered body and waited for the energy to find him. Once he felt the pulse warming his palm, Jacob withdrew his hand from the corpse and opened his palm. A rainbow of colors leaped from inside, sparking from the center of the bloodied crystal which looked just like Shadow's, which Jacob now wore around his neck.

He stared at the gem for several seconds before wrapping his fist back tightly around it. He lowered his fist and closed his eyes, feeling a massive rush of power course through his body from both the crystal in his hand and the one around his neck, as if they were working in concert. The energy was different than the souls he fed on. This was pure power unlike anything he'd ever felt, undiluted with the tainted memories of taken souls. The energy was surely part of the wizard's essence. And once he found the rest of the crystals, he'd be unstoppable.

Another four, and the world would bow to him.

TWENTY-NINE

Hannah

"WHO IS THIS?" Hannah asked.

"This is Sergei," the man said. "Who is *this*?"

"This is Hope."

Hannah didn't believe she was Hope, but needed to know more, and this man seemed to recognize her voice.

"Hope!" Sergei said, his voice ringing with excitement, like an old friend gone for decades. "It's been so long! How are you? How have you been? Where are you at? Oh, my God, Stefan is going to die when he gets back."

"I'm not good," she said, honestly. "Listen, I need to ask you something."

"What is it?" Sergei's voice shifted from hyper to apprehensive.

"How do you know me?"

"What?"

"I had an accident, and don't remember much. I need you to help me remember."

"Oh God, are you okay?"

"I'm not hurt, but my memory is spotty. I can't

remember you. Your phone number just sorta came to me."

"Oh, wow. I saw this on a TV movie of the week once." After a short pause where Sergei seemed to be thinking, he rattled off a life story fast enough to make Hannah wonder if he'd drawn a breath between sentences.

"Um, OK, you were the waitress at an Italian restaurant in St. Augustine where Stefan and I used to go to all the time back in the mid-'90s. The restaurant was called Umberto's. You were a painter, but had never sold anything. You were sweet, but super shy. Stefan and I were opening an art gallery, and helped you sell your first paintings. Then you met this man, John, and the two of you were *sooooo* in love! You moved in together — this cozy little place in the historic district — and then one day you both took off, just vanished. Rumor was you flew to Italy and decided to get married. Then you stayed there. I tried calling, but your phone was disconnected. I tried to find someone who knew how to get a hold of you, but nothing. At first, I was mad you didn't tell us, but Stefan reminded me that young love is impetuous, and I ought not be so selfish. We still have that painting you did for us, and cash from a few of your paintings that sold after you disappeared. By the way, vanishing was a great way to increase the price of your work!"

Hannah sat on the toilet, floored. She couldn't remember a single one of Sergei's stories. Yet, each wore a skin of familiarity. Like a story once told by a stranger.

After Hannah was silent too long, Sergei said, "Are you there, Hope?"

"Yeah, yeah, I'm sorry. Just trying to remember."

"Any of that ring a bell?"

"Maybe a little, I don't know."

"Where are you now? Are you okay? Are you still with John? Are you still painting?"

"No," Hannah said. "None of it."

Greg's voice was at the door, a jackhammer to her nerves. "Hannah? You alright in there?"

"I'm fine, just a bit sick to my stomach, I'll be out in a minute," she said trying to squelch her rising panic. "I'll meet you at the car."

"Um, okay."

Hannah spoke to Sergei in a hurried whisper. "I'm sorry. I've got to go in a minute. But I need you to do me a favor."

"Of course. Anything."

"Do you know John's last name? Have you seen him?"

"No, I don't think we ever knew his last name. But he did work at another restaurant, and ... oh, never mind, that place closed down a few years ago. I'm sorry, I don't know. Are you okay?"

"No. I mean, I don't know. Listen, I've got to go. Can I call you back if I need to?"

"Yes, anytime, Hope. And if you need anything, anything at all, don't be afraid to call, at any hour."

"Thank you."

Sergei seemed as if he didn't want to let her go; worried enough to keep her on the line. "Are you okay?" he asked for the third time.

"I'm fine."

"Are you in danger?"

Hannah forced herself to laugh. "Of course not, and I'll be fine," she lied. Hannah realized she should leave Sergei with something, after being gone for so long with nothing at all. "I'll call you tomorrow. And thank you."

Hannah killed the call and stared at her phone,

wrestling confusion, and the thought of some alternate version of herself that she couldn't remember. She tried to pull memories from her past, but everything was sand through her fingers. She tried again to remember her college friends, but her memory was soup.

"That's because they're not real, Hope. None of it is."

Stop calling me Hope.

She kept staring at the phone, wondering who else she could call. Her coworker and only friend Jenny?

And say what? I think I'm someone else and Greg is trying to do something, but I don't know what? Yeah, they'll put me in the loony bin, for sure. She could hear the doctor now: *"Sorry, that bump on your head in the accident was a bit worse than we thought. Turns out you're nuts."*

But nuts didn't explain Sergei knowing her voice, or the dreams and flashes of John. Nuts ignored all of Greg's mysterious phone calls. Something was happening, and Hannah couldn't afford to be timid.

She had to do something.

But what?

She thought of Greg sitting out in the car, waiting.

There's no way I'm getting in that car.

"Then don't. Go. Run."

Hannah rose from the toilet, washed her hands, and approached the restroom door hoping Greg wasn't being sweet, and waiting patiently for his "sick" girlfriend. She opened the door, saw Greg standing there waiting, and tried to retrieve her racing heart from the floor.

"Are you okay?" Greg looked Hannah in her eyes. "Wow, you seem pale."

"Stomach," she said, holding her belly and wincing. "Just puked."

"Oh, wow, I'm sorry … let's get you back to the cabin, and in bed."

Hannah swallowed, looking past Greg to the red glowing exit sign hanging over the restaurant's rear door. Every instinct ordered her to run — right past him and into the night without stopping. Surely, he wouldn't pursue her in public. Then again, it was dark. Maybe no one would notice if he did.

But rather than running, she followed Greg to the front of the restaurant, and then the parking lot. There were a few dozen cars in the lot, but no new arrivals, and no one leaving. If she ran now, or made a scene, there was no one to notice, call the police, or intervene. It would be her versus Greg, and Hannah wasn't sure she could outrun or overpower him.

Greg opened the car door and she climbed inside.

He got in and keyed the ignition.

"Get back in there! Go in, leave out the back door, and run!"

"Oh, crap, I think I left my phone in the restaurant," Hannah said, seizing on a half-baked escape plan. She could go in, run out the back, and grab a head start. "Maybe in the bathroom. I'm gonna run back inside and …

"No, no," Greg said, laying his hand gently on hers. "You're sick. Wait here. I'll go."

Shit.

Greg surprised her by leaving his keys in the ignition. He got out of the car, then leaned back inside and said. "Be right back."

"Thanks," she said, her heart pounding while eyeing the keys.

"Well, hello, Plan B. Take the car, Hope. Take it and go!"

As Greg entered the restaurant, Hannah crawled over the center console and into the driver's seat. She moved the seat higher and closer, then slowly backed out of the parking spot, darting between her rearview and the restaurant's front door.

"Go! Go!"

She floored the pedal, and tore into the night.

THIRTY

Duncan

DUNCAN SAT in the bedroom turned prison, focusing, searching, and probing through his parasite's psychic defenses. The creature was sentient, and responded to the prodding with short painful bursts to its host's brain; a message to stop, though its communication was nothing like words.

Duncan wondered if it spoke their language, or even at all. He shuddered to think of any creature existing without wants, needs, or desires besides feeding. Jacob was right about one thing: the parasitic bonding was an evolution inside him.

Duncan could feel the changes in his brain even if he couldn't figure out exactly how they happened. He was stronger, more aware, and his already enhanced senses felt sharper than ever. From dissections of feeders over the years, they'd found that the parasite connected to its host's brain, forming an inseparable bond. But when the human, or Otherworlder, died, so did the creature. So far as he knew, the reverse was also true: if someone tried to remove his parasite, they would die.

John and Caleb were the only people he knew who'd managed to pause the parasite's incursion, though both used outside intervention of magickal means. And Duncan hadn't known how either intervention occurred, or how to replicate the success, if it could be done. For everyone else, the parasite, and the Darkness it brought, were lifelong curses.

But Duncan had found its weakness. Everything had one if you probed hard enough. It had a strong aversion to pain, and that pain was shared between the parasites' psychic bonds, meaning if he hurt himself and Jacob was connected, he injured Jacob as well.

Duncan only needed to interfere briefly, long enough to allow a connection with John and warn him of the danger to Hope. He'd first sensed John after Jacob appeared demanding the list. Duncan wasn't sure why he could suddenly feel John in the world, or if the feeling was reciprocal rather than a vestige of Jacob's ability to sense his brother, passed through his parasite.

Duncan was reasonably certain the parasite would sense what he was doing once he reached out to John. Then the only question was whether his parasite would relay information to Jacob's. Duncan hoped not, but had a plan just in case.

He searched the outside world for John, unsure of what he was doing, and almost certain he was doing it wrong until he felt himself suddenly inside John's head.

John, he thought.

Then, as if he were on a phone, he heard John's voice in his head, surprised.

"Duncan?"

"Yes, I have to tell you—"

Suddenly, he felt Jacob probing.

Damn it, that was fast.

Duncan tried shoving Jacob from his mind, but the monster's power was too strong. "*Let me in,*" Jacob screamed inside Duncan's skull — a neutron bomb between his ears.

Duncan couldn't let Jacob see what he was doing, or worse, so much as try to stop him. He didn't dare push another thought out to John until he'd banished Jacob from his head.

Duncan buried the plan, his hand gripping tight around his desk chair.

Jacob sent a sharp pain through his skull trying to stop Duncan from doing anything other than obeying his master's will. But there was no stopping the chair once it was in motion, crashing through the blackened windows.

Sunlight poured into his prison, and with it, a rain of fire, erupting along Duncan's arms as he screamed loud enough to spray blood from his throat.

Jacob echoed his terror and withdrew from his brain like a scurrying roach. The moment he fled, Duncan pushed the message to John, telling him as much as he could in his scant few moments, though he was unsure how much of it made sense with pain tainting his every thought.

Do you understand?

"*Yes,*" John said. "*Where—*"

Duncan's connection to John dropped as the door to his prison burst open and two men tore inside, trying to rip him from the window. He shoved the men aside and leaped through the glass, into daylight's final hours.

Behind the roaring inferno, Duncan's life flashed before his eyes.

Most of the memories went too fast.

When they finally slowed, Duncan found himself standing on a dock overlooking the lake with Caleb as a young boy. "I can remember the flavor of ice cream you bought me at Six Flags, but sometimes I don't even remember what day it is." The boy looked up at Duncan and shrugged. "I guess what you remember depends on what you think is important."

Duncan remembered looking into the child's eyes and feeling a little less alone in the world. He might never have children, but he was lucky that he at least had the chance to feel a parent's love, even if he wasn't the boy's father. That love came with fear, and a fierce desire to protect, like lion to cub.

Duncan once believed he'd never die, and never thought it possible that he could die protecting a son.

But as fire ripped through his body, bubbling soul and flesh, Duncan found himself remembering Ed's funeral again.

Caleb had said, "This is all my fault."

"What do you mean?" Duncan had asked.

"I killed him."

"We had an argument, a big one. It was about you. He wanted me to refuse the car you promised to buy me. He said it was too much. And that if I wanted a car, I should ask him. I told him I didn't want a crap car, and that Uncle Duncan said I could pick any car I wanted. The look on his face, was just, it was like I had stuck a knife in his heart. He said, 'Duncan Alderman isn't your father. I am. And you have to do as I say.'"

Caleb had to stop before finishing his story. "And I just said the most awful thing I could. I told him that I wished he wasn't."

Caleb bawled as he fell into Duncan's chest, crying. "Those were our last words. He died that night."

"Jesus," Duncan had said, tears streaming down his face.

It was then, as he comforted Caleb, that Duncan realized he'd not lost the ability to mourn. There was still one person left in the world whose death he couldn't bear, and whom he would do anything to protect.

"It's okay," Duncan had said, hugging the boy. "He knew that you loved him. And he loved you very much."

And so do I, was Duncan's final thought.

THIRTY-ONE

Hannah

HANNAH FLOORED THE GAS, her heart pounding, pushing Greg's car as fast as it would go along the Northern California highway. She tore from El Montaña and drove north without stopping for hours, too frightened to pause her flight for more than a few minutes at a gas station about 150 miles upstate.

The station looked like it last had new pumps installed in the 30s, probably around the same time as the sign that read *Gas-4-Less!* in giant, blocky almost Art Deco letters. Though it was a full 15 minutes past "quitting time," the old man working the station was waiting for his wife Lucinda to get him. The old man asked Hannah what she was doing driving out on the roads all by herself so late at night.

"You heading out toward Ashford Canyon?"

"What's Ashford Canyon?" Hannah asked, thinking she should have simply said *yes*.

The old man mopped his brow beneath a single tuft of hair, and looked at Hannah with undiluted surprise, as if it was impossible to believe that anyone could be filling their tank at his station and not headed out toward Ashford Canyon.

Since the old man couldn't go anywhere without Lucinda, he decided to give Hannah a history lesson while waiting. He jabbed his finger at a thick swath of trees, without any general direction. "You probably know all about the gold rush, right?"

Hannah shrugged and lightly nodded. She knew a little.

"The gold rush is what changed this state. You see," he said waving his hands in a wild circle, "gold is everywhere. In every rock, believe it or not, and even ocean water. The world's always changing, and California wasn't nothing like it is now millions of years ago when it was sitting at the bottom of the sea."

The old man took Hannah's mild surprise as an invitation to continue. Despite her urgency to flee, there was something comforting in the old man's lilting voice that kept her sitting in her seat, smiling through the open window and willing to hear the rest of his story.

He thrust his thumb behind his shoulder. "The Pacific shoreline lay to the east, where Utah and Arizona are now. Hot springs along the ocean floor built up huge deposits of sulfide minerals. That makes gold, and once all that gold was sitting on solid ground instead of being stuck under water, people all around the country, if not the world, started seeing California as the end of their rainbow. Ashford Canyon was one of the state's more profitable mines, until she called it quits back in 1968."

The old man whistled, and only then did Hannah smell the whiskey. Her nerves tightened. She wanted to key the ignition and take off.

"Now it's just a ghost town people like to visit," the old man shrugged. "But the hotel is nice if you're looking for a place to stay, or at least I've heard it said. Never stayed there myself."

"How do I get there?" An out-of-the-way ghost town hotel might be the perfect place to rest her head and gather some thoughts.

"You can't miss it," he said, again pointing nowhere in particular. "Just keep driving on the road, you'll see the first sign in about five minutes, then fairly regular after that. You'll hit the canyon in about 25 miles or so. Just follow the signs."

"Thank you."

"Sure thing," the old man nodded and slapped the side of Greg's car as if giving Hannah permission to leave. "Just be careful and don't drive too fast. The roads twist something fierce up toward the canyon, and there's no light until morning, outside what you make yourself."

Hannah thanked him again, then turned the engine and gave him a small salute just as Lucinda — she assumed — pulled into the station. Hannah turned to the heavyset blonde around 60, smiling from behind the steering wheel of an ancient F150, and sent her a similar salute. The heavyset blonde returned her wave, looking uncertain.

With a full tank of gas, Hannah tore into the night, only slowing through the treacherous turns the old man had promised. She followed the signs leading toward Ashford and was now only an exit away. As the highway turned flat, Hannah floored the pedal, racing through the walls of trees and hallways of darkness around her, keeping her eyes fixed ahead on her flight from paranoia or nightmare.

Hannah didn't doubt her instincts enough to stop, or even slow, but she doubted them enough to fill her trip with self-flagellation.

What are you doing?

You stole Greg's car and left him stranded hundreds of miles from home.

Why?

She waited for her *other* inner voice, the one which prompted her haste to flee like a bat out of hell. She needed *that voice* to weigh in and assuage her guilt. Unfortunately for Hannah, that voice stayed oddly silent, thickening her doubt and decaying her resolve.

I should turn around, drive back, and say it was all just a joke, ha-ha.

Maybe I can say I forgot about him, blame it on the accident and my bump on the head. Yeah, that might work.

Despite the thought that Greg would probably forgive her, Hannah's body was in no hurry to turn the car around. She accelerated, racing toward Ashford, eager to put more, not less, distance between herself, Greg, and whatever his plans for her might be.

What was he going to do to me?

Hannah considered listening to the rest of the recording, to see if she could glean anything more. But she'd have to wait. It was too dark, and the roads too unfamiliar. She couldn't risk messing with her phone now. While nothing made sense, her fear was as real as any other instinct. Hannah now knew Greg was a danger, and maybe a threat to her life, the same way she once knew she loved him.

Loved him?

Is that now past tense?

Hannah wished her other inner voice would return to ease her mind, and assure her she was doing the right

SEAN PLATT & DAVID W. WRIGHT

thing. She felt like a rocket sent into space without any destination. Along with the fear, a small part of her also felt an undeniable tingle of exhilaration along with a welcome, much-needed freedom. That feeling made her nervous more than anything, causing her to wonder if she hadn't just imagined Greg's imminent danger to justify running from a great relationship growing too serious and fast to stop.

No, that's not it. Yeah, I could see me getting into a fight with him or thinking he was cheating, both of which did happen, yes, but I wouldn't be this creative.

Hannah wasn't sure what to do next. Maybe forget Ashford, flip the car around and head back home? If she spun it now she could probably still beat Greg, unless he'd left immediately. She could go home and pack her bags. Then what? Abandon the life she'd made for herself? Hannah's Bucket Boutique and everything else? And all for what? A *suspicion* that Greg *might* do something to her?

That's stupid! I can't run away based on a hunch!

At the same time, Hannah didn't think she should go home. Greg could find her there, *would* find her there, then what? If she was right, and he was working for someone who wanted to hurt her, as outlandish and Jason Bourne as it all sounded, it wasn't like she could defend herself from him. But if he was crazy and acting out of some sort of paranoid delusion, or something worse, then perhaps she could call the police.

No, not the police. I should call Sergei. I need to see him, to see if he recognizes me. If so, that means I'm right, and there's something weird happening. If not, then maybe I'm the paranoid one.

Hannah looked down at her speedometer — 95 mph, 35 miles over the posted 60 mph limit. She started to decelerate, but it was too late.

Bright blue lights from a police car flashed in her rearview.

Shit!

The inner voice was back in her head. *"Don't stop."*

What?

"Keep driving! Don't stop."

No way I'm running from the cops!

That was the final straw. Hannah had listened to her inner crazy long enough. In the space of a day she'd gone from being on a romantic getaway with the love of her life to stealing his car and considering a run from her life and the law.

Enough is enough.

Hannah took the Ashford Canyon exit, then pulled to the side of the road, hoping the cop car would fly on by on its way to chasing someone else instead of her, but her luck wasn't good enough to keep the cop from following her off of the highway, or from pulling up right behind her.

"What are you doing? The cop is going to run your plates, find out the car is stolen, then throw your ass in jail. Go! Go!"

I'm not outrunning a cop! I doubt I could, even if I tried. This isn't some stupid movie. Real chases don't end with people getting away. They end in arrests or horrible wrecks. There are trees everywhere and I can't even fucking see.

Hannah kept both hands on the wheel, fingers shaking around her palms as she waited for the cop to either get out of the car and approach her window, or say something over the car's speakers. She stared into the rearview, trying to see through to the cop's interior, but Hannah saw nothing beyond high beams, a flashing light rack, and blankets of black.

What's taking so long?

"He's probably being told over the radio that he's dealing with a nutcase who stole her boyfriend's car."

Shit. Shit. Shit.

"I told you to run."

I'm not running.

A stern woman's voice called out, "Get out of the car with your hands on your head."

Oh, shit.

THIRTY-TWO

John

DUNCAN'S DYING message came as the sun set, adding an urgency for John and the others to hit Cromwell's house sooner rather than later. Time was thinning. They needed answers, *now*.

They arrived just after 10 p.m. — John and Tiny waited outside the van, parked a block up from Cromwell's posh estate. The van, a white utility vehicle with a magnet on the side displaying the local cable company's logo, didn't seem like it would draw the sort of attention that might prompt a call to the cops. The pair were waiting on Larry, who was tapping away at his computer in the back of the van, accessing a backdoor into Cromwell's security system so they could control it remotely.

"Okay," Larry said over their headsets. "Everything's good to go. Head on in and make yourselves at home. I'll keep an eye out here and make sure no one surprises you."

John and Tiny casually approached the house as if they were meant to be there on a routine service call, just in case anyone was watching on closed-circuit camera or otherwise.

They stopped at the front door. Tiny held a pistol. John had no weapon other than his left hand ungloved.

"Can you sense him?" Tiny asked. "Feels like he's upstairs, sleeping. Someone's with him."

"Yeah, his wife, I'm guessing. They're both asleep."

John waved his hands over the lock, moving the pins and chamber with his mind, then turned the knob and opened the door.

They crept inside, closing the door softly behind them but leaving it unlocked. The house was gorgeous and sprawling, with high ceilings and thick moldings. It looked to John more like a model home used to sell others, rather than one where anyone lived. They quietly made their way through the front of the museum, then slowly up the stairs to Cromwell's room.

They stared at the bed, Cromwell was on the right side, sleeping on his stomach. His wife was on the left, facing the window. John nodded at Tiny to do as planned — aim the gun not at Cromwell, but at his wife instead.

John leaned over, slid his left hand over Cromwell's mouth and whispered, "Wake up."

Cromwell's eyes shot open and bugged with surprise.

John turned to acknowledge Tiny standing over Cromwell's still sleeping wife. John whispered, "Make a peep, and he blows her brains all over your sheets. Nod yes if you understand."

Cromwell looked over nervously at Tiny then back at John and nodded.

"Good, now get up."

Cromwell obeyed, slipping out of bed, dressed in boxers, a white T-shirt, and a pair of red and brown argyle socks. John pointed toward the doorway. "Go."

Cromwell stepped out of his bedroom and into the

hallway, then turned back to John in the darkness. "What do you want?"

"Just wanna talk. Got a place we won't disturb the Misses?"

"My study," Cromwell said, then led John down the hall.

As they stepped into his office, Cromwell turned to John. With an authoritative voice that harbored no fear, he said, "If anything happens to my wife, I *will* kill you."

"Nothing happens if you answer my questions," John said.

"What?" Cromwell didn't bother to turn on a light or take a seat. "Tell me what you want."

"Hope is in danger and I need to find her. Jacob is already searching. If he finds her, she's dead." John didn't bother explaining that Hope was a vessel. If Omega knew of the vessels then they'd kill her themselves, just to keep Jacob from getting the crystal. And if Duncan knew of the vessels, it was possible that someone in Omega did, too.

"Why is Jacob looking for her?"

"He wants to get to me, I guess," John lied. "But the *why* isn't important. What matters is that Hope's life is in danger, and I highly doubt you all can keep her safe."

"We're not handing her over, John. Not to you or anyone else until every last member of Harbinger, *including Jacob*, is dead. That's the deal and you know it."

"I'm not giving you a choice," John said. "Duncan Alderman is dead, and Jacob is winning his war. Hope will not become collateral damage. Where is she?"

"*What* — Alderman's dead?"

"Tonight," John said. "Jacob's men killed him. Now tell me where Hope is."

"She's safe. That's all you need to know."

John stepped toward Bob. Through clenched teeth he

said, "Don't make me find out the hard way. You won't like it."

Cromwell had balled fists and narrowed eyes. He wanted to punch John, and probably would have if it weren't for the large man waiting upstairs with a gun on his wife.

Cromwell swallowed. "She's with one of our agents."

"What do you mean?"

"A few years ago we had an agent get close to Hope, insert himself into her life. His entire job is to keep an eye on her, make sure she's safe."

"What do you mean *insert* himself into her life?"

"He's dating her. They're close."

Now it was John clenching fists and narrowing eyes. "What the hell?"

"As I said, she's safe. The agent is always with her, and if Jacob comes, he'll be around to protect her."

"Are you really that stupid? Duncan Alderman with all his wealth and guards couldn't keep Jacob away."

"Well, I'll have to take your word on that, I suppose."

"He's dead. And Jacob turned him into a vampire. So Omega's 'protection' is negligible at best."

John continued speaking, never moving his steady eyes from Cromwell's surprise. "I've done everything Omega's asked, and will continue to do so. I'll help stop whatever Jacob's planning, but you have to help me find Hope, or I'm finished, and you can all burn in hell."

"Okay," Cromwell nodded. "Let me see what I can get for you. The files are in my desk." He pointed to a switch on the wall. "Mind if I turn on the lights?"

"Sure," John nodded.

Cromwell stepped past him and flicked a switch.

The light was immediate, blinding, and painful.

The switch triggered some sort of ultraviolet lights

Cromwell must have installed as a security measure to protect himself against exactly this sort of threat.

John fell to his knees screaming, his skin burning.

A gunshot thundered down the hall, followed by Tiny screaming.

"Linda!" Cromwell shouted, running past John's burning body to check on his wife.

John's skin was seared, his flesh bubbling. Every movement further ripped his gaping wounds as he struggled to stand and move toward the switch to shut it off.

But the light was a grand piano on his body, forcing John back to the floor. He pulled his jacket over his head and pulled his hands back into the sleeves. He sat huddled, unable to stand, barely moving as he clung to life despite the bright lights above.

Tiny screamed, the giant's bellows loudly echoed by Cromwell's wife's. Another pair of gunshots ended the big man's bellows.

They killed him!

Again John tried to move, but every labored twitch brought a fresh torrent of pain.

Then the world went dark, the home's power gone.

Larry!

John heard footsteps growing louder as they approached from down the hall, then Cromwell standing over his baked body, panting. John let the jacket fall, though every move was stiff and painful. Cromwell flicked at the switch, trying to recover the lights, but nothing happened.

"You stupid fuck!" Cromwell yelled at John as he leaned down and shoved the gun into his face. "Why do you always have to interfere? I never should've listened to Duncan!"

John tried to speak, but Cromwell kept going, his pistol pressed hard into John's temple.

"I told the old bastard we should've killed you both years ago. But no, Duncan didn't listen, and now he's dead because of sentimentality for monsters!"

"Honey," Cromwell called out to his wife. "Bring me my phone."

Cromwell turned back to John. "You come into *my* house and put a gun to *my* wife's head? You fucking fool."

Cromwell pulled the trigger.

The blast sounded like a plane crashing in his ear. Impossible pain clawed through his right shoulder and sent him writhing on the floor, crying.

"Do you know how much of a thorn in my side you've been, John? How much bullshit I had to tolerate because of you and Caleb? No more, and never again. The old man is dead. We're doing things my way now. The time for your demands are over. You're going to do your fucking job, without the negotiating. No Hope. No deals. No protection for your friends. Jacob can have them all — I don't fucking care."

John, doubled over in pain, glared up at Cromwell.

The fucker is dead the minute I can stand.

Cromwell aimed the pistol at John's head. "Ah, you don't heal so well when you're hurt, do you? Neither did your big nigger friend upstairs."

John tried to reach out to see if he could feel any life left in Tiny, but his world seethed in pain and anger too much to focus. Cromwell lowered the gun, fired at John's leg, and turned his right calf to raw meat.

"Fuck!" John hollered.

"Now we're doing things *my way*, John, got that? Fail to obey my every fucking word, I'll get that little girl, Abigail, tie her up on my front lawn, and have a barbecue on her burning corpse, do you understand me?"

John said nothing, staring Cromwell in the eyes, wanting to tear him apart piece by bloody piece with his bare hands.

"I asked if you understood me!" Cromwell yelled, his face crimson. He turned and shouted back to his wife. "Honey, where the fuck is my phone?"

The phone flew across the room, skipping twice off the floor before landing beside John.

"What the … ?" Cromwell turned to see Larry with a pistol pushed into the side of his wife's head.

"Put the gun down," Larry ordered, his face stone serious. "Or I shoot the bitch."

"Okay, okay," Cromwell said, setting his gun on the carpet. "Don't hurt her."

Larry's eyes absorbed the severity of John's condition. He winced as his friend struggled to stand.

Cromwell turned to John. "I'll tell you whatever you want. Just don't hurt her."

"Yes, you will," John said, reaching out for Cromwell's flesh before the man had time to register what was happening.

John could vaguely sense Cromwell's wife screaming as he feasted, trying in vain to reach out and halt her husband's murder. Larry yanked her back, shoved her to the side, and pushed her to the ground. She tried to stand, but Larry put his foot to her chest. "Stay down!"

"No, no, no!" she screamed.

John sucked Cromwell's energy into his body, feeling his flesh stitch itself together as if someone was pouring pure life inside him. He dove into Cromwell's memories, searching for any sign of Hope.

He steered the memories toward her, first learning her

new name — Hannah Quinn — then finding the name of the agent she was sleeping with — Greg Overton.

John saw Cromwell on the phone earlier that day, instructing Mike Mathews to have Greg bring Hope in so they could wipe her again, as she was starting to remember. After that, they'd have to move her somewhere else. Or, if she became a problem, dispose of her.

John would have to get to Mathews.

He searched for more information, but found nothing. Cromwell's memories trickled to nothing, then the present surfaced and John saw what was left of the man's body lying crumpled on the floor. Larry was gone.

"Larry!" he called, afraid something horrible had happened to his friend.

John ran to the bedroom and saw Tiny laying in a pool of thick red syrup at the foot of the bed, the right half of his bald head cracked like a melon from the shot, flesh torched. His burned fists clutched at a blanket which he'd not managed to pull over himself before he was either baked into nothing, or ended by the crack of Cromwell's gun.

Jesus.

John cursed himself for luring Tiny to his death. He should never have given Bob a chance to trigger the house lights. There was no way John could've known what the man would do, but he should've suspected *something* the second Bob became Mr. Helpful.

Larry stood with his gun trained on Linda, who was sitting in a chair, crying. Larry looked like he'd been crying too, mourning his friend, Tiny, whom he'd known far longer than John had.

"What do we do about her?" Larry asked, waving the gun at Bob's wife, looking like he wanted to shoot her.

"I don't know," John said. Bob's memories of Linda

flooded his mind. He'd once loved his wife, years ago. They grew distant after their daughter went off to college, and things changed. While the passion was missing, and Linda mostly a stranger, Bob still loved her. Traces of that love coursed through John as he looked at Linda, remembering the *her* from two decades gone. The young, carefree, loving woman, eroded by years of indifference.

John hated feeling his victims' emotions, especially when clouding his practical thought. If he allowed Linda to live, she'd surely call the cops. Omega would be tipped off that much faster to John's attack, giving them a chance to do whatever they planned to do with Hope sooner rather than later.

"Please," she said. "Don't kill me."

Larry looked into John's eyes, seeking a verdict.

John shook his head. "Tie her up."

THIRTY-THREE

Abigail

ABIGAIL SAT in an overstuffed strawberry-colored chair in Katya's apartment, comfy while watching "Gravity Falls." Katya stood outside talking to her boyfriend, Derek, on the phone. Abigail didn't even know she had a boyfriend. Apparently, her last-minute visit had derailed Katya and Derek's date, meaning her newest friend was forced to soothe things over.

Katya came back inside the apartment, looking steamed.

"What's wrong?" Abigail asked.

"Nothing," Katya said, clearly lying. It was weird to see her annoyed; Katya was always so happy. Abigail couldn't remember a time when she wasn't bubbly and smiling, save for the scare Abigail gave her at the restaurant.

It was weird to see her smile missing.

"Is Derek mad?"

"He'll get over it," Katya said sinking deep into the red leather couch.

"What are you watching?" Katya asked.

"'Gravity Falls. Ever see it?"

"No," Katya shook her head. "I don't watch much TV. When I used to work for the Radleys, I didn't see anything other than Nick Jr., Sprout, and Disney Jr. Honestly, I don't even know why I have cable."

"What do you do if you don't watch TV?"

"Sometimes I try to draw clothing designs and stuff, but mostly, lately, I've been writing."

"Writing what? Books?"

"I suppose they would be books if I ever made it past 10 pages," Katya laughed. "They're pretty awful."

"I doubt that," Abigail said. "Could I read something?"

"Oh, no, they're truly, truly terrible. I swear."

"They can't be that bad."

"That bad and worse," Katya smiled. "Guaranteed."

Abigail wondered if they were really that horrible, or if maybe Katya's stories were romantic, or something else embarrassing. Abigail changed the subject.

"So, what else do you do?"

"I play a little guitar."

"Really? I've never met anyone who plays guitar."

"I'm not very good at that, either," Katya said.

Abigail frowned.

Katya pursed her lips and stood from the sofa. "Want me to play something?"

"Yeah!" Abigail said, smiling.

Katya went to her bedroom then returned a few minutes later with a large, black leather-looking case with four large metal latches on the side. The case was covered with stickers of bands Abigail had never heard of.

Katya set the guitar case on top of the coffee table then sat on the couch. Katya popped the four latches open and pulled the guitar from its home. Abigail watched, utterly fascinated as Katya plucked at the strings and adjusted knobs at the guitar's top. There was something almost magical in the ritualistic process that filled Abigail with awe.

"Any requests?" Katya asked after a few minutes spent tuning her guitar.

"I don't know. Play your favorite song."

Katya thought for a moment, then said, "I don't know what my favorite song is since there are too many good ones to choose from, but this is one I liked a *lot* a few years ago. It's called 'Elsewhere' by Sarah McLachlan. Ever hear it?"

"No," Abigail said, leaning forward in the chair, hands folded in her lap as Katya began to play.

Katya started to sing. Abigail immediately felt tears start to swell in her eyes. The music, lyrics, and Katya's voice were all beautiful by themselves, but magical together. The song was so sad, yet somehow uplifting. Abigail felt as if it were written just for her, and Katya was the first person to sing it.

Katya finished and Abigail broke down in tears. "Oh, my God," she said, wiping her eyes. "That's so beautiful."

Katya's cheeks turned salmon. "Really?"

"Yeah, I love it. What was it called again?"

Katya told her, and Abigail said, "I have to have Larry get that for me."

"Hold on." Katya set the guitar back in its case and ran to her room. She took longer than last time, but returned, clutching a CD in her hands.

"Here," Katya said. "You can have my CD. I have, like, three copies!"

Katya reached out to hand the CD to Abigail, who absentmindedly reached out to take it. Only as their fingers drew close, did Abigail remember her curse. A spark shot from her hand, causing Katya to jump back with a yelp and drop her CD to the carpet.

Abigail yanked her hand back before she could lock onto her friend.

Katya fell back on the carpet and landed on her butt. She cried out in sudden, unexpected pain. Abigail curled on the chair, shaking: covering her eyes with her fingers, afraid to see what damage she might've done.

The world was entirely dark behind her closed eyes as the room grew painfully silent. She couldn't bear to look.

Oh, God, she's dead. I killed her.

Please don't be dead, please don't be dead, please—

"Ow," Katya said. "Are you okay?"

"I'm sorry, I'm sorry," Abigail repeated.

Katya stood and stared at the fingers on her right hand, swollen and red, practically burned. She winced, looking at Abigail to see if she was also hurt. "Are you okay?" she asked again.

"I'm fine. Are you?"

"I don't know." Katya ran to the kitchen, probably to grab ice from the freezer. Abigail hopped up from the floor and followed, eager to make sure Katya was okay, and that the damage wasn't spreading up her arm or into her body.

Abigail kept a safe distance as Katya dropped her hand into a bowl of ice-cold water. She stood in front of the sink, staring at Abigail with fear in her eyes.

"What happened?" Katya asked.

"I'm so sorry."

"Why do you keep saying you're sorry? You didn't do anything."

Something in Abigail's eyes must have given her away — maybe the guilt. She stared at Katya as everything in her friend's body started to shift, from her eyes to her mouth to her look of slowly dawning understanding.

Something was wrong with Abigail, and Katya knew it.

THIRTY-FOUR

Hannah
_____

HANNAH WAS CONFUSED.

She'd been sitting in a county jail cell for a few hours, and yet nobody had said a word to her. The arresting officer escorted her to a cell, and that was that. No mug shot, no fingerprints, no anything. She'd been told to sit, then left alone.

Don't they have to charge me with something? They can't just hold me and not tell me what I'm being charged with!

Hannah decided to say something the second she saw someone. Problem was, her row of cells was empty of both prisoners and guards. It was as if the jail was a ghost town, too.

Something wasn't right.

"I told you to run," that other inner voice started to harp. *Not now.*

It was easy to lose track of time in a tiny cell without any windows. Hannah was exhausted, and wanted to sleep on the cell's only cot, but didn't dare close her eyes.

She had to stay awake — had to see what was going to happen.

Sleep finally won, and Hannah nodded off while sitting up, and desperately trying to stay awake.

~

HANNAH WOKE to the sound of her cell door opening. Greg stood beside another officer she'd not seen before, a stern looking man in his 50s.

Despite being afraid of Greg just hours before, she melted with relief as he stepped into her cell. "I'm so sorry, Greg," she said, feeling ashamed and foolish.

He hugged her tight, and his hug felt good: comfort without judgment. "I don't know what happened. I think it must be from the accident. I was confused and, I don't … "

"It's okay," he soothed, stroking her hair, "Everything's fine now. Don't worry."

The officer asked, "Everything good here, Agent Overton?"

"Yes," Greg said. "Thank you, Gene."

"No problem, sir."

Agent? Why is he calling him an agent? Why is he talking to Greg as though Greg is some sort of authority?

"I told you. He's not who he says."

Hannah kept her mouth shut as the officer escorted them out from the cell and handed Hannah the purse they'd confiscated during her arrest. Her heart pounded, confusion swirling through her head as she followed Greg outside the station and over to his car, waiting under the soft, early-morning light. Something inside Hannah screamed for her to run, but where in the hell could she go when her boyfriend was friendly with the cops? Might even *be* a cop, or something.

Agent? Who the hell is he?

He opened her door and said, "Get in." Hannah wasn't sure if she imagined the sharp edge in his voice, but sure didn't think so.

She got inside, and Greg closed the door hard behind her.

Greg got in on his side, adjusted the seat, and put the car into drive. The doors autolocked as they left the county jail.

They drove in silence, Hannah wanting to ask him why the officer called him "agent," what was going on, and even confront Greg about his phone call back at the cabin. She thought of the phone in her purse, and though she didn't dare check to see if it was still there, Hannah wondered if the police had listened to the recording, and whether they'd played it for Greg.

Hannah stared out at the passing greenery, afraid to meet his eyes. He stared at the road with gritted teeth, angrier than she'd ever seen him.

When he finally spoke, it was so loud and abrupt that Hannah started in her seat. "What the hell did you think you were doing? You really fucked things up. You know that, don't you?"

Hannah's heart was in her throat, her body trembling through his verbal assault. Greg had never been so rude. Had never said *fuck*, even in bed. His new words were a punch to her gut. If he was dropping all pretense of kindness, then anything might be possible.

"He's going to kill you."

"What's happening, Greg?" Hannah finally asked, her voice cracking. "Why did that man call you agent?"

"Because I'm with the FBI."

"What? I thought you were some kind of business analyst?" She couldn't believe her ears. Hannah wanted to know why the FBI would be interested in her, but that meant admitting to recording his call, and she wasn't ready for that. She'd play stupid — which didn't seem too difficult considering how in the dark she felt.

"I'm with the FBI, and I've been assigned to you."

"Assigned to me?" So, their whole relationship was a ruse from the beginning? He'd been lying to her for two years? She felt like she was going to puke, burst into tears, or melt down into nothing. "Why?"

"I've been assigned to protect you. But you just fucked things up for us both.

"What are you talking about? Protect me from what?"

"The man you've been dreaming of, John. Ring any bells?"

"No," Hannah lied. Flashes of the dark-haired man raced through her mind.

"I know you remember him."

"I have no idea what you're talking about," she said, her voice at the edge of a whine. While she *was* lying about not remembering John, Hannah had little more than a few scraps of scattered memory, nothing other than Sergei's conversation, which suggested the man was real.

"Whatever," Greg said, returning his gaze to the road.

Hannah stared back out the window, wanting to speak, but at the same time, pissed at Greg for being so rude. "Who is he?" she finally said.

"He's trying to kill you. That's all you need to know."

Kill me? What? Sergei said we were in love.

"Why is he trying to kill me?"

"I said that was all you needed to know. Now sit back, shut up, and don't make this any more difficult than it needs to be."

"Make *what* difficult?"

"This. *THIS!*" Greg waved his hands as if she was

supposed to understand what in the hell he was talking about.

"What?" Hannah repeated, trying not to cry. She hated crying almost as much as she hated whining.

Greg didn't respond.

What's he planning to do?

Hannah looked down at the door, remembering that it locked when they started driving. She wondered if she could open the door, jump out, and survive the fall, let alone escape into the woods alongside the highway. She looked at the speedometer. Greg was driving more than 80 mph.

Why's he in such a rush? Where are we going?

"Greg, tell me what the hell is happening. You're scaring me." Hannah finally found some force in her voice.

"I'm protecting you."

"From what?" she screamed.

Greg turned to her, his eyes wild, like he might reach out from the steering wheel and strike her at any second. Instead, he lowered his voice to one breath above a whisper and asked, "You really don't remember any of it?"

"No," she whispered back.

"You were the victim of a serial killer. He tried to kill you more than 10 years ago. You told me all of this when we met."

She stared at Greg as if he'd just told her the sky was purple and would be dropping flying saucers by sundown.

"What?" was all she could manage.

"When we met, you told me that you changed your identity, and said you were in hiding because he was still out there. So I've been investigating the killer and trying to keep you safe. And no, I didn't tell you I was FBI because I'm part of a secret division. Most people think I'm an analyst, and while I wanted to tell you the truth, I couldn't."

"Why don't I remember any of this, the stuff about the serial killer?"

"I don't know," he shrugged. "Maybe the amnesia from your accident runs deeper than the doctors thought."

"This doesn't make any sense. I would remember something like that. And I don't have amnesia. I remember my family, my friends, and ... "

"You sure?"

Hannah tried to remember her mother, or her college friends, but again she came up fuzzy, and more confused than before. She could remember *something*, but wasn't sure if it was honest memory, or fabrication.

She shook her head, waiting for her other voice to chime in with some sort of direction. Unfortunately, the silence said she was on her own, alone with her confusion.

"I don't know," Hannah said, swallowing her rising fear. It was one thing to be uncertain of Greg and his motives, another to suspect her memory's candor.

Greg moved his hand from the steering wheel and opened his fingers, waiting for Hannah to take his hand as it hovered above the center console. She did, shivering as his fingers wrapped hers. She swallowed her climbing knot while trying to bury tears she didn't want to lose.

Hannah fought a growing urge to ask Greg about the phone call. She wanted to know who he was talking to and what he was trying to do to her. Now she could barely remember what he'd said. Everything felt fuzzy, like a blur.

"Don't ask him. You need to play dumb until you can get another chance to run."

Another chance to run? Run to where? He's working with the FBI! He's trying to protect me.

"No, he's not, Hope. Don't trust him. He lied — John wasn't trying to kill you. Don't you think Sergei would've said something?"

Maybe Sergei didn't know. Or — what if the man who answered the phone was John, pretending to be someone else so he can find me now?

"You would know if it was John. Trust me, Hope. Trust yourself."

Hope. There's that name again.

"Hannah's not my real name is it?"

"No, your name was Hope Barnett. Like I said, you changed your name about 10 years ago, but no one else knows. It doesn't matter now, anyway. We have to put you in hiding. I've gotten word that he's looking for you, and that he's in town."

"The killer?"

"Yes. His name is John Sullivan. Does that name sound familiar?"

"No," Hannah lied.

Greg got off an exit roughly halfway between the vineyard and home, then pulled into an apartment building she'd never seen in a city whose name she didn't know.

"What is this place?"

"Somewhere safe," he said, as if it was. "We're going to stay here, ride things out until I hear something."

"Something about what?"

"That John is dead."

THIRTY-FIVE

John And Larry

LARRY RACED TO MIKE MATHEWS' apartment, wobbling the van with too much velocity the entire way. Neither spoke of Tiny's death, not that either had to. They would grieve when the war was over. For now, they had to focus on finding Hope, which they'd only do if they found Mathews.

As the van hit a pothole hard, and seemed like it might rip in half, Larry looked over at John. "I really ought to get a fucking sports car, as much racing around as I'm doing for you. We got that in the budget? Maybe somethin' like the Batmobile! That shit would be rad."

"I left you a ton of money. Don't even tell me you blew it all already."

"Well, not *all* of it." Larry grinned with a shrug.

"Jesus, how much Mountain Dew do you drink?"

"Enough to piss green, but that could also be because of that stripper chick I was bangin.'"

John laughed.

It felt good to laugh before dealing with Mathews. With Duncan and Cromwell both dead, Mathews would be exactly the type of loose cannon they couldn't risk working with. John had to get out from under Omega's thumb while he still had a chance to save Hope. Unlike killing Cromwell, he had no compunctions about killing Mathews. The man was on a power trip and didn't care whom he killed on the way to his finish.

Yet, even as John condemned Mathews, he realized his hypocrisy in judging the man. They were both killers. The difference, at least in John's eyes, was that his goal in saving Hope was righteous and true. Mathews' seemed like a blatant power grab.

No sense in beating myself up. We're here.

They arrived at Mathews' house at 12:16 a.m.

John was still in the van when disappointment slapped him hard in the face.

"Shit," he said. "Mathews isn't here."

"You sure?" Larry asked.

"Nobody in there but a sleeping dog."

"What now?"

"Now, Plan B." John said.

"I fucking hate Plan B," Larry said, even though he didn't have a clue what Plan B was.

But Larry was right. John was certain he'd hate it.

∼

LARRY

"THIS IS A TERRIBLE IDEA," Larry repeated all the way to The Port Hole, a dive bar in the City's seediest quarter.

"This is the only way," John had said.

Larry waited in his van, idling in the parking lot, located in a large field between The Port Hole and a fairly popular seafood joint, meaning there were plenty of parked cars to blend with. Lightning flashed overhead, flickers accompanied by a deep roll of angry thunder.

A storm is coming — a shit storm.

The plan was for John to show up at the bar as if he'd just freed himself from Shadow and his men, and would call Mathews to request extraction. From there, John would attack as soon as he could and discover Hope's location. Then they'd rescue her.

That was the plan, but as evidenced earlier at Cromwell's, and Tiny's subsequent death, plans were made for getting blown to shit. Larry waited for nearly 20 minutes before he saw an Agency van gliding black on black through the parking lot, followed by a second, and then a third.

Oh shit, Mathews didn't come alone.

"Hey, boss, you got a fucking party pulling up outside," Larry said into his mic.

"Who is it?"

"Men in black. I think they're Omega, but fuck if the good guys and bad guys aren't dressing the same these days. They've got guns, lots of 'em."

"Thanks," John said. "Cutting radio now. Over."

Larry kept his headset on, just in case, and trained his binoculars on the front door as the men stormed the bar. He wondered if any of the men were Mike Mathews. Moments later, several emerged, shoving a man in a black hood in front of them, out the door at gunpoint: John.

Shit, shit!

Larry watched them John into the back of a van and slam the doors. Then all the men returned to their vehicles.

Fuck, shit, fuck!

Larry keyed the ignition and peeled from the parking lot, chasing the vans as they headed off.

"I'm coming, John!" Larry screamed, hoping his friend could hear him, either through his earpiece or their mental connection.

Larry was driving fast, following the red lights as the sky opened and rain pelted the van in sheets.

"Really?" Larry said looking up at the invisible deity in the sky. "Really, G?"

Larry followed at a distance as the vans continued down the main avenue. There were three, their taillights the only thing visible through the rain.

Larry sighed, forced to decelerate beneath the pounding rain. His windshield was a blanket of white, headlights bouncing straight into the rain and reflecting back.

The red lights ahead gained distance and sent Larry into a panic. There were too many side roads, and the vans could turn off at any moment. He'd be fucked if that happened.

Larry sped up, trying to make sure he didn't lose Omega. The speedometer said he was going 65 in a 50 zone. That gave him two things to worry about: feds, *and* cops.

Come on, come on, where are you?

Larry leaned closer to the steering wheel, straining to see through the whipping sheets of blinding rain. Suddenly, he spotted red, both low and high — a red light, and three vans, one in each lane, all stopped. The road was too slick for Larry to slam on his brakes without flipping the van, but if he slammed into a van going as fast as he was, he probably wouldn't walk away from the crash.

With only a second to think, Larry swerved into the opposite lanes, flying past the three vans and into the intersection, praying nobody was in the cross traffic as his van sped through, sliding.

Oh, God; oh, God; oh, God!

The van miraculously made it through without leaving the road. He hit the brake once he'd decelerated enough. His eyes looked to the rearview to see if he'd drawn the agents' attention. Headlights from the vans on the right and left turned onto the cross street, one going east and the other west, while the third continued straight behind him.

Shit, which one is he in?

"Where you at, Johnny?" he asked to no response.

Larry watched as the van's headlights approached in his rearview, following for sure. Larry smiled as the van drew closer.

"Come on, bitches, just a little, ah, there we go!"

Larry slammed on his brakes, causing the van to rear end him. Larry grabbed his gun, hopped out of the van, raced up to the black van behind him, saw the driver, and whoever was sitting in the front passenger seat, both struggling with their crash bags which were taking their sweet time to deflate.

Larry raised his pistol, fired three shots through the glass, and hit both men in the head. He raced around to the back of the van, hoping like hell it wasn't loaded with more gunmen.

He pulled on the door handle and yanked it open to an empty cargo hold.

"Fuck!" Larry yelled. John was in one of the other two vans.

He raced back to the front seat, reached over the dead agent, grabbed his radio, and took it back to his van so he could listen in the off chance they'd surrender John's location.

The rain fell harder.

THIRTY-SIX

Abigail

ABIGAIL STARED AT KATYA, about to tell her everything when another voice bled back into her brain — the girl vampire, Talani, silent since the fire.

"You can't tell her."

Stay out of my head. Stop spying on me.

"She won't understand you, Abi. Humans never understand us."

Stop it — she's not like the others.

"Are you all right?" Katya had been looking at her strangely, but now she was looking at Abigail with growing discomfort.

Abigail shook her head, trying to push Talani away. She'd just appeared in Abigail's head, as if there all along, watching and listening. Waiting. It unnerved her. Abigail didn't want people eavesdropping on her thoughts, or her life.

Get out!

"Are you okay?" Katya repeated.

"I need to tell you something," Abigail said.

Talani's voice spoke again, demanding, *"Don't do it."*

Abigail ignored the warning. "It's bad."

"What is it?" Katya stepped closer, her eyes almost haunted by concern.

"I'm a monster."

"What?" Katya laughed like Abigail had delivered the punch line to a corny kid's joke.

"I'm a vampire, to be precise, but not the kind from books and movies." Abigail pushed through the words despite Talani shouting protests in her head.

Katya stared at her. The smile on her face was a stretched out shirt, awkwardly draped from its hanger. "Ha-ha, Abigail. Seriously, what do you want to tell me?"

"That's it," Abigail said. "I'm a vampire. And I kill through touch. Which is why I wear gloves and cover myself while around people who might accidentally touch me. That spark between us, that was it. There's a parasite inside me. It feeds off of other people."

Katya stepped forward, still smiling. "Don't be silly, Abigail. You're not a— " she reached out to touch Abigail's hand as if to prove her point.

No!

Abigail suddenly did something she'd never done — something she'd seen John do to Larry, but had never tried herself. Without meaning to, only from thinking it, like instinct, she shoved Katya back with a blast of energy, across the kitchen, so fast and hard that Katya's head slammed into one of the cabinet doors with a sickening crack.

Katya cried out as Abigail fell to the kitchen floor, weak and wobbly, waiting to regain her strength.

She sat across the kitchen from Abigail, burned hand on her head, looking roughed up. Their eyes met and Katya realized she wasn't joking.

"You were telling the truth?"

"Yes," Abigail said softly, ashamed.

"How? How is it even possible?"

"It's a long story," Abigail said. "And if you didn't believe the ending, you certainly won't believe the beginning."

"Try me," Katya said.

Abigail let it all out — everything she'd been stuffing inside for a year, and before then. She told Katya about her parents dying, her uncle Frank selling her, and her abuse at the hands of Randy Webster. Katya listened intently, saying all the right things, and offering something Abigail had never had before: female support.

Crying softened pressure on Abigail's soul.

Outside, rain pelted the windows, and with it, Abigail surrendered to more tears, shuddering with relief that there was finally someone in the world who understood her, or was at least willing to listen. She sobbed and spoke more, until she finally finished a thousand pounds lighter.

"Wow," Katya said, sitting just two feet across from her on the floor, looking like she wanted to hug Abigail, but now knowing better. "I don't know what to say. I'm so sorry you've gone through so much."

"You believe me, then?"

"Yes." Katya nodded.

Abigail fell into a fresh heave. Her head throbbed, feeling like she was floating in an ocean, out of control.

"I don't feel so good," she said, trying to stand.

Halfway up, Abigail collapsed, hands and elbows breaking her fall with a jolt to her brain. "Call Larry," she said in barely a whisper.

Katya stood, ran into the living room where she'd left the phone, dialing on her return to the kitchen. "What's wrong?"

But Abigail couldn't talk. She felt weak and empty. Her eyes closed, plunging her world into darkness. Her ears begged for scraps, every sound coming from beneath a turbulent sea.

"Larry, it's Katya. Something's wrong with Abigail! She's lying on the floor, passed out! I don't know what to do! I know about her real condition. Call me, please!"

Katya turned to Abigail. "I called him, but he didn't answer. I left a voice mail."

Abigail blinked her eyes back to open. Everything was a blur. She remembered John at the hotel after he'd blasted Larry, and how weak he'd become.

What was it Larry said? Oh yeah ... that John was starving and when he woke, he would attack anyone or anything he saw.

Oh, no.

The hunger stirred within Abigail. The Darkness within, uncoiling, wanting to reach out for Katya.

Abigail opened her mouth and breathed, "Go."

Katya leaned down. "What, Abi?"

Abigail felt Katya's warmth, life beckoning like garlic frying in oil.

No, no, no, not Katya.

"Run," she said, or thought she did. Truth was a haze as she faded in and out. Every time she opened her eyes, Katya was somewhere else in the kitchen. Every step echoed loudly, as if caroming between wide canyon walls.

Go, get out.

Talani was back.

"You must feed, Abigail, or you will die."

No. I'm not killing her.

"You'll die, Abigail. You don't have much time. I can feel you weakening."

I don't care. No more death.

"Take her, Abigail. She's exactly what you need. Look at her — she's lived a happy life. Think of all the miserable people you've

killed. How much of their pain you've soaked like a sponge. Feeding on her will bring you happiness."

No! She's my friend.

"You really think she can be friends with you? Look at her, Abigail. Look at her long and hard and tell me you don't see fear staring back. She'll never see you the same way after tonight. Trust me. Your friendship is over. You terrify her."

Abigail opened her eyes, and saw Katya standing at a distance, but couldn't see more than a blur.

"You're going to die, Abigail. Get up now. Feed!"

No. I'm not killing her.

"She isn't your friend. You can't be friends with humans. They don't understand you. They can't understand you. Look inside her mind and you'll see the monster that she does."

Shut up.

Abigail tried to stand, but fell again. Katya rushed over. "I'm calling an ambulance."

"You can't," Abigail tried to reply, but couldn't open her mouth. She shook her head:

Put the phone down.

If an ambulance came, she was dead. Abigail wasn't sure how she knew, but she did. They'd discover what she was, she'd be found by Omega, or she'd be passed out in a hospital bed when the morning sun rose and she burst into flames.

No, no.

"You can't call!" Abigail cried out to Katya's back. She was either ignoring Abigail or didn't hear her. Maybe she wasn't in the room. It was so hard to know up from down through the fog.

Katya blurred in and out of focus, long enough for Abigail to see her finish dialing and put the phone to her ear.

"Hello?" Katya said.

No!

Abigail sent another burst from her body. The phone flew from Katya's hand and crashed to the floor. She heard it shatter across the tile.

Katya screamed, and in that scream, Abigail heard it — the fear Talani warned of.

"She's afraid of you. How can she be friends with you when she'll always think you're going to kill her?"

I'm not going to kill her.

"I have an idea, Abigail ..."

The voice held its pause, then:

"You don't have to kill her. There is another way."

Abigail was silent, waiting for more.

"You can partially feed from her, then turn her. You can save your life, and turn her into one of us. Then you two could be friends forever, if you wanted."

Abigail smiled, or thought she did. It was so hard to tell.

She loved that idea. Abigail thought of Katya playing her pretty song again. Maybe she could even teach her to play guitar.

What if Katya doesn't want to be turned? Who am I to decide?

"Who wouldn't want immortality? She'll thank you. Trust me. You know I'm right."

I don't know how to do it.

"I'll show you, Abigail. Just get up and go to her before it's too late."

Abigail lifted her head, opened her eyes, so heavy, and saw Katya standing over her, looking down.

Their eyes met.

"Do it, Abi. Now!"

Abigail reached out, catching Katya's hand as she tried pulling away. Their eyes locked.

Energy coursed through Abigail, along with a flood of happy memories—

KATYA'S CHILDHOOD spent with her doting father; a puppy she once had named Laika, after the first dog Russia sent into space, a dog which had sadly died; and dozens more memories, all like warm sunshine melting chocolate through her body.

ABIGAIL TRIED to find Talani's voice in the current.

Help me turn her.

Talani was silent.

Oh God. Help me, Talani!

Nothing.

Oh no, no, no!

Abigail tried to break the current, but it was too late. She was riding it, high, drowning in the girl's energy and memories.

KATYA WAS SMALL, fresh from Ukraine. No friends in America, yet, so her father helped her meet some at Embassy Park, swinging and playing until they nudged their play into a circle of children.

Katya was 12 and self-conscious, smaller than her peers. Then, from nowhere, she was 14 and several inches longer, from too few to too many, again as awkward as when she couldn't get English to stick on her tongue. But still, she made friends with a girl named Rosa. They were good friends and spent a lot of time together. Sleepovers, going to the mall, and a hundred other things that normal girls did, which Abigail would never know.

Then Abigail was forced to stare into the worst memory, seeing how much Katya had cared for her, pacing her carpet for hours when she left Abigail with Larry after they returned from the restaurant, then lying in bed for several more, flipping her body like a pancake on the mattress, over and over. Something in Katya loved the little girl who seemed so beautifully big inside.

ABIGAIL FELL AWAY, the ride finally finished. Then she opened her eyes and saw Katya's ashen flesh, eyes open and sockets charred. Nothing left of her only friend.

She stared, lips trembling.

Oh God, what have I done?

Abigail screamed.

THIRTY-SEVEN

Larry

LARRY DROVE for a half hour before he thought to check his phone. He brought the screen into view, saw the red number on the green icon, then tapped it and listened to Katya's voicemail.

I hope nothing's wrong.

The pit in his stomach, deep and brimmed with acid said otherwise.

Larry played the message.

"Larry, it's Katya. Something's wrong with Abigail! She's lying on the floor, passed out! I don't know what to do! I know about her real condition. Call me, please!"

Oh shit. Abi!

Larry spun the van in the middle of the street, nearly wrecking it, and raced back to Katya's.

LARRY WAS RELIEVED to see Katya's car in the parking lot, and tried to convince himself that it was a good sign. If an ambulance had taken Abigail away, Katya probably would've followed along.

Unless they let her go in the ambulance with her — she is a kid, and Katya might insist. Say she's family.

Larry hated how his mind always found a negative response to every what-if.

Relax, everything is fine. Do you see any signs that something shitty went down?

The apartment complex was quiet. The night air was cool, and the rain had stopped. There were no sirens or police laying tape.

Larry parked in a handicapped spot and raced from the van, up the stairs to the second floor of Katya's four story building.

He knocked on her door.

It was late, but he figured Abigail would be awake — *if she's OK.*

Stop thinking negatively.

The pit in Larry's stomach tightened as his knock went unanswered.

He pounded against the door, harder and louder.

No response.

He tried the doorknob, but it was locked.

Larry pulled a Starbucks plastic gift card from his wallet, slid it between the door and doorjamb, then bent the card and forced the lock back as he pressed his weight against the wood.

The door popped open to a darkened room.

Larry turned on the light and wished he hadn't.

Oh God.

Katya's body was a withered husk.

No, no, no, what happened?

"Abi!"

No response.

Shit.

Larry called her name again and again as he ran through the house.

But Abigail was gone.

THIRTY-EIGHT

Jacob

JACOB SAT cross-legged at the top of a wooded hill, alone beneath a fat moon, staring down at Duncan Alderman's house as it was swallowed by flames in the distance. Walls of brilliant orange curled against the bright white wood — a stark contrast against the pitch black behind it, and all the dancing stars above.

Soon, the world would burn in a million fires.

His kind would claim Earth as its own, and its people as the livestock they were. Some would be spared — those deemed worthy of evolution to join his race, the Valkoer. But most on Earth were unworthy of the honor — ignorant, petty, violent, tiny-minded creatures who sickened Jacob to his core. *They* who would be cast to the ghettos, and serve as cattle for the elite as nature intended.

Why the Pioneers, who came to this godforsaken world so long ago, decided to spare the humans their appropriate fate, was beyond Jacob's understanding. He had considered inviting the Pioneers to join him, but decided not to upon further reflection. They deserved to be shackled to the humans' fate.

They had been weakened by their time on the planet, growing fond of the humans and foolishly thinking them worthy. Eventually they were weakened for their efforts. Perhaps they devolved from Humkoer to human. Jacob would be making no such mistakes. For him, it was about evolution of the species, and himself above all.

It was nearly time. He had two of the five crystals — three more would grant him the Last Great Wizard's power. Then, the walls would crumble, and Earth would be ripe for the plucking.

Jacob's mouth curled into a smile, lighting his face as he watched waves of flame devour Duncan's grand estate, a monument to misplaced arrogance. Duncan and his Guardians were trying to stop nature, not unlike how their Otherworld counterparts, the Humkoer, the ruling class who had tried to eradicate the Valkoer. On his home world, his kind were at a disadvantage. Here, Jacob's people were top of the food chain.

Humans couldn't imagine what was coming.

Jacob couldn't wait to prove his father's trust in him, to present him with the greatest gift a son could ever offer: a world for the taking, an opportunity for the King to lead his people into a new era where they were the superiors, free from the Humkoers' persecution and forcing his kind to live in a walled city.

Jacob smiled wider.

He held the crystals in a black velvet pouch, and could feel their vibration intensifying. Jacob turned to Mr. Dark as the man appeared behind him on the hill holding a similar pouch. "Sir, Elim has returned with three of the crystals."

"Ah," Jacob said smiling. He stood from his spot in the grass.

Mr. Dark handed the pouch to Jacob, who opened it

and looked inside. These crystals, like the others, were glowing bright red. They were vibrating too, as if sensing their brothers. Perhaps they did. If the crystals contained the soul of a powerful wizard, wouldn't they be sentient?

Jacob looked up at the thief standing a good distance from Mr. Dark, and nodded a *thank you.*

"Pay him," Jacob said, and returned to his seat in the grass.

The crystals hummed, lightly shaking in their pouches. Jacob opened one of the bags to look inside and was surprised when the crystals hopped out from the bag and hung suspended, hovering in the air as if held by tiny filaments. He opened the bag and watched the other three crystals fly out to join the others in midair, five crystals in squared formation, with one floating in the center.

They glowed brighter and brighter. Then, to Jacob's surprise, moved closer to one another. He thought about stopping the movement, but then thought better.

Who am I to interfere with nature?

The crystals shifted into place like a puzzle piecing itself together, brightening as the individuals fused into a single glowing crimson sphere: an almost perfect circle, save for the missing piece.

The sphere hummed, a vibration so low you could barely hear it, though it thrummed in the depths of Jacob's soul.

He felt his power emanating, and without even thinking about what he was doing, reached out to brush the sphere with his fingers. They wrapped around it, and an almost violent energy exploded through him, even stronger than the last crystal had delivered — raw, powerful, and perhaps everlasting.

It felt as if Jacob could somehow tap into and harness the power of a sun.

He closed his eyes and savored the moment, feeling as if the stars were aligned to illuminate his destiny. It was his time to conquer this world. He felt something else, too, something he'd not even recognized within himself until the moment the sphere shined its light into his brain's darkest recesses.

Jacob didn't just want to save his people, he wanted to finally prove himself worthy of his father's love. The father who had always mourned his lost sons, John and Caleb, and who had treated Jacob like less than flesh and blood. He'd always been an embarrassment to his father. But no longer, and not ever again.

Once he had the final crystal, nothing could stop him.

Where is it?

The sphere responded to his wonder, showing him a vision of the woman with the crystal: Hope.

Then it showed him where she was.

Jacob opened his eyes and gazed upon the fire consuming Duncan's estate. That signal fire a portent of what was coming.

Yes, soon, the world will burn.

THIRTY-NINE

John

JOHN OPENED his eyes to total darkness, on his feet and ready to fight by the second blink.

He was in a small holding cell with a cot, a toilet, and a door. He closed his eyes trying to feel where he was.

John was in the Building, a 12-story office structure the FBI had sanctioned exclusively for Omega's use. The ninth and tenth floors were devoted to a secret prison which no one other than the highest security clearances knew existed. Not even prisoners knew where they had been taken. They arrived with drugged heads stuffed in thick black sacks, just as John was sure he had. They left, if they were lucky enough to leave alive, the same way.

John's cell had both a camera and speaker system used to monitor the prisoner, and a row of lights behind thick bullet-resistant glass. Like the lights at Cromwell's, they were designed to kill his kind.

"Why am I in here?" John shouted, looking up at the camera.

A few moments later, Mike Mathews' voice came over the speaker.

"Hello, John. I'll be with you shortly." Then, after 10 minutes the metal door slid open and Mathews stepped into the room. He was wearing his field uniform, covered head to toe in black, and an enclosed helmet with speakers on the side designed to protect him from John's touch. He had no weapon.

The door closed.

"What the hell is going on?" John said.

"I'd like to ask you the same thing. One minute you were storming into Shadow's hotel room, and the next you two were gone," Mathews' voice said through the speakers. His visor was thick black, but John didn't need to see through to know the man's cold stare was fixed on him.

"What are you saying?" John asked, knowing exactly what Mathews was implying.

"I'd like to know how you two escaped."

"We didn't escape. He took me against my will, through a portal."

"A portal?"

"Yes," John said.

"How the hell did he create a portal? Is he working with Jacob?"

"I don't know. But it wasn't the kind that travels between worlds. It brought us from the hotel to somewhere else, some place he had set up, a well in the middle of some field."

"So, you just teleported, then?" Mathews asked skeptically.

"Do *you* have another explanation for how we got out of there?"

After a moment of silence, Mathews said, "Did you, or your Shadow friend, kill Duncan Alderman?"

"Shadow's not my friend. And no," John said, knowing

he probably should have acted surprised to learn of Duncan's death. Now it was too late.

"Why did you kill Cromwell?"

John swallowed.

I knew we shouldn't have left his wife alive. Shit.

"Well?" said Mathews, tapping his foot.

"It was an accident."

"That's not what Cromwell's wife said. She said you were there looking for information. Specifically, you were looking for Hope. Tell me, John, *why* would you be looking for Hope? You know we have our eye on her, and that everything is fine. She's safe so long as you cooperate. So why the search? Were you planning on ending our arrangement?"

John wanted to tell him she was in danger, but couldn't tell Mathews that Hope was a vessel without him dragging her in, and probably ordering her killed to prevent Jacob from getting the crystal.

John told Mathews the closest thing to the truth he could afford.

"Jacob's back, and he knows my weakness is Hope. He will target her, and though you, and some others, are top-notch agents, I can't say the same for everyone in the FBI. You can't guarantee her safety; I can."

Mathews leaned closer, probably trying to read John's honesty through the visor's scanners. "Send Skinner in," he said, but not to John.

Skinner was the son of an Otherworlder, gifted Half-worlder with powers to probe people's minds. He'd been co-opted to work for Omega to avoid detention. Suppos-edly, he'd taken to betraying his kind with glee, though there were plenty, such as Shadow, who accused John of the same thing.

The door opened and Skinner stepped inside. He was

tall and thin, a creepy nightmare with closely cropped, jet-black hair and dark circles ringing cavernous eyes. He seemed mid-fifties, but John figured he had to be a century older at least.

"Not too close," Mathews said, warning Skinner to avoid John's touch.

"I know," Skinner said in a light German accent.

"Find out what he's hiding."

John tried not to appear nervous. It was possible that Skinner couldn't probe him, in which case he might be able to escape further interrogation.

"Okay," Skinner said, closing his eyes.

John felt the man's touch as if he were laying fingers inside his skull, probing for fault lines in his brain. He erected psychic barriers inside his mind, keeping his defenses high and hiding Hope's secret.

Mathews said, "So, what was your plan, John? Find Hope and run away together, live happily ever after while Jacob went about killing whomever he wanted? Was that it?"

John knew what Mathews was trying to do — distract him with discussion so he couldn't maintain his defenses. John was far too skilled in psychic warfare, able to carry on full conversations while fending off attempted intrusions for Mathews' tactics to matter.

"I hadn't thought it out that far. My priority is keeping Hope safe. After I gave her shelter, I meant to continue tracking Jacob. I *will* continue."

"How do I know you're not working *with* him?" Mathews asked.

"I'm not responding to stupid questions."

John continued resisting Skinner's attempts to crack his mind until Skinner finally turned to Mathews.

"He's fighting me."

"Oh, is he? Well then, our friend John must have something to hide."

"I'm not hiding anything."

"Then why don't you open wide and let Skinner in?"

"Sorry," John said. "I don't let anyone in my head."

"We'll see about that." Mathews reached into his pocket and pulled out a small black rectangle — a remote of some sort.

Mathews thumbed a red button on the remote and the rows of special lights blazed on above.

John fell to his knees in agony as his skin caught fire from inside. "Stop!" he screamed.

Mathews clicked off the lights. John stayed on his knees, body shaking in torment and pain. Skinner had shattered the gauzy wall at the edge of his defenses. John clenched his fists and squeezed his eyes tight trying to repel him, but the burning was rot to his resistance.

Skinner was in.

John felt the man seize upon the information he was most trying to hide. And then Skinner was out.

As his pain receded, John watched the crimson skin on his arms slowly heal.

Skinner turned to Mathews. "He's searching for vessels — people with crystals stuck in their flesh. Five crystals holding the soul of the Last Great Wizard from Other-world. The person who pieces them together controls the wizard's power. Jacob is hunting the vessels, then killing each to retrieve the crystals. Hope is on the list."

John glared at Skinner, wanting to sink his fingers into the bastard's flesh.

"Thank you," Mathews said. "You're excused."

"Yes, sir." Skinner nodded, the German accent crisp on his lips. He left the room, not daring to meet John's stare.

Mathews stepped closer to John, looking down at him,

almost daring him to make a move. John considered it, but the man's finger was on the button, and the man had grown sadistic enough to fry him for laughs.

"So, *that's* why you want to find Hope. It's all so perfectly clear now. Interesting."

"You have to bring her here," John said. "If Jacob gets to her, she's dead."

"Yes, yes, good idea. She *should* be here."

Mathews fell several steps from John, then spoke into his helmet radio. "Get me Agent Overton." Moments later, Mathews was talking to Agent Overton, instructing him to bring Hannah to The Building. "If she resists in any way, kill her immediately."

John went to strike, but wasn't fast enough. Mathews pushed the button again and flooded the room with lethal light, sending John back to the floor in crippling pain.

Mathews clicked the lights off, then leaned down to John and calmly said, "Your free ride is finished, John. You had exactly two friends in the Agency looking out for you, and, as it so happens, both Duncan and Cromwell are now dead. That means a new boss. Are you familiar with Bernard Walsh? He's now in charge of The Guardians, and unlike his predecessor, Walsh understands that this job leaves zero room for misplaced sentimentality."

John rode out the pain, rocking back and forth on the floor as Mathews continued. "None of this would have happened if Duncan had done the right thing when it had to be done. But I assure you, John, you'll not see the same mistake from me. When it's time to choose between one life and millions, I won't falter."

John forced himself into action through the pain. He tried to reach out, but his attempt fell pathetically short.

Mathews stepped away from John, as if trying to evade a swatting old cat. "Goodbye, John. I'd like to say it was

SEAN PLATT & DAVID W. WRIGHT

great working with you, but we both know a lie when we hear it."

Mathews left just as John managed to stand.

The door closed and locked.

John wondered why Mathews hadn't simply killed him, and figured he either still needed him alive, or Mathews wasn't able to make the call for John's death — *yet*.

But there was also a third (ugly) option: The torture was too fun for Mathews to end.

FORTY

Hannah
_____

HANNAH WAS SITTING on the apartment couch where she and Greg were sequestered, trying to relax despite her frayed nerves, when Greg got a call from his bosses. He left the apartment to take it. She pressed her back into the cushions, waiting through the anxiety that sat like lead in her stomach.

As her foot tapped the carpet a thousand times, waiting for Greg to return and tell her what was going on, Hannah expected her inner voice to chime in with more doomsaying. But that voice was uncharacteristically quiet, and had been since their arrival a few hours earlier.

The door finally opened. Greg said, "We've gotta go. The Agency wants us in Washington immediately."

She wasn't sure if it was the look in his eyes or a simple fear of the unknown, but Hannah felt as if she were about to be strapped into a long and terrible ride without any escape.

"*Washington?* For how long?"

"Washington State, not D.C. My division is headquartered up there. As for how long, I don't know."

"But what about the shop? I need to call Jenny and update her."

"Jenny's not expecting you back until next week, so we can wait until we arrive before doing anything else or making any other decisions. Okay?"

"Okay," Hannah agreed. "Why are we going to Washington? Did something happen with John?"

"I don't know. Nobody's saying much, but they were insistent that we leave immediately. That means they think you're in danger."

◇

THEY DROVE to a private airfield where a small private Agency jet waited.

They sat with an Agent Henry, a tall Marine-looking black man with a charcoal suit, a granite jaw, and no trace of a smile.

They rode in silence as Hannah tried to calm her jangling nerves, both from the flight, and all that was happening so quickly. The world was a web of confusion around her, each second another sliver of proof that everything was wrong and nothing would ever be right again.

She drew long breaths, in and out and over and over, trying not to cry as she gently dug fingers into her thighs and lightly bounced her heels against the floor. Through every mile of her fear, she tried to find the voice. But Hannah's inner whisper, that other voice that had led her down this path, was silent.

You sure had a lot to say before!

I know you're there because I'm here.

Why won't you answer me?

If something happens to me, then it happens to you, too. And if something happens to US, it's all your fault.

262

Hello?

Even after Greg spoke, Hannah's whisper stayed silent through his story.

"How are you doing over there?" Greg asked, friendly.

"Fine. I guess."

"I'm sorry about all of this." Greg looked at the clouds outside the window rather than her, but it was hard for Hannah to doubt the apology lining his voice, despite his many lies.

She was tempted to answer his sorry with an, "It's okay," but she was far from fine, and didn't feel obligated to protect his feelings. So Hannah said nothing.

His eyes held the clouds as he spoke. "I didn't plan for any of this."

Hannah stared down at her hands in her lap, still silent.

It was hard to separate truth from its opposite. There was so much of Greg to love, but knowing what was real now felt impossible. The meaning of *true* had softened, and truth told with ill intent could be worse than a lie.

Hannah thought back on the years of Greg's countless compliments; the many times he practically sang gospels about how lucky he was to have a girl like her in his life. He would compliment the way she looked, the way she smiled, the way she could turn any handful of flowers — from garden to bucket — so beautiful. He would stare into her eyes, steal glances at her face and body, hungry to kiss her through the length of his gaze. He always went out of his way to make her happy, like the way he slipped notes into her lunch bag, which she often found stuck to the bottom of her see-through microwavable containers. At first she would only see them after she finished her lunch, but Greg had done it so often that Hannah was now trained to look first.

The hardest part about their flight, besides heading into her nightmare's next chapter, was that every affectionate gesture, kiss on the cheek, or midnight nibble now seemed somehow premeditated or possibly insidious, down to the day they met.

Clouds thinned, and snowy ground and city came into view below. Greg kept staring out the window while Agent Henry read *Popular Science*.

Something jarred inside her, what felt like a memory, or a glimpse from a remembered dream, loose in her mind.

They were standing on the beach, the warm sunshine kissing her skin, the cool, salty breeze blowing his long hair. His eyes met hers. She asked what he was thinking about. He was always so quiet and distant, his thoughts far away. He'd usually answer with *nothing*, even though she never believed him. This time he said something different.

"You. It's weird. I never really felt like there was something missing from my life. I never felt like I was waiting for the right person to come along. But now I realize just how empty I was before I met you. And how even though I didn't know it, I was waiting for someone — you, Hope."

A chill ran down her spine as Greg's voice dragged her back to reality.

"You okay?"

"I'm fine," Hannah said. "I guess."

THEY TOOK a truck from the airfield to a nondescript office park with a 12-story mirrored building that seemed like a thousand other such buildings, seen back home and during their drive. Yet, Hannah felt cloaked in an overwhelming sense of déjà vu.

There was something about the office park, the building itself, or …

Hannah swallowed, realizing it wasn't the park or the building or anything else.

It was John.

Her inner whisper returned.

"He's here."

"You *sure* you're okay?" Greg asked, pulling the car into a space in front of the building.

"Positive," Hannah said.

FORTY-ONE

Abigail

ABIGAIL STOOD FROZEN in horror after she killed Katya. She panicked, not knowing where to go or what to do. She had now murdered four innocent people, five if you counted Karen McKenna, which, of course, Abigail did.

I'm a monster.

Abigail thought about calling Larry, telling him what had happened, but the thought of his probable response was terrifying. He would be furious, and worse, afraid of her. She could feel his fear after she'd killed the family down the street and set their house on fire. Larry would never hurt her feelings by saying so out loud, but part of him had to be wondering when she might kill him. Abigail wouldn't be surprised if Larry started locking his door when he went to sleep.

I wouldn't trust me.

Abigail tried calling out to John in her head. He might understand, and be able to tell her what to do next.

John?

John, please, I need you.

She wondered if their connection was broken, or if he

was simply too busy to respond. Abigail sobbed, staring down at the remains of her only friend.

"I'm so sorry," she said, lying on the floor beside Katya, hugging her corpse.

Suddenly, Abigail felt someone in her head.

John?

"*No,*" the voice said. It was Talani.

"You made me kill her!" Abigail screamed. "She's dead."

"*Dead?*" Talani said, seeming surprised. "*What happened?*"

I did what you said. And then when I tried to save her, to turn her, you left me! Now she's gone!

"*Oh God, Abigail, I'm so sorry.*"

Why did you leave? Why?

"*Our connection broke. I couldn't feel you anymore. I didn't do it on purpose, I swear. I thought you had pushed me away.*"

Abigail said nothing, just stared at Katya's body, wishing she could reverse the energy and put breath back into Katya. She would gladly surrender her life to bring Katya back.

She was nice. She shouldn't have died. I should have.

"*It's not your fault.*"

Yes, it is!

"*No, Abigail. You were trying to help her — trying to share your gift.*"

Gift? You call this a gift? It's a curse! I wish John had never brought me back.

"*You don't mean that, Abigail. You're just scared.*"

I do mean it. I don't want to live like this. I don't want to be a monster.

"*You're not a monster. You're just with the wrong people. They don't understand you. It isn't their fault. It's not that they don't love you. They just can't understand you.*"

John understands me. We're the same.

"But he's not there, is he?"

It's not his fault. He has to work.

"Sounds like my father. Always working. Never had time for me. I never would've been turned if he had been home when the man tried to kill me."

What man? What are you talking about?

"It was a man who lived next door to us. He knew my parents were never home. He came over and tried to … touch me. I fought back and he stabbed me. Sixteen times before he left me for dead. I crawled out onto the street. An old woman saw me. She called an ambulance once she stopped screaming. I died while being wheeled into the hospital. Someone brought me back."

Who?

"A woman who happened to be at the hospital when I was brought in. She snuck into my room and saved me. Now I'd like to save you, Abigail, to offer you a place with others of your kind."

There's more? How many?

"There are four of us like family. But there are even more out there, an entire community of people like us. Like you."

All vampires?

"No, not all of them. But all are different, and all are people you can feel safe to be yourself around. People who won't look at you as the monster you're not. Come, Abigail, please. Let me introduce you to them."

I don't know.

"Listen, Abigail, I won't speak ill of your friends. But I will ask you if they are there when you need them most? Where are they now?"

Talani had a point, even if it hurt Abigail to see it.

Larry and John were off fighting monsters, or whatever it was John had to do for the government. What was to say he would ever have time for her? If she was losing control of her abilities now, then surely she would hurt Larry soon, or someone else John cared about. She thought of John's love, Hope. What would happen once they were reunited? Would John try to become human again? If so, they wouldn't have room for an out-of-control vampire child in their life or home.

What was I thinking? That we could all be one big happy family?

Abigail felt foolish.

Everyone would be better off without me.

"*You don't need to be alone,*" Talani reassured Abigail from inside her head. "*Come, meet my family. Then decide if you want to stay. If not, I'll bring you back home.*"

Okay, Abigail thought back, though she wasn't sure she even had a home, not once Larry found out about Katya.

Abigail grabbed her coat and was about to head out the door. But realizing she had no money, Abigail went back, grabbed Katya's purse, then dug for her wallet, phone, and credit cards. She took them all, shoved them into her coat, and headed out to find the voice in her head.

ABIGAIL WALKED to the corner gas station, called a cab, then took the taxi downtown following Talani's directions. She arrived at a cyber café located at the far end of a strip mall with a grocery store, bar, bank, and few other places, all closed. The café was small, lined with a dozen or so surfers, all sitting at cramped desks, lining each wall and running down the small shop's center aisle. Most of them seemed to be playing some sort of car game or another.

Near the shop's rear sat an old black woman in a bright pink floral dress, looking up from behind a larger desk with a computer and register. In front of the woman sat a romance novel, face down and open to the center, a long haired man's bare chest gleaming from the cover.

"Ask for me," Talani had said. *"Edith will bring you to the back room."*

Abigail approached the old woman, nervous, feeling as if she were doing something criminal by asking for Talani.

"Hi," Abigail said, her quivering voice betraying her timidity. "Is Talani here?"

The woman eyed Abigail up and down, as if trying to determine if she belonged. The woman, probably Edith, nodded then pointed to a door behind her. "In there."

"Thank you," Abigail nodded, then went to the shop's rear and tried the doorknob. At first, it didn't budge.

Edith pushed a button behind her desk and the door clicked unlocked. Only then did Abigail spy the shotgun sitting on a shelf under the desk, within Edith's easy reach.

What kind of place is this?

Abigail turned the knob and slipped through the doorway, into a narrow hall with another three doors on either side, plus one at the end with tinted glass leading outside. She saw a camera above the rear door with two lenses, one aimed at the door below and the other directly at the door where she'd entered.

Before Abigail reached the hallway's end, one of the doors opened and a thin, black girl with long, dark hair and a stylish, black coat and dress stepped out, studying Abigail. She seemed maybe 16.

"Abgail?" the girl said, her voice the same as the one in Abigail's head.

"Yes. Talani?"

"Good to meet you," Talani smiled, a big, genuine-looking smile, walking toward Abigail and reaching out to pull her into a hug, as if they were long-lost friends freshly reacquainted. Abigail pulled back out of instinct, forgetting she was harmless to a fellow vampire. Talani smiled and Abigail relaxed into her embrace. Her newest friend wore the scent of a faint but sweet perfume which Abigail instantly liked.

"Come," Talani said, "there's someone I want you to meet."

Talani led Abigail back through the door and into a small storage room piled high with cardboard boxes. Abigail looked around, confused, seeing no one.

"Just back here," Talani said, leading Abigail back past the boxes and through a doorway leading to a second storage room, also filled with boxes. She opened a door which spilled into a much larger room, the boarded up storefront beside the cyber café.

Is this some kind of secret place that you can only get to by passing through their security in the cyber café?

The room was lit by a solitary candle sitting in the center of a table. Several folding chairs surrounded the table as if it were a regular meeting place of some sort. At the table sat a short, blonde with medium length hair who appeared mid-30s. She wore thin, round, red-framed glasses. "This is Judith," Talani said. "She saved me."

"Hi," Abigail said, standing at a distance and waving.

"Sit," said Judith in a friendly voice, waving her hand at the other chairs.

Abigail sat across from Judith. Talani took a seat to Abigail's right. Abigail looked around, "What is this place?"

"A special sort of meeting place. Talani tells me you're one of us? A vampire?"

"Yes," Abigail said.

"And so young." Judith sighed. "Who turned you?"

Abigail felt protective, and didn't want to give John's name. "A man who saved me after I was shot."

"And where is he now? Why is he not taking care of you?"

"He was, but he has a busy job. He has to travel a lot."

"Yes." Abigail thought she might have heard the slightest hiss in Judith's word. "I heard he works for our enemy."

Abigail wondered how she knew that. Abigail hadn't told Talani. The girl must've been poking around in her head and found out about John. Abigail felt a chill run down her spine, afraid she'd made a bad mistake meeting Talani.

"He's not a bad man," Abigail said, shifting nervously in her seat.

"It's okay," Judith smiled. "I'm not interested in perse-cuting your friend. We all make our choices, and who is anyone to judge another's decisions until they've walked in their proverbial shoes?"

"Good," Abigail said, fidgeting, uncertain what she should say and feeling like she might have offended the woman, though she had no plans to apologize.

Judith smiled. "You're among friends now. We run a meeting for our kind here twice a week at 8 p.m. on Mondays and Fridays."

"What kind of meeting?"

"Support, Abigail. We offer a place for outcasts to come and feel accepted. It's sort of like church, but without a false God to pray to."

"Oh," Abigail said, not sure what else to say. She was feeling uncomfortable and wished she'd called Larry rather than following Talani's call.

"Show her the place," Talani said.

"Oh, I don't know," Judith said.

Abigail wondered what place Talani was talking about.

"You have to!" Talani pleaded, for the first time sounding like a teenager instead of the authoritative voice

Abigail had somehow grown almost used to hearing in her head.

Judith met Abigail's eyes. "Would you like to see something only five others on Earth have ever seen?"

"Okay," Abigail agreed, again shifting in her seat, still uncomfortable behind the thick curtain of uncertainty.

Judith held her hands out in front of her, cupping them as she muttered and whispered into her palms. Abigail could barely hear, and the few words she could make out were foreign, and somehow *off*. It was a language she'd never heard, and yet it seemed vaguely familiar.

A dim light was born in Judith's palms, then glowed brighter as an image hovered above them. It jumped and flickered, like video seeking reception, until it cleared enough for Abigail to see the rich, green mountains, a waterfall larger and bluer than any she'd seen even in the glossiest pictures, and something flying high in the richly purpled sky. As the image closed in on that something, Abigail saw that it wasn't a bird, but rather the impossibility of a Pegasus instead.

"Whoa!" Abigail breathed, lost inside the beauty of a winged horse, so rich with details it couldn't be fake.

Judith closed her hands around the image, and Abigail watched as it faded into ashen wisps of nothing.

"What was *that?*" she asked, mesmerized.

"That is the world I'm from," Judith said. "Home to our kind, the Valkoer."

Valkoer? That's what we're called?

"It's so beautiful," Abigail whispered, wondering if that was where John was from, too. And the world his brother, Caleb, had gone off to. It had to be. John and Larry didn't speak much of the world in front of her, or Caleb. She'd only picked up on bits and pieces. But they had never described it so beautifully, or mentioned something so mythic as winged horses.

"Yes," Judith said. "Those are my final memories of home. I've not been back in thousands of years."

"Thousands?" Abigail said, shocked. "How old are you?"

"I stopped counting long ago," Judith smiled. "How old are you?"

"I'm almost 13. Well, I stopped growing when I was 11. So, I guess eleven."

"Do you like being 11?" Judith asked.

Abigail looked at Talani who smiled sweetly, then back to Judith. "Not really. Everyone treats me like a kid."

"Yeah, I imagine that's rough," Judith said. "Given a choice, what age would you choose to be?"

"I don't know," Abigail shrugged. Memories from Katya flashed through her mind — the girl's twenty-first birthday in particular. A large party with many friends, a cute boyfriend who wore his hair long. He liked to laugh and loved her a lot. The party had been one of the best nights of her life, and memory said she thought of it almost every day.

"I think I'd like to be maybe 20. Or 21?"

Judith smiled. "Ah, yes, those *are* good years."

Abigail turned to Talani. "How old would you choose?"

"I like being this age. I'm young enough that people are still nice to me, and it's easy to take advantage of nasty old men." Talani laughed.

Abigail joined her, though she didn't think the comment was *that* funny.

"Tell me, Abigail," Judith said. "What would you do if I said you don't have to be 11 forever?"

"What do you mean?"

"What if I said you can choose your age?"

"I can? Nobody ever told me that."

"Of course not. Men who turn girls into vampires want to be needed. They don't like when girls grow into women and find their independence. If they could have their way, they'd keep us all in boxes on shelves, serving only their whims."

Abigail shook her head. "No, that's not John. He loves me. He didn't even *want* to turn me. He saved me after I died."

Judith smiled. "Well, perhaps he doesn't know the spell."

"The spell?"

"The spell that allows us to alter our age. You can be any age you want to be, Abigail. Any age at all."

"How?" Abigail whispered.

"I'm glad you asked," Judith said, her smile growing wider, reminding Abigail of the Cheshire Cat.

FORTY-TWO

Hannah
_____

HANNAH WAITED for Greg in the small office, furnished with a chair and desk, but no phone, computer, or any other sort of communication device. She wondered what sort of work was done in such an empty office. She considered opening the desk drawer to see if there was anything inside — maybe the office wasn't assigned, or it was an office for field agents to temporarily use — but she didn't know if there were cameras, or if she was somehow being watched. She probably was, so Hannah fought the urge to investigate, along with the one to nod off as her head grew heavy. She wasn't sure what time it was, but they'd been there a few hours, and it felt late.

Hannah was tired, hungry, and wanted to be anywhere other than the FBI building where Greg had brought her — a place that didn't say FBI anywhere outside, but instead looked like any of the typical buildings Hannah filled with flowers each Monday for the week's standing orders. Yet, inside everyone looked like agents, straight from a movie, and she was surprised to see the number of people working so late.

Since their arrival, Greg had barely been there, off talking to his bosses or doing God only knew what, while Hannah's patience was disappearing. When Greg finally returned, he wasn't alone.

He stepped into the office behind one man and in front of another. The first man — introduced as Commander Mike Mathews — was about 10 years his senior. His jaw was chiseled like a G.I. Joe, though his body was short, and slightly soft. He looked like any number of asshole frat guys Hannah thought she remembered from college. He gave her a big fake smile and extended his hand. "Hello. It's such a pleasure to meet you."

"Likewise," Hannah said, shaking his hand. She tried not to laugh as he showed the strength of his handshake. *What a tool.*

The second man was older. Tall, thin, and pale looking, with dark hair and darker circles blotting the skin beneath his nose. He reminded Hannah of a cartoon villain, enough that she had to suppress a smile.

"Hello, ma'am," said the cartoon villain in a German accent, making him seem even more like a cliché, nodding toward Hannah but not offering his hand, as if too shy to shake.

Okay, he's not weird at all.

"This is Mr. Skinner," Greg said. "He would like to examine you."

"What?" Hannah couldn't hide her alarm. "What do you mean, *examine* me?"

Mathews took a step forward wearing his big fake smile. "It's nothing like you're thinking, Ms. Quinn. Mr. Skinner isn't a doctor. He's something of a specialist, here to help us find something."

Not a doctor; oh, that's a relief.

"I'm confused. What's happening, Greg?"

"Just relax," he said, his voice reassuring as he stuck her in the neck with something. She could barely register what it was before seeing the needle.

"What the … " Hannah fell back before she could finish her sentence.

Greg caught Hannah and set her gently back in the chair.

What the hell are you doing?

She could barely feel her body, or his touch. Hannah could only sense it as if it were happening to someone else. She felt as if she were swimming through the middle of a weird dream that barely belonged to her. She turned to Greg, their eyes meeting for a breath, but focus was difficult. She tried to ask why but Hannah's mouth ignored her mind.

The tall German leaned closer and placed his hands over Hannah's chest. She tried to move, repulsed by the thought of the strange man touching her, but she couldn't even twitch with her entire body, which was numb and unresponsive.

The man continued to hold his hands over Hannah, moving them back and forth, hovering centimeters above without touching herb body. He turned back to Mathews and pointed directly at Hannah's chest. "It's here. Next to her heart."

Mathews pulled the phone from his pocket, mashed his thumb on the glass, waited a few seconds, then said, "How quickly can we get a surgeon here?"

Surgeon?

After a painfully long silence Mathews said, "Tomorrow's too long. We'll just cut her open."

What? Cut me open? Why? What's happening?

Hannah's heart raced; a crashing plane between her ears, her mind desperate to find sense in her surroundings.

But she couldn't cut through the chaos, no matter how hard she tried. She wished her inner whisper would chime in and offer a clue, but it was inconveniently silent, leaving her alone and afraid yet again.

"What?" Greg said, clearly alarmed. "You can't just cut her open. She'll die."

"Not my concern," Mathews said. "She has what I want, and I'm not waiting until tomorrow. Who knows how long until … "

A high pitched buzzing ripped through the room, and somewhere, Hannah heard what sounded like gunfire erupting.

What's happening?

A voice crackled on Mathews's phone. "Harbinger is here!"

Harbinger? Who?

Mathews pointed at the creepy German. "You, stay with her. Make sure no one comes in." He handed the man a gun. "And make sure she doesn't leave."

Mathews grabbed Greg's arm and they raced from the room. Greg looked back at Hannah as if it was the last time he'd see her.

Hannah was suddenly alone with the creepy man, her heart pounding so hard she thought it might explode.

FORTY-THREE

John

JACOB IS HERE.

John thought it moments before the first rounds of gunfire cracked from somewhere in the building. He stared at the door, waiting for it to burst open and for Jacob, or worse, his henchmen or monsters, to come storming through to kill him once and for all.

More gunshots, followed by screaming.

John tried reaching out to feel what was happening, see how many enemies Jacob brought with him, but too much chaos made sense of nothing. The world on the other side of the door bubbled with fear, screams, and pain — the writhing anguish of many. To dip in without losing himself in the flood would be impossible in John's current state, drugged and weakened, his body still slowly stitching from its earlier burning at Mathews' hands.

John wondered how well he'd be able to fight when death came to claim him. Maybe he'd get lucky and the first to attack through the door would be caught unprotected and unaware. Then, John might be able to feed from their souls and use the power to finally kill Jacob.

280

A sudden horror struck him.

Perhaps he's not here for me. Maybe Hope is already here.

That thought sent John into action. He ran at the door and slammed his body hard against it.

"Jacob! I'm here, you fucker. Come and get me!"

John closed his eyes and tried reaching his brother, finding him, somewhere on the bottom floor, killing agents with glee.

Jacob stopped for a moment, turning his thoughts to John.

"Well, hello there, brother, fancy meeting you here."

"I'm on the 10th floor, you fucker, come and get me," John said, knowing his words would travel to his brother alongside his thoughts.

"Perhaps, I'll visit you later, John. Right now, I'm here to see someone else. Maybe you've heard of her. She shares her name with something of yours which will surely continue to dim by the second."

Jacob laughed like a monster.

"You fucker. Stay away from her!"

"Aw, Johnny, you amuse me so with your bravado. Ta-ta, brother. Be seeing you soon. Is there any final message you'd like me to give her?"

Jacob killed the connection before John could respond.

"Jacob!" John screamed into the silence.

He paced his cell, determined to find a way out. "Mathews!" John looked up at the camera, screaming. "Let me out! Now, goddamn it!"

"Mathews!"

The screams outside seemed almost louder than the gunshots. John closed his eyes and tapped into streaming thoughts, searching for Hope in the din.

So much death. Despair. Horror.

John's door suddenly clicked and began to slide open.

Here comes death.

He balled his fists, waiting to spring on anyone who entered, hoping he was up to the task and wouldn't be staring down a squad of armed, suited men immune to his touch.

Skinner stepped into the room, carrying an unconscious Hope in his arms.

"What did you do to her?" John stepped closer, cautiously, hoping she was okay.

"She isn't hurt," Skinner said. "I took her away when hell came raining. I'll help you escape into the service elevator and then to the roof. You can jump from there, yes?"

John nodded as Skinner set Hope lengthwise on the cot. "I'll need some more clothes so I don't touch her."

"Take my coat," Skinner said, removing his suit. It was long on John, but fine for the moment.

"Thank you," said John, slipping his arms through the sleeves. He moved closer, desperately wanting to touch Hope, to open her eyes and say "Hello."

It had been so long since he'd seen her. And despite Adam saying that he'd change her appearance, she looked just as he remembered her, and not a day older. *So beautiful. So sweet.* His heart melted, ached, and exploded. He wanted to pause the moment so it was only them in the world, and the ensuing violence outside could never permeate their bubble of forever.

But the continued gunshots killed John's hope and sent urgency into his limbs.

He turned to Skinner. "Why are you helping us?"

"Because Mathews is drunk with power. Now that Jacob is here, you are the only one standing between him and the end of this world as we know it. Come, we must go. Are you strong enough to carry her?"

"Yes," John said, unsure if he was, but knowing as he stared down at his love that he'd find a way no matter what.

~

JOHN WASN'T sure if there was something different about Hope, or whether he was simply too weakened to properly handle her. She felt far heavier than she should have. Hope should have been a pillow in his arms, but John was limping heavily from his cell into the hallway, then every step after that as they crossed the long hallway, strides behind Skinner.

"We have to go faster," Skinner urged, his eyes wide and panicked. "Are you sure you're okay? I'd be happy to help you carry her."

John could hear the kindness through Skinner's thick accent, which surprised him considering how eager the German had seemed to help the bad guys a short while before.

"No, I'm fine." John took a second to readjust Hope in his arms. It was awkward since he had to keep her body up past his forearms and away from the naked flesh of his hands in case they slipped from Skinner's long sleeves. He tightened his grip and walked faster, quickly closing the distance between them and Skinner.

"That corner," Skinner pointed toward the end of the hallway. "The elevators wait around it."

Great. Let's hope I can make it that long.

John felt the promise of growing strength as they neared the corner, and dared to hope for recovery. His eyes were on Skinner's back as the German approached the corner.

Skinner screamed and stopped dead in his tracks.

John fell an involuntary step back, clutching Hope tighter against him, before rounding the corner and seeing the source of Skinner's cry.

A monstrosity charged at them, a monster unlike any John had ever seen, though his humming déjà vu suggested otherwise. The monster wasn't tall, though its hulking bulk gave that impression. It was 5 feet high, thick, like a giant tree with dark skin to match, tiny legs, and long arms ending in sharp, black pincers that looked like they could shear metal like grass.

In the center of its mass were what appeared to be dozens of eyes, some blinking and each ringed with a wet dark circle. The blinking eyes opened to a softly glowing amber. Beneath them, a wide open maw filled with hundreds of teeth jutted in every direction like quills.

The monster paused its charge and seemed to study them, its hesitance saving their lives. John was weak, Hope still in his arms, and Skinner frozen, staring at the creature as if hypnotized.

John pulled strength from somewhere and set Hope down against the wall. Then he ran toward the monster and Skinner, not knowing what the hell he'd do until he got there.

Skinner drew his gun but the beast batted it from his fist with a blur — fast considering the creature's mass.

The monster leaped toward Skinner, but John was faster, throwing himself between Skinner and the beast. John thrust his hand up at the creature's face, expecting to pull the soul from inside it.

Nothing happened.

John felt the creature's soul calling out, which meant it should have been his for the taking, but its bark-like body was a protective armor. Momentarily dazed, John stood rooted with a weakness in his body wanting to force him down to the floor.

It did, and the monster fell on top of him. Its dozen or so eyes were all open, staring at John as it opened its mouth, ready to feast.

Six deafening shots rang through the hallway, then the monster's body grew suddenly still and heavier on John's.

"Thanks." John said, looking up at Skinner as he ran to them and pulled the monster off of John, and rolled it aside, black ooze pouring from its wounds.

Skinner nodded and reloaded his clip. He pointed to the elevators. "Let's go."

John scooped Hope up from the wall and into his arms. Twenty feet from the elevator, the wall exploded beside them and another of the tree-like creatures barreled into the hallway. It seemed the same size, but that was an illusion given that the beast was hunched over.

Standing it revealed itself to be at least 7 feet tall, and almost twice as wide as its fallen brother.

Shit.

Skinner fired two shots, then three before the monster swung, sending him flying back, almost into John. The creature shrieked, a loud, bird-like shrill, almost metallic in tone.

John set Hope on the ground, and looked up in time to see the monster running toward him.

One of the monster's eyes seemed larger than the others, a deeper amber bleeding from behind its barely open lid. The larger eye made John think of something he should have thought of before.

He brought his fingers together in a point — a rough and ready shiv — then ran straight at the beast, shoving his hand into the monster's barely open eye.

The creature shrieked, screaming with something that

sounded like a train scraping off the side of the rail as everything it ever was or would be shot inside of John.

Its memories were raw, animalistic, a life of brutality and carnal lust, with nary an intelligible thought beyond its primal urges. But the power was immense, coursing through John, recharging him more than any human ever could. He released the beast and stared down at his hands, trembling with energy he longed to spend on Jacob's destruction.

Hope stirred on the floor, softly moaning, looking like she was about to wake up. But when John went to gather her into his arms, she fell back into unconsciousness. With the monster's strength, John could now carry her easily. With any luck, they would soon be far from the Building.

Skinner stood looking down at the beast and then back at John until a smile cracked through his lips. He walked over to the elevators, made the top button glow, then turned back to John and said, "Very impressive."

"Eyes are windows to the soul," John half-smiled. "I just had to break one."

They stepped inside the elevator, Skinner first. John's heart pounded on their way to the roof.

Come on, come on, come on.

He stared down at Hope, flashing back to their last kiss. The final nights they'd spent together before the world flickered and changed. A decade gone felt like a lifetime apart.

Jacob was responsible, for every pain that John had ever felt — from the death of his true mother, to the chain of events that sent his brother to Otherworld, forced Hope to have her memory erased and to live apart from John, and turned an innocent child into a vampire.

Jacob was a cancer that destroyed everything he touched.

There's no way in hell I'll let him do it again. John stared at Hope and vowed.

The elevator dinged open and John carried Hope onto the rooftop, watching her face the entire time, hoping, and fearing, she might wake. Wind whipped through her hair, and John longed to touch it, to run his fingers through it again.

Skinner followed closely behind, pointing ahead to the building's southern edge which looked down on a smaller six-story bank building. He had to shout over the howling wind. "If you jump over to that roof, you should be able to escape unseen."

"What about you?"

"Don't worry about me, I'll stay here until the smoke clears. Nobody's looking for me."

"Thank you," John said.

Skinner's eyes suddenly widened at something behind John. The German opened his mouth but was launched through the air, thrown back 10 feet and slammed to the rooftop before he could utter a word.

John turned and saw Jacob floating in midair, holding a glowing red sphere in his right hand, wielding it like a power stone. Jacob thrust the sphere hand forward, sending John and Hope both flying back to the ground. John tried holding onto Hope, but lost his grip, crying out as she flew four feet farther than John, tumbling across the rooftop.

He scrambled to his feet and ran to Hope, but didn't make it four inches before he was frozen in place, then lifted from the ground by Jacob and his powerful orb. John tried fighting, to push back with his telekinesis, but Jacob's power had grown too strong.

"Is that any way to greet your brother?" Jacob grinned a lunatic's smile and spun John to face him.

John wanted to spit in Jacob's face, to reach into his chest and pull out his heart, then shove it down his fucking throat. But he was impotent in the stone's hold.

"You can't fight me, John. I have the wizard's power now. Well, *nearly* all of it. I've just one small piece to get."

"The hell you will," John grunted, pushing with all his strength to raise his hands, trying to reach out and strangle his brother.

Jacob laughed at John's hands fluttering helplessly at his sides. Jacob clucked his tongue. "We're such a stereotypical family, always trying to murder each other. Why must we quarrel so?"

"Typical families don't kill their mothers and try to murder their brothers."

"Okay," Jacob laughed. "So, we're a *bit* eccentric. But hey, we live and learn, right? Your brother finally came around after all."

"What are you talking about?"

"Oh, you didn't hear?" Jacob raised his eyebrows in mock surprise. "Caleb finally saw the light, and realized the righteousness of our cause. He is now sitting at the throne beside Father."

"Liar."

"I'm many things, but a liar is none among them. Who do you think created the portal to bring me back here?"

John swallowed. "No. Bullshit."

"Last chance, brother. And may I point out how overly generous I've been with my many offers for you to join me, and fight by my side? I'd say that makes me a damned nice, and *forgiving*, brother, wouldn't you?"

John said nothing.

"Very well," Jacob spun John around, just in time to see Hope rising from the ground, blinking as she stood, rubbing a bloody gash on her forehead.

She looked up with haunted eyes, staring as if at a ghost, ignoring the floating man behind him.

"John?"

She remembers!

The crystal in her chest glowed with a bright enough red to see through her skin.

Jacob cackled.

Hope looked down, staring at her glowing skin, eyes wide in horror. She clutched at her chest, screaming in pain as the crystal moved under her flesh, pressing up, trying to rip free of her body.

"Stop it!" John screamed, unable to move, or turn to face Jacob — helpless to do anything but watch. He could feel Jacob sucking his life from him, weakening him the longer he held him in his grasp. The more John tried to break free, the more energy Jacob withdrew.

The crystal ripped through Hope like a gunshot, the gem flying through the air and leaving a bloody arc behind it on its way into Jacob's orb. Hope stood momentarily, stunned, or in shock, before her eyes closed and she collapsed to the ground.

John screamed.

Jacob released his hold of John and allowed him to fall to the ground as the orb turned crimson, pulsating as wind swirled in a growing tempest around them. John tried to stand, to reach Hope, but was sent to the ground by a gust of wind that knocked his feet out from under him. Rolling thunder exploded, each boom louder than the last, as if the world itself was exploding.

John looked up to see a swirling darkness gathering above and blotting out the stars, sliced by bolts of bright purple lightning crackling in an ever growing circle, starting small but quickly spreading, splitting the world behind Jacob into an ever wider aperture. Another portal opened.

John managed to get up, scrabbling to Hope's side as she lay in a spreading pool of blood.

"John?" she said, confused, and lips trembling.

Tears streamed down John's face as he looked at Hope's wound. She was losing too much blood. And too fast. She'd die if he didn't do something.

He thought of the healing spell he once taught Larry, but shook his head knowing Hope's wound was too deep for a spell. He would need it, plus everything he had inside his own soul. If he had to drain himself to death to save her, he would.

And if he failed, he didn't want to live, anyway.

John, ignoring Jacob, recited the spell, holding his hands high above her chest. Behind him, he heard Jacob say, "Goodbye, brother. Until we meet again."

The portal closed and Jacob disappeared, taking the weather with him.

John continued reciting the spell, holding his hand over Hope's chest, trying to summon the energy, but nothing came. He was too weak, drained by Jacob and the drugs before that.

"Please, God!" he screamed into the heavens.

John tried healing her again, repeating his incantations which hit the charred and still slightly purple air as only words.

Suddenly, Skinner was standing beside him, staring down at Hope, his black ringed eyes filled with sorrow.

"Here," he said, holding his hand out to John. "Take my soul."

"What?"

"Take my soul. You are the only one who can save the world. I have family here. If Jacob returns, they'll be slaves or cattle. Please. You can't allow that to happen. Take my soul, save her, then go slay the monster."

"Thank you," he said, meeting Skinner's eyes.

John reached out to take his hand.

Skinner's soul followed.

FORTY-FOUR

Larry

LARRY PACED THE HOUSE, waiting for Abi.

He'd driven all over town searching for her. He'd even put out word to Tiny's crew, after telling them that their boss was dead, a fact they were none too happy to hear.

Larry didn't know what to do. John and Abi were gone, and he couldn't take a chance that one or both might appear at the house in need of his help.

Still, he felt helpless.

Larry looked at his watch for the hundred-thousandth time, wanting to punch something hard, or kick something harder.

"FUCK!" he screamed to no one.

The sun would be up soon, and Abi might be dead when it was. She had no way of protecting herself out there, wherever she was. John might be a dead man, too.

Larry shuddered.

"*FUCK!*"

He imagined Abi injured, lying in a gutter as the sun came up. Or …

Then Larry realized with a disturbing certainty —

maybe she was chasing death, out there waiting for the sun to come and put an end her misery. Katya had been such a happy part of Abi's life. It must've been an accident, just like the neighbors.

He remembered when he asked to join Johnny and Tiny on the trip to Cromwell's. Abi had begged John not to go, said she was scared.

What if she killed again?

That's exactly what happened. She can't control it.

Jesus, I've got to find her.

A voice in his head: *"Larry!"*

It was John.

"Larry, I need your help, now!"

FORTY-FIVE

Hope

THERE WAS LIGHT, sound, and some sort of memory, but everything mingled into a muddy sludge. The white light turned brighter, until it was almost painful, then softened to a kiss.

Hope saw something impossible — a monster who looked like a tree with way too many eyes — and the tall skinny German, then ...

Nothing.

Then she saw John. Standing in front of her. They were on a roof, up high. She called out his name, confused. Then she saw the bald man in black robes, somehow floating behind him.

She remembered him, too.

She flashed back. He'd called himself a detective a long time ago, had come to her house, asking questions. He'd wanted to talk to John. And when she told John, he freaked out. That's when he told her everything — what he was. And what he had to do.

She remembered.

Everything.

Suddenly, she felt a hot pain in her chest, looked down, and saw a red glowing in her skin.

What the hell?

Then unimaginable pain, worse than anything she'd ever felt. Her chest an explosion turning everything to black, until the white light finally returned, bringing with it her true name.

"Hope ... "

Again and again it repeated.

"Hope, Hope, Hope ... "

She opened her eyes to John's hazy face staring down at her.

"It's you," she whispered, remembering both her past decade as Hannah, and her life before, when she lived in Florida with John.

She remembered their parting, and what he had told her — that he was a vampire, and that her memory would have to be erased.

She sat up, her head spinning, in pain.

"You? You did this to me?"

He looked wounded or confused, she wasn't sure which. Then he spoke, "Oh, God, I've missed you so much, Hope."

She swallowed, tears welling in her eyes. She missed him, too, even if she hadn't realized it until now. She reached out to John, to touch his face, but he pulled back as if horrified.

"If we touch, you'll die," he said.

"What?"

John explained that he fed through his touch, without any control. She remembered something, vague from before, but the memory didn't make it any easier to believe.

"What happened here?" She sat up and looked down

at the ashen corpse.

"It'll have to wait," he said. "Right now, we need to get out of here."

"Hannah!"

Hope turned and saw Greg slowly approaching, his pistol out but not aimed. Beside him was Mike Mathews — the man who had wanted to cut her open. There were another three men behind them, all dressed in black gear with weapons drawn.

Greg screamed at John: "Get away from her!"

FORTY-SIX

John
___

JOHN STOOD and placed himself between Greg, Mathews, and Hope.

"You're too late," he shouted over the screaming wind. "Jacob got the crystal and he's gone back to Otherworld."

"Bullshit," Greg said then fired a shot.

It ripped into John's chest.

"Stop!" Hope screamed, running to put herself in front of John.

In John's mind he saw Greg fire his second shot, then watched the bullet sing through the night in slow motion, sailing past its intended target and finding Hope instead. Another wound so soon was a risk he couldn't allow.

No fucking way.

John reached inside himself, gathered every bit of his Darkness, then screamed, unleashed it in a giant blast of energy directed at the huddle of men, sending them stumbling like trees ripped from the ground in a hurricane.

Two of the men sailed over the roof as John raced towards the remaining three, quickly disarming the final man in black, reaching into his visor and sucking his life in a quick spurt.

John turned to the last two men on the rooftop, Greg, still doubled over in pain, and Mathews, aiming his gun at John, rage boiling his face into an ugly shade of red.

Mathews fired three rounds. One hit John in the jaw and blasted part of his cheekbone off.

The other two bullets sank into his chest and shoulder, but John was too amped on adrenaline and raw energy to feel anything other than anger, hate, and a bottomless thirst for vengeance.

John flashed back on Mathews shooting the poor woman, Emilia, who had lost her daughter. He felt her memories, the pain of losing Kayla, and the betrayal of a man who had sworn to protect the nation. John locked his eyes on Mathews. He wanted no part of the man's vile recall, or any of his destructive past. He only wanted him dead.

John grabbed Mike's gun, breaking free before his touch could kill the man, then turned the weapon back on Mathews, aimed straight between his eyes. He pulled the trigger twice, blowing Mathews' face and brain to bits.

"Fucker." John dropped the gun in disgust and turned to the last man standing: Greg, the liar who had been sleeping with Hope. And he'd brought her here to do what? Turn her over to Mathews and his corrupt regime?

Greg dropped his gun, sliding it past John, and pled for his life. "Please, please," he begged, hands up, palms out in front of him. He turned to Hope. "Please, Hannah, I love you."

John looked back at Hope, having almost forgotten her presence in his moment of rage. He felt like a kid caught killing a bird. Her eyes were wide, scared, and filled with tears, many falling freely down her face.

John could only imagine what she was thinking about him right now, wondering what sort of monster she'd been stupid enough to love. He wondered if she would beg him to spare Greg.

He didn't want to. John wanted to sap the man's life to nothing, to pluck the memories from his head, memories of a life stolen with Hope, so he could live through those lost years, even if only vicariously.

"Please, Hannah, I love you," Chris cried. "I'd never let them hurt you."

Hope approached them, her eyes locked on John as if trying to reconcile the man she loved with the monster he was, staring as if seeing inside him, right to the Darkness, the part of himself he'd buried for so long.

She'd never seen this side of him. His creature unleashed, the feeding frenzy, the destruction, the horror. Yet, here he was, raw and exposed as the monster he was. John felt more vulnerable than he'd ever been, as if a single word from Hope could destroy him.

"Please," Greg begged again.

John, having heard enough of his whining, turned to Greg and yelled, "Would you shut up?"

A gunshot punctured the pre-dawn.

John turned to see Hannah holding the pistol Greg had dropped to the ground. John turned from Hannah and back to Greg, just in time to see the bloody hole in his face.

Greg fell to the ground.

"My name's not Hannah," Hope said, then fell to her knees, staring at what she'd done, stunned and silent.

John stood still, uncertain, wanting to comfort his love, but not knowing if she was disgusted by him, or maybe by what she'd done.

John looked around, waiting for more men, either Omega or Harbinger to storm the rooftop, but no one was coming. He looked down at the bank building. They had to make a run for it, and soon. He prayed that Hope would come with him.

He closed his eyes and tried to feel Larry was nearby, hoping his friend would arrive.

Epilogue

JOHN WATCHED in the predawn darkness as Hope slept in the queen-size bed. He sat in a chair beside the bed, where he'd also spent the night before. A blue nightlight in the corner cast the room in a somber, cold glow.

He longed to be beside her, to touch her, hold her, kiss her, but he couldn't so long as he was cursed. Nor did he even know if she would *want him* to touch her. She was still hurt by his betrayal more than a decade ago. He'd lied to her, had her mind wiped, never giving her a choice to stay and fight alongside him. He'd tried to explain things, but his words all felt stupid, and her patience was thin.

So they'd spent most of the past day in silence interspersed with moments of small talk. He wanted to reach out, to make things right, to find the right words to say, but part of him was too distracted by Abigail's disappearance.

Though he couldn't feel her, which concerned him deeply, he knew Abigail was out there, somewhere, hurting.

It had been two days since any of them had seen the child.

Hope, John, and Larry were staying in one of Larry's safe houses in east Washington. It was slightly too small, but far enough from the Guardians, or anyone in Harbinger who might be left looking for them.

The world hadn't ended, yet. The FBI had buried the story of the Building's destruction. As for how the Agency was going to recover from their ample losses, John had no idea. Nor did he particularly care.

He only cared about being with Hope and finding Abigail.

Hope had remembered mostly everything, though John didn't dare tell her she wasn't from Earth. Not while she was trying to sort out her life. A decade of false memories, ten years of a new life built, all of it now meaningless.

She stirred in the bed and opened her eyes "You all right?"

"Yeah, just thinking."

"About what?" She turned toward him and pulled the comforter tighter around her body.

"You. Wondering what's next."

"Ah," she said, not offering more.

"You know you can't go back to Hannah's life, right? There will be people looking for you."

"Ye. Though I'm not sure I was ready to live a lie, anyway. So, what's going to happen?"

"With us? Or everything else?"

"I can't even think about us, right now," she sighed. "I mean with Jacob. What will he do with the crystal? How did it even get inside me?"

"I don't know." John hated lying to Hope, yet again. But if he told her that she wasn't even who she thought she was, wasn't even human, it might be too much for her to handle.

Hell, it's too much for me to handle.

"But as for Jacob, I don't know. He's stronger than ever. The Guardians felt that if he got all the crystals he'd be too powerful to stop — that he might come back to our world and bring the vampires with him. It will be open season on humans."

Hope swallowed and sat up, visibly shaking. "I wish I could go back to thinking I was Hannah. The world was so safe then."

She swiped at her welling tears. He thought to ask her about Greg, wondering how she was coping with killing a man she'd loved. Ending anyone's life had to be devastating for her, but killing a man she'd known, trusted, and had been intimate with — it had to be soul shaking, the kind of thing you may never recover from. But he didn't dare take that dark road. He wished he could wipe her mind of the past 24 hours, or maybe everything since they'd left Florida.

A strangers' silence stretched between them, and every minute felt like an hour.

He wanted to break the silence, but didn't know how, or what to say.

She spoke, instead, "I dreamed of you. I'd gotten into an accident and began remembering you."

He smiled.

"I really loved you, you know?"

"Loved, as in past tense?" he asked.

She was quiet. He looked down at his hands, unable to meet her eyes. He heard her swallow.

A knock on their bedroom door shattered the silence.

"John?" Larry said in an urgent whisper. "You awake?"

Hope looked up at John and nodded, giving permission for Larry to enter.

"Come in," John said.

Larry burst into the room holding his MacBook Air, open and bringing its bright light to John's side.

"You have to see this! I got this from one of Tiny's men, who have been sitting watch on the portal in Anchor Harbor."

He handed the laptop to John and pressed a button to start the movie.

The video showed the portal, or at least the surrounding tent , with four armed soldiers standing guard.

A timestamp on the recording read one night ago, 2:31 a.m.

John watched, waiting to see what Larry was so excited about. He glanced up at Larry.

"Just keep watching," he said.

Hope stood, came to their side, and looked down at the screen.

Dark blurs raced by, and the soldiers were down in seconds, never having a chance to fire their weapons.

It was a massacre, over in seconds, four vampires attacking four guards. Seconds later, the tent came down, as if ripped away by thought alone. The portal swam bright in the darkness and the four figures started toward it.

As they drew closer to the portal, the light illuminated them better so John could finally make out their shapes — three women and a man.

No, correction: A man, two women, and a child.

"Abigail!" John stared at the screen, trying to will what had already happened from happening.

Who is she with? Are they Harbinger?

The woman and man entered the portal and vanished. The other woman, who John now realized wasn't much older than Abigail, held out her hand for Abigail.

She took it, and they disappeared into the portal.

John's heart sank.

"What was that?" Hope asked.

"That's the girl we've been looking for. And she just went to Otherworld with people I don't even know."

"Oh, my God," Hope said, the gravity of what they'd seen sinking in.

John began watching the video again, trying to glean something useful. Larry looked down at John, "We have to go after her."

John looked up at Larry, and then at Hope. He couldn't bear to be apart from her again. But at the same time, Larry didn't need to argue on Abigail's behalf. The girl was in more danger than ever, especially if she was with Jacob's people.

"Yes," John said.

"I'm going with you," Hope said.

John shook his head. "No, it's too dangerous. I'll come back for you — *I promise.*"

"No," Hope snapped, her voice firm and eyes serious. "I'm tired of running. I'm tired of hiding. I'm tired of not knowing what's happening." Her eyes welled up, but she fought back the tears. "You asked me before if I loved you, as in past tense, or still love you. I love you, John. And always will. But you can't do this again. I can't lose another decade living a life that isn't mine. I want to come with you."

There was no way John could allow her to come.

"It's too dangerous. God only knows what lays on the other side of the portal. Jacob is there. My father, the king of the vampires, and my brother, Caleb, who has turned to the Darkness, if Jacob is to be believed. It's a suicide mission if I go alone. I can't even fathom what would happen to you."

"If you die," Hope said, "then we die together."

"Make that three," Larry said. "Let's take a trip."

The story continues...

Want to find out what happens next? The adventure continues in *Available Darkness: Book Three*.

About the Authors

Sean Platt is an entrepreneur and founder of Sterling & Stone, where he makes stories with his partners, Johnny B. Truant, and David W. Wright, and a family of storytellers.

Sean is the bestselling author of over 10 million words' worth of books, including the Yesterday's Gone and Invasion series. Sean is also co-author of the indie publishing cornerstone, Write. Publish. Repeat. and co-host of the Story Studio Podcast.

Originally from Long Beach, California, Sean now lives in Austin, Texas with his wife and two children. He has more than his share of nose.

David W. Wright is the co-author of edge-of-your-seat thrillers including the best-selling post-apocalyptic series *Yesterday's Gone*, the paranoid sci-fi *WhiteSpace* series, and the vigilante series, *No Justice*, as well as standalone thrillers *12*, and *Crash* which was recently optioned for a movie.

David is an accomplished, though intermittent, cartoonist who lives in [LOCATION REDACTED] with his wife and son [NAMES REDACTED.]

He is not at all paranoid.

He is "the grumpy one" on *The Story Studio Podcast* with fellow Sterling and Stone founders, Sean Platt and Johnny B. Truant.

You can email him at <u>david@sterlingandstone.net</u>

We swear, he almost never bites. Unless you feed him after midnight.

Also By Sean Platt

The Dead World Series

Dead Zero

Dead City

Dead Nation

Dead Planet

Empty Nest

The Beam Series

The Beam Season One

The Beam Season Two

The Beam Season Three

Robot Proletariat Series

En3my

Robot Proletariat

The Infinite Loop

The Hard Reset

Cascade Failure

Reboot

The Tomorrow Gene Series

Null Identity

The Tomorrow Gene

The Tomorrow Clone

The Eden Experiment

Karma Police Series

Jumper

Karma Police

The Collectors

Deviant

The Fall

Homecoming

Yesterday's Gone

October's Gone

Yesterday's Gone Season One

Yesterday's Gone Season Two

Yesterday's Gone Season Three

Yesterday's Gone Season Four

Yesterday's Gone Season Five

Yesterday's Gone Season Six

Tomorrow's Gone

Tomorrow's Gone Season One

Tomorrow's Gone Season Two

Tomorrow's Gone Season Three

Available Darkness

Darkness Itself

Available Darkness Book One

Available Darkness Book Two

Available Darkness Book Three

WhiteSpace

WhiteSpace Season One

WhiteSpace Season Two

WhiteSpace Season Three

Stand Alone Novels

Burnout

The Island

Crash

Emily's List

Pattern Black

Devil May Care

The Secret Within

The Sleeper

Last Night Never Happened

I Am John Tidor

Also By David W. Wright

Cold Vengeance

Cold Vengeance

Cold Reckoning

Cold Retribution

Hidden Justice

Hidden Justice

Hidden Honor

Hidden Shame

Hidden Virtue

No Justice

No Justice

No Escape

No Hope

No Return

No Stopping

No Fear

Karma Police

Jumper

Karma Police

The Collectors

Deviant

The Fall

Homecoming

Yesterday's Gone

October's Gone

Yesterday's Gone Season One

Yesterday's Gone Season Two

Yesterday's Gone Season Three

Yesterday's Gone Season Four

Yesterday's Gone Season Five

Yesterday's Gone Season Six

Tomorrow's Gone

Tomorrow's Gone Season One

Tomorrow's Gone Season Two

Tomorrow's Gone Season Three

Available Darkness

Darkness Itself

Available Darkness Book One

Available Darkness Book Two

Available Darkness Book Three

WhiteSpace

WhiteSpace Season One

WhiteSpace Season Two

WhiteSpace Season Three

Stand Alone Novels

12

Crash

Emily's List

Threshold
The Secret Within

www.ingramcontent.com/pod-product-compliance
Lightning Source LLC
Chambersburg PA
CBHW011449100726
47899CB00010BB/3217